The Fo

Rachel McLean writes thrillers that make your pulse race and your brain tick. Originally a self-publishing sensation, she has sold millions of copies digitally, with massive success in the UK, and a growing reach internationally too. She is also the author of the Detective Zoe Finch series, which precedes the Dorset Crime novels, and the spin-off McBride & Tanner series and Cumbria Crime series. In 2021 she won the Kindle Storyteller Award with *The Corfe Castle Murders* and her last five books have all hit No1 in the Bookstat ebook chart on launch.

Also by Rachel McLean

Dorset Crime series

RACHEL McLEAN

THE FOSSIL BEACH MURDERS

hera

First published in the United Kingdom in 2022 by Ackroyd Publishing

This edition published in the United Kingdom in 2024 by

Hera Books
Unit 9 (Canelo), 5th Floor
Cargo Works, 1–2 Hatfields
London SE1 9PG
United Kingdom

A CIP catalogue record for this book is available from the British Library.

Print ISBN 978 1 80436 765 0

Look for more great books at www.herabooks.com

Printed and bound in Great Britain by Clays Ltd, Elcograf S.p.A.

1

CHAPTER ONE

PC Douglas Anderson was having a bad day.

He'd been woken at 4am by his daughter Poppy, and despite Naomi getting up and sending him back to bed, he hadn't found sleep afterwards.

At 6:30 when he'd eventually given up, he'd discovered that the boiler was on the blink and there was no hot water for a shower.

And now, despite the skies being clear when he left home, raindrops the size of gumdrops were splattering his police uniform.

Douglas yawned and tried to shake himself out as he ran from his car to Lyme Regis police station, but it only made water run down the back of his neck.

Ugh.

He didn't need this. Not now. Not with his brain running on empty for the fifth time in as many days.

"Dougie!"

He looked up to see his partner, PC Wendy Sharman, running towards him. She skidded to a halt in front of him, leaning over to ball her fists on her knees.

"Dougie," she said. "No time to come inside. There's been a landslip up at the Spittles."

"What?" he asked, his brain not yet woken beyond Neanderthal mode.

"A landslip. Didn't you hear me the first time?" She straightened up and rolled her eyes "You've had another broken night, haven't you?"

He yawned. "Babies."

She punched his arm. "I did warn you. Come on, I'll drive."

He followed her to their panda car, an underpowered Astra that often rebelled against the hill that led from the station to the main road.

"Where was it again?" he asked her.

"The Spittles," she said. The cliffs north of Lyme Regis.

He rolled his shoulders to relieve the fatigue, and strapped himself in. He watched in a daze as Wendy backed out of their space. On mornings like this, Douglas sometimes wondered whether the laws that banned driving under the influence of alcohol and drugs should be broadened to cover the effects of living with four-month-old babies.

Ten minutes later they were at the Charmouth Road car park.

"Is this the closest we can get?" he asked as Wendy unfastened her seatbelt.

"Sorry, mate," she told him, "you know it is."

He did. In the event of a landslip, they approached from below, not above. And even then, they would come at it from a distance. They kept powerful binoculars in the car so they could assess the damage from the beach.

The Coastguard would have already been alerted. They were sometimes able to get a better angle, come in via helicopter.

But everyone in this town – at least everyone who wasn't a tourist – knew that you never tackled the coastal

2

path after a landslip. Not unless you wanted to start another one.

He knew the drill. Approach from a sensible position, keep your distance, take photographs, assess, and wait for the coastal protection boffins to decide what needed to be done.

The council employed civil engineers, specialists in assessing the impact of a landslip and working out a new route for the coastal path. They'd been planning ground stabilisation measures in this area, but hadn't started work yet. The engineers were miles away in Dorchester; they wouldn't be here until lunchtime.

Douglas pulled up his collar as they took the steps down from the car park. The steps were slippery and the wind bit at the exposed skin of his face. Where the steps ended wasn't all that far away from where they'd begun at the police station, but they needed a car as close as possible.

Wendy looked up at him.

"You on a go-slow?"

"Oi." He picked up pace, hurrying down after her as fast as he could without slipping. At the bottom, they turned towards the Spittles, the cliffs outside town that were famed both for their dangerous walking conditions and their fossil finds.

Douglas could see it as they approached, a scar on the land. Fresh clay marked the spot where the last two weeks' rain had weakened the cliff face and finally sent it tumbling down to the sea. He winced, hoping to God nobody had been up there when it happened.

"What time was it reported?" he asked Wendy, panting as they ran.

"Six am."

He nodded. At 6am he'd been lying awake, about to give up on sleep. Had he heard anything?

No, his cottage was on the other side of Lyme Regis, past the Cobb. He'd slept through landslips in the past.

He scanned the cliffs ahead of them. The nearest houses were behind them, beyond the car park. The nearest with a view of the cliffs were towards Charmouth.

"Who was it that made the call?" he asked.

"Old Samuel Waller, up at Black Ven."

Douglas nodded. Samuel was eighty-six, but had hearing like a feral cat. He'd reported landslips before.

"He didn't come out here, did he?"

"Not that I know of," Wendy replied, raising her voice against the wind.

Good.

The heavy rain was thinning and the sun was doing its best to put in an appearance over the sea to the east. But an ominous gloom hung over the bay.

"We should stop here," Wendy said.

Douglas almost crashed into her as she ground to a halt. "Sorry, mate."

"You need to convince that baby to sleep some more."

"That's what babies do," he replied. "Sleep in the day, keep their parents up all night."

Wendy had the binoculars to her eyes. She peered towards the landslip.

"That's why you won't catch me having one," she said.

Douglas would have said the same thing himself five years ago, when he'd been Wendy's age. But things changed.

"What can you see?" he asked.

"Give me a minute." She frowned and scanned the cliffs slowly.

The tide was out, and they were on the beach below the concrete walkway that led out from the centre of Lyme Regis. Here, the beach was a mix of rocks and sand, striations clear from the actions of the tide over millennia. This was the stretch of beach where the tourists came fossiling in the summer, where Mary Anning had famously found her Ichthyosaurs.

Wendy held out a hand to shush him. Douglas hadn't been speaking.

"What can you see?" he whispered.

"Shush. I don't know yet." She took a step forward.

"Thought it wasn't safe to go any further," he said.

"Yeah, but…" She lowered the binoculars and looked at him. "Take a look through these. Tell me what you see."

The binoculars were high-powered, worth a fortune. The first line of defence against the landslips was to see what damage they'd already done.

Douglas looped the strap around his neck and brought the eyepiece up to his face.

"What am I looking for?"

"I'm not going to tell you," Wendy replied. "I want you to say what you see."

"Fair enough."

He scanned the cliff. It didn't take long to pinpoint the spot where the land had fallen. Slowly, he panned downwards from the clifftop towards the beach. He followed the line that the earth would have taken as it fell towards the sea. He frowned.

He panned up again and stopped halfway.

"What's that?" he asked.

"I know what I think it is," Wendy told him. "But what do you think it is?"

"It looks like…" He felt his chest clench. "*Shit.*"

He lowered the binoculars and looked at Wendy.

"Was somebody up there?"

"At six in the morning?" she replied. "It would have been dark."

"Dog walkers can be hardy types."

She whistled. "I bloody hope that's not a dog walker."

He brought the binoculars back up to his eyes and found the spot.

"There's two of them," he said.

"What?" Wendy grabbed the binoculars, yanking his head down with the strap. He unlooped it and let her take them.

"Put it around your neck," he told her. "We don't want to drop them."

"Yeah, yeah." She looped the strap roughly around her neck and brought the binoculars back up to her eyes.

"You're right," she said. "There's two of them."

Douglas swallowed. There were two bodies up there. Right in the middle of the landslip.

She looked up at him, her eyes wide. This was Wendy's first landslip since qualifying. Sleep deprivation or not, he needed to take charge.

"We need to get search and rescue up there," he said. "Right now."

CHAPTER TWO

DCI Lesley Clarke looked up at a knock on her office door.

She made a gesture and DS Dennis Frampton, her second in command, entered.

"Boss," he began. "I've got bad news."

She leaned back in her chair and scratched her chin. "Go on."

"Local police in Lyme Regis have found two bodies after a landslip this morning." He paused.

"That it? Any more information?"

"The landslip uncovered them. They could have been there ten years, or just a couple of days." He sniffed. "Or thousands of years."

"So it might not be a crime scene."

He shrugged. "I'm waiting for them to get a closer look."

She waved for him to sit down. "Landslip. What exactly do you mean?"

He pulled out the chair opposite her. "It happens frequently along that stretch of coast. The cliffs aren't stable, so if there's enough rain the land slips. It uncovers all manner of things. That's why Lyme Regis is full of fossil hunters every summer."

"So normally these landslips just uncover old bones?"

"Fossils. Trilobites, ammonites, bits of ichthyosaur if you're lucky."

"You're making that up."

He gave her a smile. "No."

"So," she sighed. "You say local police?"

"PC Douglas Anderson and PC Wendy Sharman, Lyme Regis police station. They would have been sent out to ensure no members of the public got too close to the danger zone."

"And do they think we have a crime on our hands? Anyone gone missing over there recently?"

"No one they know of, boss. And Lyme Regis is the kind of place where local police know everything that happens."

She stood up. "OK. I want to follow it up. Beats this paperwork."

"It's not exactly round the corner."

"No?"

"No," he said. "You live in Bournemouth, right at the east of the county. Lyme Regis is in the west. Smack bang on the border."

"A drive will do us good, Dennis."

He coughed. "If the A35 is kind to us, it'll be an hour and a half."

"You can survive that long with me, cooped up in a car?"

"There *and* back."

Lesley laughed, imagining Dennis saying something like that to her when she'd started here eight months earlier. He'd certainly mellowed. "We can catch up, Dennis. Tell me about your hiking exploits."

He pursed his lips. "I'm sure you don't want to…"

"I'm sure I don't. But you can tell me more about Lyme Regis en route, and we can get the team to research links to possible missing persons while we're driving. Come on."

He stood back to let her pass. "You're approving the overtime?"

"Overtime?" She looked at the clock: 2pm. "Dear God, yes. Tell Pam you'll be late home. I'm sure she can keep your dinner warm."

He flushed.

"And I imagine I'll need to pick up a sandwich for myself from the canteen. You want one?"

"Er, no, boss."

"Good. Come on, let's brief the team."

CHAPTER THREE

Douglas Anderson stood on the beach, gazing up at the side of the cliffs. The CSIs had arrived about an hour ago. A short, dumpy woman, and a tall, willowy man in an unmarked van. It had taken them three quarters of an hour just to get to the site where the bodies were. Wendy was already up there, cordoning it off, trying to make it safe. He was down here on the beach, making sure no members of the public tried to get up there. A crowd had gathered behind him, growing by the minute. He was trying to ignore the muttering and speculation.

"Dougie!" called out a voice. "D'you know who they are, mate?"

He shook his head, not looking round.

"Not yet," he replied. "Let's just keep speculation to a minimum until we know what's happened."

"That's bollocks."

Douglas turned. "I'll thank you not to…"

The speaker raised an eyebrow. It was Tom Harrison, Dougie's best mate from school.

"Tom," he said, "What are you doing here? Shouldn't you be at work?"

Tom was the manager of one of the town's two remaining banks. Normally he'd be pushing a pen around his office.

"Why *aren't* you at work?" Douglas asked.

"Day off. Looks like I picked the right day, too. Plenty to keep me occupied."

"You'll soon get bored."

"They're going to need to reroute the path again," Tom replied, ignoring the comment.

Douglas nodded. "Not until the CSIs have finished."

"And it'll take the council weeks to get round to it."

"I wouldn't be so sure," Douglas replied. There were just four weeks to go until Easter. The tourists would be arriving, and the council would want to make sure they had access to the path. Safe access.

"What's Wendy up to?" Tom asked.

"She's making it safe."

"What you doing, letting a girl do that for you? You should be up there."

Doug gritted his teeth. Wendy liked to go rock climbing in her spare time. She was sure-footed and had insisted on going up alone. And she knew the cliffs along here as well as anyone.

Besides, one of them needed to stay down here. Otherwise, Tom, and all the other gawkers would be up there. Taking photos, trying to identify the bodies.

"Is it anyone local?" a woman asked. Anita Hampshire, who'd retired to a cottage in Uplyme six years ago.

"I'm sorry, Mrs Hampshire," Douglas said, "but we don't have an identity yet. I'm sure they'll—"

"Are they definitely dead?" Tom interrupted.

"Tom," Douglas said. "I've already said, let's not speculate."

"I still think you should be up there instead of Wendy."

Douglas pulled in a breath.

"Does Naomi know about this?" asked another woman.

Douglas turned to her, feeling the tension ebbing from his shoulders. It was Annie Abbott, his mother-in-law. He softened.

"Hi, Annie," he said. "I called her when we found it."

"I'm glad you didn't go up there." She gave Tom a sidelong glance. "Can't have Poppy's dad putting himself in danger."

Douglas smiled. "Nobody's in danger."

She pointed beyond him. "Doesn't look that way to me. Tell Wendy to be careful, won't you?"

"Wendy doesn't need me to—"

"Besides, I can't watch." Annie's eyes were on Wendy anyway. She shook herself out and turned to Douglas. "How's the sleeping coming along?"

He yawned. "Not good."

She tapped his arm. "It gets better. You hang on in there. And don't let my Naomi do all the night feeds, alright?"

He gave her a mock-salute. "No, Annie."

Annie blew out a breath. "Brings back memories. Tina was a bloody nightmare." She turned to him. "You heard from Tina lately?"

Tina Abbott was working at Dorset Police HQ these days, a fancy DC. She didn't get in touch with the likes of him, even if they were family.

"Sorry," he said. "Haven't heard from her in months."

"She owes me a phone call. Not to mention a visit with that baby of yours." His mother-in-law screwed up her nose, watching Wendy on the cliffs. "She'll be coming, you know. Major crime investigations team. They'll need Tina and her colleagues to look into this one."

A murmur went through the crowd. Annie was probably right, but Douglas didn't like the idea of civilians telling him how the job was going to be done.

"Let's just wait," he said.

He turned to look up towards Wendy and the two CSIs. Wendy had managed to string tape around the perimeter of the landslip. She was moving slowly, her centre of gravity low. She scanned the area in front of her before each step, checking the ground was stable. He'd been right to let her go up there instead of him.

The council would arrive at some point to assess the slip and work out how far back they needed to take the path. It would be Easter in a few weeks, and the tourists would be flocking down here. They'd need to get a shift on. Wendy stood up and waved an arm wildly to get his attention. He waved back.

His radio crackled.

"PC Anderson, PC Sharman here," came Wendy's voice.

"How's it going, Wendy?"

"PC Sharman, you mean."

Wendy liked to keep things formal when using the radio.

"Sorry, PC Sharman. Report."

He looked up at her as he spoke into the radio. At this distance he couldn't make out her face, but he knew she'd be smiling at his sarcasm.

Or maybe not, given what she was doing.

"Can you move away from the crowd?" she asked.

He shuffled forward, holding up an arm to keep the crowd from following. He heard Annie admonish someone: *Let the lad do his job.*

13

Wendy was standing up on the cliff, facing him. "Bodies look as if they've been here a while," she said. "Significant decomposition. CSIs reckon it could be years."

Douglas stepped further forward and cupped his hand over the device.

"Years?" he muttered.

"Yes, Dougie," she replied, all thoughts of formality forgotten. "Years."

CHAPTER FOUR

Lesley opened the door to her office. "Can you all come in here, please?"

Tina was on the phone. She raised a finger and Lesley nodded. Mike and Stanley stood up from their desks and walked into the office.

"Boss," Stanley said as he passed.

She gave him a smile. Stanley had been made a permanent member of the team, replacing Johnny Chiles. With Tina's promotion, that gave them an appropriately sized team.

She watched Tina hang up the phone and stand. The young woman was wearing a green jacket, one of two she'd bought since moving to CID. The maroon jacket she'd used in earlier days when not required to wear uniform had been relegated to the charity shop.

"What was that?" Lesley asked her.

"Lyme Regis Police," Tina replied. "Just getting an update."

"So you know."

"Yes, boss."

"Come in. Let us know what we've got."

Lesley went to the board, which was empty for now.

"Right," she began. "Two bodies were discovered early this morning following a landslip in Lyme Regis. Dennis?"

Dennis grunted.

Tina raised a hand.

"Tina." Lesley sighed. "How many times do I need to tell you?"

"Sorry, boss."

"What have you got from Lyme Regis Police?"

"PC Douglas Anderson, he was the one who spotted them. Well, him and Wendy Sharman."

"She's another PC?" Lesley asked.

Tina nodded.

"Dougie is my brother-in-law."

Lesley raised an eyebrow. "You come from Lyme Regis?"

"My mum still lives there."

"Good," Lesley said. Local knowledge would be useful. She'd never been to Lyme Regis, didn't know anything about it.

She leaned against her desk and picked up the packet of biscuits she'd left there earlier. She popped one in her mouth, then saw Mike's gaze and offered him one. When the packet had worked its way around the room, she looked at Tina. "You might as well take over, DC Abbott. Tell us what we've got."

Tina rubbed her hands together and grabbed a marker pen. She drew a quick plan of Lyme Regis on the white-board: the harbour, a road curving towards it, and the beach to the north.

She pointed to the beach. "This is called the Spittles. Frequent location of landslips. It's been raining the last two weeks, and that would have weakened the ground. The cliffs finally gave way last night and uncovered two bodies."

"Who reported it?" asked Mike.

"No idea. I'm sure Dougie's on it. PC Anderson." Tina smiled. "This is going to be weird."

"How far up?" Stanley asked.

Tina jabbed her pen into the drawing. "About halfway, but they were probably higher up when they were originally buried."

"Local police think they were buried?" Dennis asked.

"That's the theory," Tina said. "Dougie says there's evidence of them being interred for quite some time."

"How long?" Lesley asked, leaning back in her chair.

Tina shrugged.

Dennis turned to Lesley. "Gail Hansford and her team are already over there, they'll be examining the scene thoroughly."

Lesley was impressed. The journey from Gail's house in Swanage to Lyme Regis was probably the longest you could take around here without leaving the county. But then, Gail seemed to have a sixth sense that got her to crime scenes quickly.

"But so far," said Tina, "it's looking like they've been up there for quite some time."

"What does quite some time mean?" Dennis asked.

"Sorry, Sarge. A few years at least."

Mike whistled.

"Very well," Lesley said. "So we could be looking at a cold case. When will we know exactly how long they've been there?"

"The pathologist is on his way," Tina replied. "Hopefully, he'll be able to identify how long the bodies have been there with more accuracy."

"Not much more," Dennis said. "Even the best pathology examination won't be accurate beyond months after death."

"They're calling in a specialist," Tina told him. "A forensic archaeologist. Specialist in the soil composition of that stretch of coast. It'll have had an impact on decomposition."

"And then there's old cases," Lesley added. "Mike, Stanley, I want you going through HOLMES. See if you can find any double missing persons cases."

"Right, boss." Mike made a note in his pad. "Lyme Regis area."

Dennis rolled his eyes. "No, Mike. Bournemouth area."

Mike grimaced. "Sarge."

Dennis looked at Lesley. "We need to get over there, find out what's going on, talk to the people at the scene."

Lesley nodded. "Change of plan, Dennis. I want Tina with me. You stay here and head up this side of the investigation."

He frowned. "Tina? Surely——"

She gave him a stern look.

"Tina's local to Lyme Regis. She knows the local police and population and if I'm not wrong," she looked at Tina, "she'll be familiar with the terrain."

Tina nodded. "I've been walking those cliffs since I was a little girl."

"Good," Lesley said. "That might help us identify where the bodies were originally left."

"Right, boss," Tina said.

"Dennis, somebody will need to be in charge of collating evidence and following up on the forensics and pathology." She checked her watch: gone 3pm. This would be a late one.

"Come on, Tina," she said. "Let's get moving."

CHAPTER FIVE

"Do you want me to drive, boss?" Tina asked as they made for the DCI's car.

"It's OK, Tina," Lesley told her. "I'll drive, you can make some calls."

"OK."

Tina slid into the passenger seat. She didn't enjoy being a passenger. In Uniform she'd spent four happy years driving fast response vehicles, and she relished the sense of control that being behind the wheel gave her. Sitting next to another driver just made her itch to take over.

By the time they hit the A35, Tina had already made her first call. She put her phone in her lap.

"That was Dougie. PC Anderson. There are no developments."

The DCI sniffed. "We'll be there soon. Can you call Gail, find out what's happening with the forensics?"

"You think there'll be any?"

"Forensics aren't just about objects left behind. The siting of the bodies is important, too. She might be able to find evidence of where they were originally left."

"Are we assuming this was a murder?"

The DCI glanced at her. "If it was suicide, they'd be at the bottom of the cliffs, or washed up by the tide. Accidental death is a possibility, but unlikely. They'd have been found years ago. I'm pretty sure these bodies were buried."

Tina nodded. "At the top of the Spittles."

"The what?"

"That's the local name for the cliffs."

The DCI shrugged her shoulders.

"You want me to take over the driving for a bit, boss?"

"Let's swap at the next lay-by. Tell me about your family. Douglas Anderson is your brother-in-law?"

"He's married to Naomi. My sister." Tina bit her lip. "Boss, will I be able to take ten minutes out to visit her while we're over there?"

She still hadn't met Naomi's baby, Poppy. What with work, and the CID exam, she just hadn't had the time. The child was four months old, most likely unrecognisable from the photos that Naomi had sent her in the early weeks. Tina's mum was cross that she hadn't been over to visit yet. She hoped Naomi would be pleased to see her.

"I can't promise anything," the boss said. "But seeing as your brother-in-law's involved with the case, I'm sure you can sneak ten minutes in if you need to."

"Thanks." Tina clenched her fist in her lap. She'd been avoiding Naomi, dodging her calls.

"What does your sister do?" the DCI asked.

"She's a teacher. Currently on maternity leave."

An eyebrow went up. "Now I know why you want to visit her. How old's the baby?"

"Four months." Tina felt heat rise up her neck. She wasn't in the mood for baby talk right now. "I'll try Gail again." She grabbed her phone before the DCI could ask any more questions about her family.

"Good," the DCI said. She drove past a lay-by.

Tina watched it disappear behind them as she dialled.

"Gail, it's Tina Abbott."

"Good. Are you with Lesley?"

"We're on our way over. We'll be…" she looked at the satnav, "about twenty-five minutes."

"Ask her about the pathologist," said the DCI.

"I'll put it on speaker." Tina placed the phone in her lap.

"Lesley, how much do you know?" Gail asked.

"The bodies have been there a few years. Are you any closer to knowing exactly how long?"

"I've been searching for indications as to where they were left, but I'm not getting very far. They're in a bad way. I'm waiting for the pathologist to tell us more."

"Is it Whittaker, or Fiona Brightside?"

"Neither. We're closer to Exeter. They're sending someone."

The boss frowned. "That's outside the county."

"Closest morgue," Tina said.

"Pathologists don't work on the same boundaries we do," Gail added.

"Fair enough," the DCI said, as they passed another lay-by.

"Boss," Tina muttered. "I thought you were going to let me drive."

"We're nearly there now. You can drive back."

Tina shrugged and twisted her hands in her lap.

"She bossing you around, Tina?" Gail asked.

"Of course not."

Gail laughed. "I know Lesley. Don't take any shit."

Tina blushed. The DCI was her commanding officer. If there was shit to be taken…

"She's right," the DCI said. "You've got local knowledge on this one. Don't hang back, if there's something you need me to know about. People, locations…"

"No, boss."

"You tell her, Lesley," said Gail. "Tina, we'll be glad to have you here."

Don't patronise me, Tina thought. She gazed out of the window.

"Let me know if anything else comes up," the boss said, raising her voice to be heard over the phone. "We'll tell you when we're close."

"Thanks." Gail hung up. Tina left her phone in her lap.

"So what's it like, Lyme Regis?" the boss asked as they turned left at the roundabout to avoid Bridport. "Small town?"

"Very. Close-knit, the kind of place where everyone knows each other. Except in the summer."

"Touristy?"

Tina smiled. "That's not the half of it. Population quadruples in the summer. Naomi keeps trying to convince Dougie to go away during August, escape it all, but he likes to stay put. And you know what it's like. When the grockles are in town, that's when the crime goes up. Dougie says they can't spare him. I think he just likes nicking drunk out-of-towners."

"He grew up there too?"

Tina nodded. She'd been at school with Dougie. They'd dated for three years, until she'd decided local policing wasn't for her. He'd stuck with the local police force, and switched to dating her sister. And now they were married, with the baby.

She turned to look out of the window, wiping a tear from her eye.

"This going to be difficult for you?" The boss was looking at her. "Please don't tell me you and PC Anderson don't get along."

Tina shook her head. "He's fine. No, it's just…"

The last time she had been home for any length of time had been last spring. For her dad's funeral. She'd visited her mum since, but not enough.

Would she be forgiven?

"Anything I need to be aware of?" the DCI asked.

"No." Tina rubbed her eyes. Her mascara would have run. "Just family stuff. Dougie's fine, he's a good copper. I'm glad it was him who found them."

"Good. Ten miles now, where will I need to park?"

"I'll give you directions."

"Good."

Tina's phone rang. She hit hands-free, glad of the distraction.

"DC Abbott," she said, resisting a smile. She was still getting used to the *DC*.

A male voice came down the line: deep, accentless. "Are you the right person to talk to about the bodies that have been found outside Lyme Regis?"

Tina straightened in her seat. "Yes. I'm with DCI Clarke, the SIO. We're on our way. Are you the attending pathologist?"

Tina waited for the DCI to speak. She didn't.

"I will be," the pathologist replied, "once I get out of this traffic jam. I just wanted to let you know I'm on my way."

"When do you expect to arrive?"

"Hang on… oi, you can't go there! Sorry, that was just… I'll be half an hour or so, but I really can't be sure."

"OK. Thanks."

He hung up.

The DCI looked at Tina. "Glad to hear we've got a pathologist with a bit of initiative."

"He's stuck in a traffic jam."

"I heard."

"Hopefully he'll be able to date these bodies, give us a more specific age."

"Hopefully."

The DCI slowed the car as they approached Lyme Regis. Tina felt the thrill of familiarity run across her skin. *Home.*

"OK," the boss said. "Give Mike a quick call, tell him and Stanley to look further back in the cold cases. If we can find something that might be a match, it'll help corroborate whatever the pathologist says."

"Yes, boss," Tina replied.

She dialled Mike's number as they passed the *Welcome to Lyme Regis* sign. She needed to bring him here, too. She'd like to show him where she'd grown up. But she wasn't ready to introduce him to her family. Not yet.

CHAPTER SIX

"So, lads," Dennis said. "What have you managed to find so far?"

Mike looked up from his desk.

"Not much I'm afraid, Sarge."

Dennis stood up and stretched his arms above his head. He'd been sitting for too long. He'd rather have gone to Lyme Regis with the boss. He could see the logic in taking Tina, but still... the most inexperienced member of the team, number two on a double murder inquiry?

He shook out his frustration and walked around to Mike's desk.

"Any unsolved cold cases?" he asked.

"Only one with two people involved." Mike pointed at his screen. "A couple. Edgar and Dorothy Williamson, went missing from Bournemouth six years ago. CID suspected their son had killed them, but they never found the bodies and weren't able to pin it to him."

Dennis wrinkled his nose. "That's a fair way from Lyme Regis. We've got nothing over in that direction?"

Stanley raised his head. "Can I make a suggestion, Sarge?"

"Go on."

"What about Devon? They might know more."

"Good idea," Dennis said. "Anything on the system?"

"Sorry, Sarge." Stanley's shoulders dropped.

"Very well," Dennis replied. "We need to get onto the Devon and Cornwall force. Find out if there's anything they know about that's not on the system. Stanley, given that you suggested it, can you make that call?"

"Yes, Sarge. Who do I need to speak to?"

Dennis frowned.

"I'll let the boss know. In fact," he said, feeling a shiver run across his skin, "I should probably run this past the super too. Devon and Cornwall might want in on this, given how close we are to their patch."

"It's not far at all," said Mike. "The beach at Lyme Regis is what, a couple of miles from the border with Devon?"

Border. Dennis smiled. It wasn't as if they were talking about an international border with customs officials and body searches before you crossed, although he'd met people who wouldn't have complained if the council had introduced such measures.

"Keep looking through the system," he said. "Try press reports as well as HOLMES. I'll speak to the super."

CHAPTER SEVEN

Tina directed Lesley to a car park on the road leading into Lyme Regis. They were high above the beach, the sea stretching out below them.

"So how far are we from where you grew up?" Lesley asked as they left the car.

"Not far. Mum's in Anning Way, down there." Tina pointed towards the town.

"Your mum still lives there?"

Tina smiled. "Moved in on her wedding night, she'll leave in a box. She loves it here."

Lesley wondered what it would be like to spend your entire adult life living between the same four walls. She'd had three addresses in the last year alone.

They walked to a gate leading to a pathway down to the beach. Lesley could see Charmouth in the distance, but Lyme Regis was obscured by a hedge.

"Is this where the bodies are?" she asked.

"It's the closest we're able to park," Tina told her.

She pushed open the gate and Lesley followed her down the path, which was followed by a steep flight of steps.

"You say your brother-in-law's already here?"

"He's with the CSIs."

Lesley nodded. How Gail had beaten them over here, she wasn't sure. But she was glad of it.

At the bottom of the steps a raised concrete walkway led in both directions, parallel with the beach and high above it. It wasn't what Lesley had been expecting.

"Not exactly scenic."

"It's not that kind of beach, at least not this section. It's shallow, the tide comes up a long way. They built these defences in 2013."

"I bet the locals loved that."

Tina sucked in a breath. "It was… controversial."

She turned left and Lesley followed. Beyond an ugly metal barrier, another flight of steps led down to the sands, concrete this time. Beyond that was a cordoned-off area. Figures moved around: three uniformed officers, and two white suited CSIs. *Good*.

At the bottom of the steps, Lesley strode ahead in front of Tina. The DC's local knowledge was useful, but she was the SIO.

The first PC she came to was a short woman with a shock of matted black hair. Lesley held out a hand.

"You must be PC Sharman."

The woman bobbed, almost as if in a curtsey.

"Yes, Ma'am. Are you DCI Clarke?"

Lesley raised her eyebrows.

"I am. Who's in charge?"

The PC gestured behind her. "Gail Hansford's the crime scene manager. And my sarge, PS Connor, he's keeping an eye on things for you."

An older man was approaching. He was slim, with thinning hair and a sergeant's badge. Lesley walked towards him.

"DCI Clarke," she said. "I've been sent over from Winfrith to head up the investigation."

"Sergeant Connor," he replied. "Glad to have you here, Ma'am." He looked past her at Tina. "And PC Abbott."

"DC Abbott. I passed the detectives' exam."

The sergeant's eyes widened. "Why didn't Dougie tell me? Well done, *DC* Abbott." He smiled, then looked back at Lesley, his smile disappearing. "Sorry, Ma'am."

"You don't have to *ma'am* me."

He frowned. "I'd rather... if you don't mind, Ma'am."

Lesley gritted her teeth. *Fair enough.*

"So what have we got?" she asked.

"Follow me, Ma... please."

He led her to the cordon and stopped.

"I'll brief you here. The less time we spend on the other side of this tape, the better."

"Is it still not safe?" Lesley asked.

She heard voices behind her. A uniformed PC was with Tina, their faces close together. Tina's brother-in-law?

"It's not, I'm afraid," Sergeant Connor told her. "We're not entirely happy about the CSIs being up there, but they insisted they need to examine the scene."

"What can you do to make it safer?" Lesley asked.

"There's a team already at the top of the cliff examining the land up there. They'll do an analysis, estimate how damp the ground is above the spot that's fallen. They'll try to work out the probability of it happening again."

"Is that common?"

"It can be. We don't want to take the risk."

"No."

Lesley watched the CSIs, wondering where the pathologist was. If the man was coming from Exeter, he should have beaten them.

"Gail!" she called out to her friend.

One of the two CSIs straightened up. She put her hands in the small of her back and stretched, then turned towards Lesley and waved. She walked carefully towards them, her footsteps hesitant and her eyes on the ground.

"Lesley," she said. "So they put you in charge?"

"They have," Lesley replied. "These bodies, they've been here a few years?"

Gail nodded.

"We're looking at their clothing. Watches, that kind of thing, trying to work out how old they are. The pathologist and the forensic archaeologist will be able to analyse the bodies themselves. Sergeant Connor doesn't know of any recent disappearances."

"Not just recent," said Connor. "I've worked from Lyme Regis station for thirty-two years and we don't have a single unsolved disappearance."

"That's a good record," Lesley said.

"Unsolved, Ma'am. I'm not saying people don't go missing around here. Just that we've found them all." He hesitated. "Normally at the bottom of the cliffs, after a high tide."

Lesley looked past him, towards the disturbed ground. "So they've been here longer than thirty-two years?"

Gail shook her head. "I think they've been preserved by the soil, but not that long. You're looking at a few years. But probably not a local disappearance."

"Great," Lesley said. "So we're looking for a cold mispers case, from anywhere outside Lyme Regis."

"Sorry," said Gail.

"It's fine." Lesley looked round at Tina. "We like a challenge, don't we?"

CHAPTER EIGHT

Gail had retreated beyond the cordon, and Lesley and Tina were watching, when Lesley heard movement behind them. She turned to see a tall, dark-haired man approaching. He wore a beanie hat and a fleece over a grey suit and carried a large holdall.

"Where do you need me?" he asked.

"I'm sorry?" Lesley replied.

"Sorry," he said, "I came here in a bit of a hurry. I'm Dr Bamford, the pathologist. Where are the...?" He looked ahead and spotted the CSIs in their white suits. "It's alright. I'll go and speak to the CSIs."

"Hang on a moment," Lesley said as he made for the cordon. "I'm DCI Clarke, SIO on this investigation. You might want to talk to me first."

He stopped and turned to her. "DCI Clarke." He held out a hand. "Er, oops. Looks like we got off on the wrong foot."

She shook his hand. "Hopefully we'll make up for it." She eyed him. Was this pathologist going to be like Henry Whittaker, brusque and rude, or Fiona Brightside, crisp and efficient?

He leaned back, smiling at her. "I haven't met you before. Did they send you from Exeter?"

"Winfrith. Dorset Major Crimes Investigation Team. We're still in Dorset, in case you hadn't—"

"So we are. That'll make things interesting."

"How so?"

"Well," he gestured at her, then the cordon, "what with…" He frowned. "It'll be fine. What have you got for me?"

"To be honest, DC Abbott and I have only just got here ourselves. Gail Hansford is the CSM, she tells us there are two bodies and that they've been there for some time."

He nodded. "How long?"

"I think that's for you to determine."

"Of course." He looked towards the CSIs.

"Are you going to head over there, then?" Lesley asked, sensing Tina shifting from foot to foot behind her.

"Er… yep, of course. After you." He held out a hand.

"I've been told to stay this side of the cordon." Lesley looked at Tina again. "But I want to observe. Tina, you stay here."

She pulled up the cordon and ducked beneath it. Up ahead, Gail's colleague grabbed her arm.

Gail turned. "It's not safe!"

Lesley pointed at Bamford. "I've got the pathologist with me. I'm the SIO, Gail, you have to let me observe."

Gail looked at her colleague, then at the ground behind her. Lesley could only see one of the bodies; the other was almost entirely obscured by earth.

"I'm sorry," Gail said, "I know you're impatient to take a look. But I can't let you up there until we get the all-clear from the guys on the clifftop."

"How long will that take?"

"It takes what it takes."

"But you're up there," said Dr Bamford. "Surely it's just as unsafe for you."

Gail shrugged. "We're restricting numbers. Look, I'll give them a call, see what the verdict is."

"Good." Lesley plunged her hands in her pockets. Gail gestured towards the cordon behind her and she retreated, Bamford following her.

"Is she always like this?" asked the doctor as they arrived back with Tina.

"Gail?" Lesley asked.

He was watching the CSM on her phone. "Yes."

"I thought you'd worked together before."

"A few years ago. She hasn't stopped ordering people about."

"Gail is careful. She's thorough. If she tells us what to do, it's because that's her job."

He shrugged. "It's not the first time I've examined a body on these cliffs. I do know what I'm doing." He eyed Lesley. "Have you ever even been here before?"

Lesley felt heat rise to her face.

"I grew up here," Tina said. "I know these cliffs like the back of my hand."

Lesley noticed Tina's accent had strengthened. It had been growing stronger since they'd arrived, but now, talking to the pathologist, she sounded like a proper local.

"Lesley!"

Lesley looked up to see Gail beckoning.

"It's safe?" she called.

"All-clear. Just you and the pathologist. And be careful."

"I'm always careful."

Gail said something unintelligible. Lesley lifted the cordon again and waited for the pathologist to go ahead.

"I've called Bea," he said. "She's a forensic anthropologist. If these bodies are as old as you reckon, then she'll be able to date them more accurately than I can."

"Bea?"

"Professor Beatrice Steadman. Imperial College London."

Lesley nodded. Hopefully they'd be able to match these bodies to a missing persons case, and the professor's help wouldn't be needed. But she appreciated the pathologist's initiative.

Gail approached them. "Dr Bamford. How are you?"

He gave her a thin smile. "Very well. And you?"

"Impatient to get you two out of here and reduce the risk of making the land slip again."

He shook his head. "It's dry today. The water's done its job. We'll be fine."

Gail grunted. Lesley wondered when she'd worked with the pathologist and what had happened between them.

"Anyway," Gail said. "We've got two bodies. Emerged following the landslip last night. My reckoning is that they've been there at least five years."

"I know," Bamford said, "I read your email."

Gail pursed her lips. "And you've contacted a forensic anthropologist?"

"I have."

So it had been Gail's idea, Lesley thought.

"Good," Gail said. "You'll need to be careful, the land still isn't steady. Really, we shouldn't be up here."

"I'll be fine," he replied. "I'll take a quick look, then we can remove the bodies."

"Yes," Gail replied. "Although, given that my jurisdiction is Dorset and yours is Devon…"

He laughed.

"Can we just get on with it?" Lesley asked.

Gail looked at her. "Sorry." She raised her eyebrows at Dr Bamford, who made for the bodies and crouched down. Lesley followed him.

"Well, Gail's right," he said. "They've been here some time. Advanced desiccation." He turned and called to Gail. "Do you know which section of cliff they started off in?"

"We won't be able to determine that until it's safe to go up there. My theory is that they were in dry soil, it preserved them."

Lesley looked at the first of the bodies. A few scraps of fabric clung to it, the remnants of clothes. The skin was remarkably well-preserved: dry and brown, but still holding the corpse together. The flesh had sunk and the form was little more than a skeleton encased in a leathery shell.

"One man and one woman?" she asked.

"Yes," Gail replied.

"You've removed the clothes?" asked the pathologist.

"There weren't many to remove."

He grunted and shuffled over to the second body. It was surrounded by rough earth and sand. One side of it was covered by earth, obscuring the side of the face, one leg and half of the torso. Clinging to it was the remains of what looked like a purple fleece.

"Can we determine what they looked like from these remains?" Lesley asked.

The pathologist shook his head. "It's not going to be easy. We can get a DNA analysis done, and look for dental records." He pointed to the mouth of the first body. "Teeth are still intact." He turned to her. "But with bodies that have been here this long, your best bet is going to be matching them to an old case."

"I know that," Lesley replied. It wasn't his job to tell her how to run her investigation. "Can you determine a cause of death?"

"Not from what I can see so far," he said. He cleared some of the soil away from the second body. "No sign of wounds, but with bodies this old, it's always going to be difficult to… Hang on a minute." He pushed more soil aside and leaned back. Lesley could see the other side of the second body now, including the neck.

"You see that?" he asked her.

"I do." Lesley swallowed.

The neck was twisted, the head skewed to one side. Beneath the shoulder she could make out an object. It looked like rusting metal.

The flesh of the neck itself had a wound. A neat hole in the side that had been obscured.

Lesley sucked in a breath. She looked at the first body; no corresponding wound.

Dr Bamford stood up. "I can't say for sure it's the cause of death until I've done the post-mortem," he said. "But at least one of this pair was stabbed."

CHAPTER NINE

Dennis knocked on Superintendent Carpenter's door and waited to be summoned. One advantage of being a DS was that he rarely had to deal directly with the superintendent. The last time he'd had to do so was during the investigation into DCI Mackie's death, and that hadn't gone well.

"Come in," came a voice.

Dennis cleared his throat, pulled his shoulders back, and opened the door. The super was sitting at his desk, a pile of paperwork in front of him. Dennis approached.

"DS Frampton," Carpenter said. "DCI Clarke not here today?"

"She's had to go to Lyme Regis. Two bodies were found after a landslip."

Carpenter nodded. "I heard about that. They've been there some time, yes?"

"At least five years."

A grunt. "So what do you need from me, then?"

"We've been looking into old case files," Dennis said. "We can't find anything that matches. Given that Lyme Regis is right on the boundary with Devon, it makes sense that we speak to Devon and Cornwall police, find out if they have any cold cases."

"You've not checked HOLMES?"

"We have, Sir. But sometimes, local knowledge can be more helpful."

Carpenter nodded. He closed the file that he'd been reading.

"Very well. I'll speak to my opposite number in Devon, get someone to give you a call."

"Thank you, Sir." Dennis backed away from the desk.

"One moment," Carpenter said. "How are you, DS Frampton?"

Dennis stiffened. "I'm fine, Sir. Busy on this case."

"You know I don't mean that. Your state of mind? You were seeing a… a psychologist?"

Dennis felt a flush work its way up his neck. "Yes."

"Still seeing the shrink?"

"We're down to once every three weeks now."

"Good. So you've been making improvements." It wasn't a question.

"I have, Sir."

Every muscle in Dennis's body felt taut. Discussing his mental health with the DCI had been bad enough, but with Carpenter…

"If that's all, Sir?"

"Yes." Carpenter opened the file again and waved Dennis away. "You'll get a call from Devon and Cornwall police, don't worry."

Dennis left the room, aware that he was sweating.

CHAPTER TEN

Lesley and Gail stood together, surveying the crime scene from the safety of the beach beyond the cordon. Gail shrugged her shoulders and shifted her weight between her feet.

"Kills your back, bending over like that for so long," she said.

Lesley looked at her. "Are you sure you're safe working up there?"

Gail shrugged. "Somebody's got to do it."

Lesley gazed up the hill. The pathologist was up there with his assistant, who'd arrived ten minutes earlier. Gail's colleague Brett watched on from just inside the cordon, and two uniformed officers were observing from the beach. A crew from the council with a digger had arrived on the beach. Lesley needed to find out what they were here for.

"The object that was below the victim's shoulder…" Lesley began.

"Brett's going to make sure it's disturbed as little as possible. If we can keep it intact, then we may be able to match it to the wound."

"It was rusted."

"We have cleaning solutions, didn't you hear?" Gail gave Lesley a nudge.

"Of course. I don't suppose you'll be able to get prints from it, though."

"It's unlikely, but you never know."

Lesley watched as the pathologist's assistant and Brett covered the first body in a protective bag.

"I need to get up there and help out," Gail said.

"Uniform can do it." Lesley gestured to Tina and pointed to the two Uniforms on the beach.

"No problem," Tina said and walked towards them.

Now that she and Gail were alone, Lesley could finally say what she'd been itching to. "So what's with you and Dr Bamford?" she asked. "The two of you don't seem to get on."

"Sorry, was it that obvious?"

There was a cry from up on the cliff. Lesley could see Brett shouting at Bamford's assistant.

"What the hell's going on up there?" she said.

"Brett's got it in hand. Maybe you shouldn't watch."

"I think I bloody well should. So… you and the pathologist? He pissed you off on an old case?"

"No. He's fine. Slow, like everyone over here, but he knows his stuff."

"He's good?"

"Bloody brilliant. He worked in Dorset until eight years ago, transferred to Devon, preferred the beaches there apparently."

Lesley scoffed. "What, like this one?"

"We're still in Dorset, remember?"

"True."

Gail put hands on her hips and twisted from side to side. "If you must know, I used to go out with him."

Lesley turned to her friend, forcing herself not to gasp. "You and him?"

"Don't tell Brett. It was before I met Bob, my ex. Not long after I qualified. It ended badly."

"So that explains the atmosphere between you."

Gail twisted from side to side. "I'll make sure it doesn't get in the way, Lesley. I'm sorry you noticed. It was unprofessional of me."

"Don't be daft. You're never anything short of professional."

Lesley watched the team up on the cliffs. The pathologist kept looking down at them. He was observing Gail, she realised.

She hoped this wouldn't cause problems.

"Shit," said Gail. "I think I'm going to need to get some physio."

"Your back giving you problems?"

"Yeah. Maybe it's my mattress. I don't know. Sorry, I'm getting distracted. But yes, if anybody's going to work out the cause of death on such tricky corpses, it'll be Gaz Bamford."

"Gaz?"

"Gareth."

"That's reassuring," Lesley replied. "Is it going to cause a problem him being from Devon?"

"No," Gail told her. "With anyone else it would. If it was Whittaker… but no, you're fine."

"The clothes," Lesley said. "The victim with the stab wound, the woman. She was wearing a fleece. Can you use those to help us get an ID?"

"We can try. If you're lucky, we'll be able to match the fibres to a manufacturer. If you're really lucky, there'll be an M&S label."

"I'm never that lucky."

"No."

41

The female victim's body was bagged up now and Brett was bringing it down the cliffs with the help of Bamford's assistant.

"I need to go up there again," Gail said. "Take a better look at that potential weapon."

Lesley nodded. "Bring it down, yes? And tell me if you find anything else."

"Of course."

CHAPTER ELEVEN

DI Hannah Patterson had been a DS in Dorset CID until five years ago, when she had moved to Devon for a promotion. Dennis vaguely remembered the woman. She was competent, if not outstanding.

"Ma'am," he said. "Thanks for calling. Do you have anything that could be pertinent to our investigation in Lyme Regis?"

"We might have," she replied. "Cold case six years ago, a couple who went out walking and never arrived at their destination."

Dennis frowned. That kind of thing happened in the Australian outback, or the Peruvian jungle. Not on the South West coastal path.

"They never arrived?" he asked.

"The Coastguard scoured the beaches below the path, and the cliffs, but never found anything. They didn't arrive at the B&B they'd booked for the next night and they didn't make contact with their families. We assumed that they must have fallen into the sea and been washed out."

That made little sense. People who drowned were invariably washed in by the tide, not washed out. But a cold case with two bodies six years ago... It could be a match.

"Are you able to send me the details?" he asked.

"There's a problem," she replied.

Dennis felt his chest slump.

"What kind of a problem?"

"I'm sorry, DS Frampton. This is above my paygrade, but the politics of the situation. I'm sure you understand…"

"No, Ma'am," he replied. "I really don't understand. What's the problem?"

"My bosses want me brought into this investigation to work alongside your DCI."

Dennis clutched his phone tighter. "Really?"

"Sorry."

"And I won't be given access to your cold case file unless we do this?"

"Not my decision, Sergeant."

"As you know, my DCI is the SIO. It's not for me to decide who's a member of the investigating team."

"Above your paygrade too?" she chuckled.

It's not funny. Dennis took a breath.

"I'll speak to my DCI," he told her. "In the meantime, I'd be grateful if you could send me the case files."

"Sorry, mate," she said.

Dennis bristled at the *mate*.

"I can't do that until we've sorted out this problem."

Problem, he thought. Why couldn't people just do their job?

"Very well," he told her. "I'll speak to my DCI. Hopefully, we'll be able to come to a solution."

CHAPTER TWELVE

Lesley plunged her phone into her pocket and sped up. She and Tina were walking across the car park of Lyme Regis police station.

"Everything alright, boss?" Tina asked.

Lesley grunted. "That was Dennis. Devon police are being a pain in the arse."

"How?"

"They've got a cold case, a couple who went missing six years ago on the coastal path. They're not sending us the file unless we bring one of their DI's into the investigation."

Lesley looked at Tina, who was nodding slowly. "Her name's DI Patterson. Heard of her?"

"Sorry, boss," Tina said. "I've not had any dealings with the Devon and Cornwall force."

Lesley sighed. Bringing in another force would complicate things. It would annoy Carpenter, she knew.

But the reality was, the crime scene was less than three miles from the boundary with Devon. There was a good possibility that evidence would turn up on the other side of that line. Maybe it would make sense to involve this woman.

"I'll need to speak to the super," she said. "I can't see any problem with it, but…"

Tina gave her a look. "You think the super won't approve?"

Lesley put her hand on the door to the police station. She pulled it open and gestured for Tina to go in first.

"To be honest, Tina," she replied, "I have no bloody idea what Superintendent Carpenter will say."

Tina smiled and went inside, glad she didn't have to deal with inter-force politics.

Inside, a young man with neat, dark hair and a face that looked as if it had been battered by the elements was waiting for them.

"PC Anderson," Lesley said. "Thanks for meeting us."

"No problem, Ma'am."

"I need to know more about what you and your colleague discovered this morning," she said. "Can we have a chat?"

"Of course, Ma'am. I'll fetch Wendy. We can use cell number two."

"A cell?" Lesley asked. "Surely you've got a meeting room."

His jaw tightened. "Sorry, Ma'am, meeting room's having work done. There was a leak in the roof. Only private space is the cells and the first one's occupied."

Lesley glanced at Tina, who shrugged.

"Fair enough," she told him. "Lead me to your cells."

Lesley was about to follow the PC through to the cells when the door behind them opened, and a woman flew in.

"Tina!" she cried, flinging herself at the DC.

Tina turned and caught the woman. "Mum!" She pushed her away. "I'm working."

The woman let go of her daughter and turned to Lesley. "You must be DCI Clarke, I've heard all about you."

"You have, have you?" Lesley gave Tina a smile and held out a hand.

"Oh, I don't do handshakes." Tina's mum leaned in for a hug. Lesley stiffened as the woman wrapped her arms around her. At last, she pulled away.

"Stay at my house," she urged. "Tina, you know your room's always there for you, And DCI Clarke. You can sleep in Naomi's old room."

"It's fine," Lesley said. "We'll be making our way back to HQ after we've—"

"Oh no, you won't." Mrs Abbott gave her daughter a stern look. "My Tina hasn't been home for nearly six months. I'm not letting her go now."

"Mum," Tina said, her voice low. "Just let me do my job. I'll talk to you when we've finished here." She hesitated. "If there's time."

"Time? There'd better be time." Mrs Abbott gave Lesley a stern look. "I expect you to release her for an hour to come and see her mum."

"I'll see what I can do. Now, if you don't mind…"

"Annie," PC Anderson said. "Why don't I get someone to make you a cup of tea and you can wait here?"

"You'll come and find me, when you're done?" the woman asked Tina.

"Yes, Mum." Tina didn't make eye contact.

"You'd better. It's been too long, and I want to know why."

Tina took a step away from her mum. Lesley noticed that she hadn't once looked the other woman in the eye.

It was none of her business.

47

"Come on, DC Abbott. We've got a case to work on. Very nice to meet you, Mrs Abbott."

"Likewise." Tina's mum beamed at Lesley as a uniformed PC appeared from a doorway and led her to a chair.

Tina turned away from them and pushed open the door they'd been about to enter. "Sorry, boss." She pulled the door closed as soon as Lesley and PC Anderson were through.

"She's just worried about you, Tina," PC Anderson said.

"I know. And I'll thank you not to get involved."

"I got her off your back, didn't I?"

"She's going to be sitting in your reception drinking that cup of tea for hours."

"Unless you go and talk to her."

Lesley put a hand on the DC's shoulder. "I can spare you for half an hour."

Tina looked up at her, her forehead wrinkled. "Can you?"

"Of course. She's your mum."

"OK. Thanks." She looked at the PC. "Not yet, though. Dougie, let's get on with this chat."

CHAPTER THIRTEEN

Elsa Short was about to leave the office when there was a knock on her door. She looked up and gestured for her visitor to come in.

Aurelia Cross, her partner in the firm of Nevin, Cross and Short, took the chair opposite her. She leaned back, her arms resting on the chair arms, her fingers splayed. She was the picture of relaxation.

Elsa knew Aurelia better than to trust that body language. Something was wrong.

"What is it?" she asked.

Aurelia gave her a wry smile. "Who's to say I'm not just coming in for a friendly chat?"

Elsa checked her watch. "It's quarter past six, you're normally gone for the day by now."

"That predictable, am I?"

"I'm a lawyer, Aurelia. I'm paid to notice detail. You leave here at five to six on the dot every day. You go and visit your mother."

Aurelia tensed. She sat up in her chair and frowned.

"How do you know that?"

"Harry told me."

Harry Nevin had been murdered by his mistress six months ago. Lesley had been the senior investigating officer and it had been more than awkward given that

49

Elsa and Lesley's relationship had been in its infancy at the time.

"I'm sorry," she continued. "Was he not supposed to have told me?"

Aurelia sighed. "It's no secret. It's just something I prefer not to talk about in the office."

"OK." Elsa surveyed the other woman. "I was about to head home. What can I help you with?"

"I don't imagine you're in a hurry to get home. Your girlfriend's over in Lyme Regis."

"How do you know that?"

A smile. "I keep my eye on things. Anyway, I wanted to talk to you about your special client." Aurelia raised her fingers in air-quotes.

"My 'special client'?"

Elsa knew exactly who Aurelia was referring to. They didn't like to mention Arthur Kelvin by name. He brought in a lot of money for the firm, but Elsa knew that one day he'd also bring a lot of trouble. She'd been trying to extricate herself from her role as his lawyer since Harry had died and handed over the reins, but it was proving tricky.

"You told me you were making progress," Aurelia said.

"On what?"

"You know." Aurelia looked back towards the door.

"We shouldn't be talking about this here."

Elsa pulled her bag out from under her desk and placed it on her knees. She started piling paperwork into it, hoping Aurelia would get the hint.

"Are you going to be more specific?" Aurelia asked.

Elsa paused, her hand inside her bag. "Not yet," she told her colleague. "I'll tell you when I'm ready."

"You'd damned well better," Aurelia said. "I'm not having this firm dragged through the mud. It was bad enough when Harry died."

"Are we any closer to finding another named partner?" Elsa asked.

"It's not easy. Deciding not to promote an existing junior partner reduces our scope somewhat. Bournemouth isn't exactly heaving with people we can trust right now." She leaned forward. "Which is why I need you to hurry things along."

Elsa nodded. She knew that it would be easier for the firm to find a new partner when her *special client* was no longer on their books. There were things Harry had done for the man that would be preferable not to tell a newcomer about.

Elsa stood up. She slung her bag over her shoulder.

"Well, if that's all?"

Aurelia stood and looked into her eyes.

"Keep me updated," she said. "Yes?"

"Of course." Elsa gave her a pleasant smile.

Aurelia grunted and turned to leave the room.

CHAPTER FOURTEEN

"So you didn't see anybody up there, after the landslip?" Lesley asked PC Anderson.

He sat across the cell from them, in a scuffed wooden chair, his colleague PC Sharman beside him. Their voices echoed in the cell and Lesley was shivering. Somebody had brought in a fan heater and it was struggling to fill the space with warm air.

"No, Ma'am," said PC Anderson. "There was nobody up there. It was early, and the weather wasn't good." He looked at PC Sharman, who nodded.

"Still," Lesley said, "I imagine you get walkers up there at all times of day in all weathers."

"Generally, yes," PC Sharman said. "But not on a Wednesday in March."

Lesley nodded. "Normally we'd be looking for evidence of someone having been up there recently."

"But with the bodies having been there so long…" Tina added.

Lesley looked at her. "Yes. But there is a chance that whoever originally buried them might have gone back. If they'd known there'd been a landslip, they might want to check it hadn't dislodged the bodies."

"And it did," PC Anderson said.

"It wouldn't have been possible for someone to move them, with them having slid so far. I'd like to know if anyone was seen up there. Who reported the landslip?"

"Samuel Waller," PC Anderson replied. "He lives towards Charmouth, there's a clear view of the Spittles from his front windows."

"Good," Lesley said. "We'll need to talk to him."

"He's a bit... odd."

Lesley raised an eyebrow. "Odd doesn't phase me, Constable."

"No." Anderson glanced at Tina in what looked like a conspiratorial way.

Tina's phone rang.

"Do you mind if I...?"

"Take it." Lesley wondered if it would be the DC's mum, checking when she'd be home for her tea.

"Detective Constable Abbott," Tina said, emphasising the 'Detective'. Lesley smiled: four months in CID and Tina was still proud of her achievement.

Tina nodded. She put her free hand on the table and tapped it with her fingertips.

"Yes, Sarge," she said. "Do you want to speak to the boss?"

Lesley put out a hand, waiting for the phone to be handed to her.

"Oh, OK." Tina put her phone down and turned to Lesley.

"That was the sarge."

"I gathered that, what's happened?"

"The super's given his OK for us to bring DI Patterson in."

"Good. And?"

"She'll be here in the morning."

Lesley looked at her watch: 6pm. "Looks like we're staying over, then."

Tina shifted in her chair. "My mum'll be over the moon."

"Hmm." Lesley wondered whether it would be rude to book herself into a hotel instead.

Yes. It would. And Annie Abbott had been very welcoming.

"Call your mum, Tina. Looks like we'll be here a while."

"Will do. The good news is that DI Patterson's bringing the case file with her."

Lesley clenched a fist. "She's not sending it over?"

"Sorry."

Lesley shook her head. "What's this woman's phone number? If we can go over the file tonight, it'll give us a head start in the morning."

"I'll get it for you."

"Good." Lesley stood up and looked at the two constables. "Can one of you make contact with Mr Waller, tell him we'll be coming to see him in the morning."

"Will do," said PC Sharman. "He's an early riser."

"Good. Maybe we can chat to him before our Devon friend turns up."

CHAPTER FIFTEEN

Dennis, Mike and Stanley sat in the DCI's office. Mike and Stanley had been reconstructing the Devon case from press clippings and what they could glean from HOLMES. Stanley was pinning photos to the board: the two missing people. They were still trying to find out more about them, including an exact address and details for next of kin. But they did know where the couple had last been seen, thanks to the local press.

Dennis perched on the edge of one of the two chairs opposite the DCI's desk, Mike beside him and Stanley at the board. No one had taken the DCI's chair.

"So," Stanley began. "This couple. David and Carmela Stubbs. They went missing from Axminster almost exactly six years ago."

"Almost to the day," Mike added.

Stanley wrote on the board. "Six years and four days ago. Do we think it's relevant?"

"It's not," Dennis answered. "The landslip is what dislodged them. No one could have predicted that."

"But what if someone went up there, caused the landslip?" Mike suggested.

Dennis scratched his cheek. "It's a possibility. But why six years and four days? Why not go back on the six-year anniversary?"

"Six years and four days is when they were last seen," Stanley pointed out. "It might not be the date they were killed. Or when they were buried."

"Let's not get ahead of ourselves," Dennis said. "We don't even know if it's the same couple yet."

"Hell of a coincidence," said Mike, paling when he caught Dennis's look.

Dennis surveyed the board. Tina and the CSIs had sent photos from the crime scene. Close-ups of the bodies, and some more distant shots of the landslip. It was a big one.

"OK," he said. "So walk me through what we know about this case."

Stanley touched the photo of the missing couple with his pen. It was black and white, taken from a newspaper. "They were last seen on the third of March. He didn't turn up for work the next day, and she was expected at a church meeting that evening."

"How long before they were reported missing?"

"Four days," Mike said. "His employer assumed he was off sick, and her church group... it was voluntary, so I guess they weren't too worried."

"And we're getting all this from the local press?"

"No case file yet," said Mike.

"No." Dennis wrinkled his nose. "We have to consider that the story we're piecing together from press reports might not be entirely accurate."

"Probably isn't," snorted Mike.

"Not necessarily," Dennis said. "This is the Dorset Echo, not the national press reporting on a missing celebrity."

"No reason for them to make stuff up," added Stanley.

"No," agreed Dennis. "But they may not have had access to all the information."

Stanley let his pen fall. "It's all we've got to go on, Sarge."

"I know. And it's a start. I just wish Devon and Cornwall Police were being more helpful."

The two DCs said nothing.

"Right." Dennis shook himself out mentally. They didn't need a case file to start piecing together the disappearance of the Stubbs couple. "So they were last seen on the third, then reported missing four days later. Was a search conducted?"

"Not until the sixth day," Stanley said. "They were adults, low risk."

"What kind of search?"

"We can't be sure," Mike said. "I've found a couple of photos on Facebook, but there isn't much detail of how big the search was, or where it covered."

"No. Do we know who the police interviewed?"

"Not the police," said Mike. "But the newspapers did interview a neighbour."

"Go on."

"Elsie Timmins, next door neighbour. She talked about unusual activity in her road two days before they went missing. Cars going back and forth."

"Relevant, or just a witness trying to make herself more important to the press?"

Mike shrugged. "We won't know until we have interview transcripts."

"How far was their home from where the bodies were found?"

"Six miles," Stanley said. "I've got a map."

He pinned up a map on the board. It showed the location of the bodies on the Spittles, plus an address in Axminster that had been circled.

"So, did the police, or the media, talk to anybody further afield? Family, friends?"

"Not that we know of," Mike said. "We've got these news reports, the interview with the neighbour, and lots of speculation. It petered out after about a week."

"Not surprised," Dennis said. "Two adults going missing, nobody bats an eyelid."

"There's no record of them turning up anywhere," Stanley said. "I've trawled through the local papers, can't find any mention of them after the dates they disappeared."

"Electoral register? DVLA?"

"Nothing."

"Hmm. So David and Carmela Stubbs never resurfaced, as far as we know. It certainly sounds like it might be the same couple."

"Hell of a coincidence," repeated Mike, forgetting himself.

Dennis gave him a look.

"Sorry, Sarge."

"Right," Dennis said, "I'll call the DCI and let her know what we have so far. Then we'll need to wait until she's spoken to the Devon and Cornwall force. I think that's all we can do for today."

"Sarge." Mike nodded and closed his laptop.

"Thanks, Sarge," said Stanley.

Dennis watched the two DCs file out of the room. He stood up from his chair, his eyes on the board. They didn't have enough. A few snippets from social media, some press cuttings... nothing. He hoped that the Devon police would be cooperative, and the boss would be able to find out more than he'd managed.

CHAPTER SIXTEEN

Lesley walked out of the police station. The building was situated in a side road, half a mile from the sea. She could hear seagulls and smell the tang of salt.

She wondered what it would be like to grow up somewhere like this, within spitting distance of the water. Surrounded by people who knew your business.

She needed to make a call. She leaned against her car and dialled.

"DCI Clarke. Have you got news for me?"

"I was hoping you might have an update for me," she told him.

"Sorry," replied Matt, "I haven't heard from her recently."

Matt Crippins was a producer at the local BBC TV station. He was the manager of Sadie Dawes, local reporter and sometime thorn in Lesley's side.

"You really haven't heard from her?" she asked Matt. "How long has it been?"

"A month."

"Surely if somebody doesn't turn up to work in that long, you start disciplinary proceedings?"

"Things are a bit different with Sadie."

Sadie had been investigating the death of DCI Mackie, Lesley's predecessor. A death that the coroner had declared a suicide. She'd claimed to have information, then gone to ground. Sadie had done this before. She'd gone AWOL before Christmas, then popped back up again. Lesley still didn't know what had brought her back.

"I can imagine." Lesley sniffed. "So do you need to open another missing persons investigation?"

"Shit, no," he said. "Sadie told us to leave her alone, she's working on something and it'll be big."

Lesley dug her fingernails into the palm of her hand. That's what she was worried about.

"Have none of your team heard from her?"

"Not that they're telling me."

"You keep secrets from each other?"

"No, DCI Clarke. Stop judging us."

"I'm not judging anybody. I'm just worried."

He laughed. "You don't need to worry about Sadie, she's done worse than this in the past."

"If she turns up," she told him, "I'd like to know."

Silence.

"Matt, are you still there?"

"Thinking."

"About what?"

"Considering whether I'll tell you if she turns up."

Lesley turned so she was facing away from the station. She thumped the roof of her car. "You had us open a missing persons case for her last time, Matt. If she turns up, you need to let us know." She chewed her lip. "Because if she doesn't, then we might just suspect you of having something to do with her disappearance."

CHAPTER SEVENTEEN

Tina's mum hovered next to Lesley as she guided her into the living room.

"DCI Clarke," she said, "take a seat. I'll make you a cup of tea."

"Coffee, please," Lesley told her, perching on the end of a long sofa. "And you can call me Lesley."

Tina turned to look at her boss. The DC opened her mouth, but said nothing. Lesley raised an eyebrow at her.

"The boss likes her coffee strong, with milk, Mum," said Tina. "I'll help you."

"It's OK," Lesley told them. "You don't have to wait on me, I'm not visiting royalty."

Annie gave her a look. "You're a very important woman in my daughter's life. Without you, I don't think she'd have passed the CID exam."

"That's not true," Lesley said, wishing she hadn't sat down now. She felt at a disadvantage with the two of them standing over her. "Tina's a very capable police officer. She'd have passed the detective's exam, with or without me."

Annie looked from Tina to Lesley. "You're a positive role model, DCI Clarke."

"Please," Lesley said, "it's Lesley. And you too, Tina, if we're going to be staying together here, I don't want any of this boss, Ma'am or DCI business. Call me Lesley within these four walls."

Annie gave a nod and quietly left the room, leaving Lesley and Tina to continue their conversation.

"You sure, boss?"

Lesley cocked her head. "What did I just tell you?"

"Are you sure, *Lesley*?" Tina blushed. "It just doesn't feel right, boss. I've never known a senior officer ask me to call them by their first name."

"Well, I'm not your average senior officer, am I?"

"That's certainly true," laughed Tina.

Lesley stood up, brushing down her skirt. "Is it indeed?"

Tina's flush crept further up her face.

"Oh God, boss. No, I'm sorry. I didn't mean…"

Lesley put her hand on her shoulder.

"It's alright, Tina. You can relax."

She looked around the room. It was cosy, filled with photographs of Tina and her sister, as well as some old wedding photographs, she assumed of Tina's mum and dad. She wondered where Mr Abbott was, but wasn't about to ask.

"It's a nice home your mum's got," she said. "And it's very kind of her to put us up."

Annie appeared at the door with two mugs. "Here you are DCI… Lesley." She placed one on a side table. "Strong with milk. If that's not right, you can blame Tina."

"Thanks, Annie." Lesley picked up the coffee and drank. It had been a long day, she needed the boost.

She also needed to speak to Elsa.

"Do you mind showing me where my room is?" she asked.

"I'll do it," said Tina. "Mum, stop fussing."

62

Annie gave her daughter a nervous smile. "Just trying to create a good impression, love."

"You're creating the impression that I come from a family of paranoid idiots."

Lesley laughed. "Oh, I know what that feels like."

Tina looked at her but said nothing.

"So, do you have any family?" Annie asked, standing in the doorway.

"A daughter," Lesley told her. "And a girlfriend."

A shadow briefly crossed Annie's face. "That's nice," she said, her voice uncertain. "Does she live in Birmingham?"

"My daughter does. Sharon's seventeen, in the sixth form. She's talking about moving down here after the summer."

"That would be lovely," Annie told her.

Lesley nodded. It would be good to have Sharon with her, but she still hadn't researched the schools. She didn't want Sharon compromising her future.

"And what about your... your partner?" Annie asked.

"My girlfriend lives in Bournemouth, with me. We've got a nice flat, not far from the sea."

It was the first time Lesley had referred to Elsa's flat as her own. It still didn't come naturally, and with the tension between the two of them right now...

"Anyway," she said, downing the last of her coffee, "if you don't mind showing me to my room?"

"Of course," said Annie. "Tina, you do the honours."

"Follow me, boss."

"Ahem."

"Sorry, Lesley." Tina shook her head. "I'm never going to get used to that, boss. Please don't make me do it."

"Try. It'll make me feel a bit more relaxed while I'm here."

"It won't be long, surely?" Tina asked. "We'll go back to the crime scene tomorrow, meet with DI Patterson, and then head back to the office."

"I wouldn't be so sure," Lesley told her. The two of them mounted the stairs, their voices echoing in the narrow hallway. "Cases like this have a habit of turning out more complicated than you think."

CHAPTER EIGHTEEN

Tina sat in her usual spot on the sofa and stared at the TV. It was as if the last five years had never happened. Sitting on her mum's settee, feet up, blanket over her knees, cup of tea in front of her, and EastEnders on the telly.

Her mum walked in with her own cup and sat down beside her. She placed a hand on her knee.

"How was Naomi?"

Tina smiled. "Happy. Tired, but happy. The baby's cute."

"Babies tend to be cute," her mum replied. "The pair of them aren't getting much sleep, but that's par for the course. I remember you, kept me up every night for six months."

Tina shifted her knee out from under her mum's grip. "If I had a quid for every time you told me that story…" She felt her stomach rumble and stopped talking.

Her mum laughed. "I like to remember you when you were little. I miss you. It's a long way to Winfrith."

Tina took a sip of her tea. On the screen, two people yelled at each other. Tina hadn't watched EastEnders for a while. It didn't change.

"How's that new boyfriend of yours?" her mum asked.

"Not so new," Tina replied. "We've been together for four months now, Mum."

"You think it'll last?"

Tina gritted her teeth. *All the questions.* "I hope so."

"You think it might not?"

"That's not what I said."

Annie had a way of bending what Tina said, catastrophising every situation.

"So is there any particular reason you hope it lasts?"

"No, Mum."

Tina bent over, turning her back to her mum and placing her mug on the table beside her. She stared into a photo of herself from 2004. Ten years old, wearing her school uniform with her hair brushed to within an inch of its life.

"No reason at all. Everything's fine. Mike's lovely."

"Good," her mum said. "I'd like to meet him."

Tina turned to her mum. "You might do on this case. If he needs to come down here."

Her mum raised an eyebrow. "I don't want to meet him because he's got work requirements in Lyme Regis love. I want to meet him because you bring him round. Come for a weekend, stay here."

Tina glanced up at the ceiling. She could hear the boss moving around in the bedroom above. How would Mike feel about staying in this house? The walls were thin, the beds lumpy. For Tina, it was home. But she wasn't so fond of it that she couldn't picture it through someone else's eyes. She wondered what the DCI was making of it.

"I'll ask him, Mum," she said.

Mike would have to visit Lyme Regis, would have to get to know her family. She owed it to her mum and her sister.

She leaned back on the sofa. EastEnders was finishing, a cookery programme coming on.

"It's nice to be here, Mum," she said.

"It's nice to have you." Her mum gestured upwards towards the ceiling. "What's she like?"

"She's got a name."

"What's Lesley like?"

Tina laughed. "I can't get used to calling her that, even if we're sleeping under the same roof."

"She's got a girlfriend?" Annie asked.

"Yes, Mum." Tina felt a note of exasperation creep into her voice. "Her name's Elsa. She seems OK, she's a lawyer."

Annie put her mug down and stood up.

"No business of mine," she said. "I just hope she treats you well, is all. Not many women at her level in the police force."

"Mum, this is the twenty-first century."

"Only saying. Just make sure she treats you well."

Tina watched her mum leave the room. She didn't have much control over how the DCI treated her, that was up to the DCI. But so far, the boss *had* treated her well. She knew she wouldn't have made detective without the other woman's encouragement.

Would that continue now she was a permanent member of the team, or would she just be one of the lads? She'd have to fit in.

She leaned back and let the TV wash over her. Tomorrow would be an early start, she should go to bed. But for now, sitting here, reliving her youth on her mum's sofa, she was happy enough.

CHAPTER NINETEEN

Lesley cupped her hand over her phone. This house was small, and the walls were thin. She didn't like the thought of Tina's mum listening in on her conversation.

After three rings, the call was picked up.

"Hey."

"Hi Els," Lesley said. "Everything OK? Did you get my text?"

"You're in Lyme Regis, overnight stay."

Elsa's voice was stiff.

"Look," Lesley said, "About the conversation the other night—"

"Stop," Elsa interrupted. "I don't want to go over it again."

"But we need to," Lesley replied. "I don't want this getting between us."

There was a sigh at the other end of the phone. "It's just work. Why can't we ignore it? Pretend it doesn't exist."

Lesley leaned back against the pillows. They were pink and floral.

"We can't ignore our work, Els. I'm a detective, you're a lawyer. We come into contact too often."

"We both agreed we'd be professional when we started this," Elsa said.

"I know, but this is different."

"It's not. I'm sorting it."

Lesley swallowed. "You told me that months ago."

"I really am this time. I've spoken to Aurelia. I've got a plan."

"Do you want to share it with me?"

"Just let me do it and I'll tell you when it's over."

Lesley ran a hand through her hair. Since she'd discovered that Elsa had been in contact with her predecessor DCI Mackie, there'd been a tension in their relationship. She'd tried to discuss it with her girlfriend, find out what was going on. Elsa was cagey, citing client privilege and refusing to provide more details. But DCI Mackie wasn't Elsa's client. He would have been a retired detective, perhaps a witness on a historic case she was defending. Why couldn't Elsa share that with her?

"Do you trust me, Lesley?" Elsa asked.

Lesley gripped the phone harder. "Yes," she said, after a moment's hesitation.

"You don't, do you?"

"I do," Lesley replied. "I'm sorry, I do, honest."

A grunt. "Good. You'll trust me to sort this out then. Let me know when you'll be back, yeah?"

"Of course."

"Where are you staying?"

Lesley smiled and glanced towards the door.

"Tina Abbott's mum's house."

"Fancy!"

Lesley laughed. "And get this: it's on Anning Way."

"Are all the roads named after Mary Anning?"

"Just this one."

"Next thing, you'll be telling me the crime took place in Ichthyosaur Street."

"Not far off," Lesley replied. "The crime scene is the cliffs where those ichthyosaurs were found."

"I've seen it on the news," Elsa said. "A landslip."

"They uncovered two bodies," Lesley told her. "We still don't know who they are, or how long they've been up there."

"So you could be there a while?"

"I hope not." Lesley sighed. "I'll be going to Exeter in the morning, speak to the forensic anthropologist. Hopefully they'll help us get to the bottom of this."

CHAPTER TWENTY

Elsa hung up, her stomach clenching. She hadn't noticed that she had been twisting her hair through her fingers. She winced as she extricated them.

She didn't like talking to Lesley about her work. She'd known there'd be risks if she got involved with a police detective. But with what she was planning right now... she hardly dared think about it, let alone talk to her girlfriend.

She plunged her phone into her pocket and raised her arms above her head. She'd been leaning against the kitchen island during the call, twisted at an angle that made her shoulders ache. She needed air.

She left the flat, hurrying down the stairs and towards the beach. It was quiet. Early spring, nine in the evening. Chilly, too; she should have stopped to grab a jacket. A distant dog walker tugged on his dog's lead about a hundred metres away, but apart from that, there was nobody.

Even so, she didn't want to risk being overheard.

She jumped down to the sand and walked towards the sea's edge. Swallowing, she pulled the phone out of her pocket, dialling before she had a chance to think too hard.

"Elsa," came a familiar male voice. "Why haven't you been answering my calls?"

"Sorry, Arthur," she said. "Things have been a bit hectic in the office lately, what with us still having just two partners."

Arthur Kelvin. Her least favourite client. The man no one in her firm apart from her and Aurelia ever got the chance to meet.

"That's not my problem, is it? I need to talk to you about that *favour* you said you'd do for me."

She shivered, turning her back to the sea. The dog walker had disappeared and there was no one in sight.

"Arthur," she said, "You know I don't feel comfortable about this."

"I don't give a fuck what you feel. You're my lawyer and you're paid to do as I tell you."

"Well, that's not entirely—"

"Just fucking do it."

She hesitated. She'd known her answer before making the call. She wouldn't have made it otherwise. "OK."

"The case file on Bobby Henderson," he said. "That's the one."

"I know," she told him. "Leave it with me."

He grunted. "There's something else I've been meaning to ask you about."

"Go on." She felt damp lick at the back of her foot. She edged forwards, further up the beach. "What is it?"

"You heard of a journalist called Sadie Dawes?"

Elsa frowned. She turned to walk along the sea's edge. "Sadie Dawes?"

"You heard me. BBC. Been asking questions she shouldn't be."

"What kind of questions?"

"I'll worry about that, you worry about that file. You sure you haven't come across this Sadie woman before? She's not been onto your firm, sniffing around there?"

"Definitely not," Elsa replied.

She knew the name. The journalist had gone missing before Christmas. Lesley had been looking for her, and then she'd suddenly stopped. Elsa wondered if that was connected with Sadie asking questions about Arthur Kelvin's business.

She paused. The dog walker was back, heading in her direction. Elsa turned away from him, making her way up the beach.

"I'll let you know when it's done," she said.

"Send me a text. Do it quickly, yeah?"

"Tomorrow," she told him.

Not waiting for a response, she hung up and stared at her phone. She had an urge to fling it into the sea. Instead, she clutched it in her hand and walked back to the flat, glad that Lesley wasn't waiting for her.

CHAPTER TWENTY-ONE

Lesley and Tina were up early, but not as early as Annie. The woman was already in the kitchen when Lesley descended, breakfast laid out on the table.

Lesley surveyed it: toast in a rack, a jug of milk, pots of jam and marmalade, butter in a butter dish. All on a practical PVC-coated gingham cloth.

It felt like she'd been transported back in time.

"This is very kind of you," she said. "But I really haven't got time for breakfast."

Annie raised an eyebrow. "There's always time for breakfast," she replied. "I know what your job's like, running around all day, never getting time to eat. Tina was a nightmare when she was in Uniform. Sit down, eat some toast. It'll only take you five minutes."

Lesley stared back at the woman and then down at the table. She checked her watch. She could spare five minutes, and there was no sign of Tina yet. She pulled out a chair and grabbed a slice of toast.

"I've got filter coffee, too," Annie said. "None of that instant rubbish. Do you want a cup?"

"Please," Lesley replied, trying not to spit out toast crumbs.

She watched as Tina's mum poured coffee from a filter machine and placed a mug on the table. She stood back against the sink, arms folded, eyes narrowed.

"I hope you won't be expecting Tina to go up on those cliffs."

Lesley shook her head. She took a few chews then swallowed her toast.

"I can't talk to you about the details of the investigation."

Annie scoffed. "I'm not a suspect, you know. I'm Tina's mum. I just want to keep her safe."

"I know," Lesley said. "But we conduct risk assessments, we're very careful."

A snort. "Risk assessments, my arse. I know those cliffs, I know how dangerous they are. Those bodies getting moved. How far did they go?"

"We're not sure yet," Lesley told her. "The CSIs and the engineers are still investigating. But really, I shouldn't be talking about this with you."

"Investigating." Annie cocked her head. "You got any locals working on it?"

"The engineers are from Taunton."

"That's not local. People who live here, they know those cliffs like the veins on the backs of their hands. Ask them, they'll tell you what happened."

Lesley heard footsteps behind her and turned to see Tina in the doorway.

"Mum. I told you we just needed coffee. We haven't got time for all this." She waved her hand at the table.

Annie reached behind her and grabbed a tinfoil-wrapped parcel. "I took the liberty of making you toast and jam. You can eat it in the car on the way to wherever you're going. Lesley here says she's going to keep you safe."

Tina rolled her eyes. "Of course she's going to keep me safe, Mum."

"Good. Right." Annie clapped her hands. "I imagine you two have work to do, I'll see you later."

She stepped towards Tina and pulled the young woman in for a kiss. Tina looked over her mum's shoulder at Lesley, shrugging. Lesley smiled. Would she be like this with her own daughter one day?

CHAPTER TWENTY-TWO

Samuel Waller lived in a squat, detached house on the edge of Charmouth. The gutters were rusting, and the front windows looked all but rotted through. Lesley was amazed the whole structure hadn't tumbled down the cliff.

She stood back as Tina knocked on the door.

"Do you know him?" she asked the DC while they waited.

Tina shrugged. "I've met him a couple of times. But I wouldn't say I know him. He's got a bit of a reputation, though."

The door opened and Tina clamped her lips shut. An elderly man stared at them. He had thinning hair that straggled over his ears and pale, rheumy eyes.

"What do you want?"

Lesley held up her ID. "I'm DCI Clarke, this is DC Abbott. We're investigating two bodies found after the landslip that you reported over on the cliffs."

"The Spittles?" he said, staring at her with an eyebrow raised.

"That's correct," Lesley replied. "Can we come in, please?"

"S'pose so."

He stood back and let them pass, waving his arm towards the door at the back. He smelled of stale urine and dog hair.

"Go in the dining room," he said. " 'S the only room that's tidy."

Lesley exchanged glances with Tina and walked through.

The dining room was cramped, with just enough room for a scuffed mahogany table and six chairs. Lesley shuffled around its edge, squeezing between the table and the wall. She took a chair, checking it first for stains. She nodded for Tina to do the same.

Mr Waller appeared in the doorway.

"Made yourselves at home, I see," he said as he took the seat opposite Lesley and placed his hands on the table.

"Mr Waller," she began. "I wanted to ask you some questions about what you saw yesterday morning."

"I already spoke to PC Whatsisface." He pointed at Tina. "Your mate, the one that's married to your sister."

"Dougie?" Tina replied. "PC Anderson, I mean."

"Tha's the one. Haven't you spoken to him?"

"We have," Lesley said. "But we'd like to get it straight from you if you don't mind."

He pursed his lips. "Fair enough. What d'you want to know?"

"You were out walking on the cliffs," Lesley said. "What time was it?"

He screwed up his face. "Six o'clock, quarter past? Early, it was still dark. Hettie wanted a piss."

"Who's Hettie?" Lesley asked.

"My dog. Who else d'you think needs a piss on the cliffs at that time of day?"

Lesley bit her bottom lip. "So you went out with your dog at a quarter past six in the morning. Was it the dog that saw the change in the ground?"

"Nah. I spotted it in the distance. The ground had changed colour, moved in the night, that storm we had."

Lesley nodded. "Was it still raining at that time?"

He shook his head. "Wouldn't have gone out if it were. Nah, it'd stopped. Bloody freezing, though. Sometimes I wish Hettie were a cat, I could get 'er a litter tray."

Tina laughed, then clapped a hand over her mouth. "Sorry, boss."

The man looked at her. "That's alright. Dogs is funny, ain't they? 'Specially Hettie."

Lesley wondered where the fabled Hettie was. Asleep somewhere, probably. There were enough hairs on the dining chairs to attest to her existence.

Tina nodded, still squirming with suppressed laughter.

"Yeah," he said. "I saw the ground had moved, I went as close as felt safe, had a bit of a look. Didn't hang around, not safe."

"Did you notice any sign of people up there?" Lesley asked him.

"People? No."

"But you saw the landslip," Lesley said.

"Had me torch, didn't I? Hettie 'as this thing about wandering off, sometimes I need to find 'er. Got 'er a sparkly collar last year, stupid bitch lost it in the bushes."

Tina suppressed another snort. Lesley flashed her a look and clenched a fist under the table.

"So you saw the slip. You approached, realised what it was, and then what?"

"I came back home. Ring it in, didn't I?"

"You called 999?"

He shook his head. "Nah, I called Tim at the Coast Guard. I've got his mobile number, just in case. When you live out here like I does, sometimes you spot ships.

79

You don't call 999 if you see a ship in trouble. Quicker to call Tim, he sorts it. D'you need me to go out there with you, show you where I was?"

"No thanks," Lesley told him.

Based on his description, she was confident that the spot where the man had stood to look at the landslip would be within the police cordon. She was amazed he hadn't slipped down the cliff himself.

"Is this the first time you've seen the ground move in that section of cliff?" she asked.

He looked at Tina. "She can tell you that. Course it is."

Tina looked at Lesley. "He's right, boss. That section of cliff hasn't moved, not since before I was born."

Ted snorted. "Not since before I were born, neither. And that's a damn site longer than this kid."

Tina's cheek twitched.

"And how long have you lived up here?" Lesley asked him.

He wrinkled his nose. "Thirty years, thirty-five? Longer than them bodies 'ave been there."

"Do you remember seeing any unusual activity up on that section of the cliff? Possibly some time ago?" she asked him.

"Maybe six years ago?" Tina added.

"Nah," he said. "Nothin'."

"You've never seen anyone up on that part of the cliff, or above it, maybe looking as if they were burying something?"

"You think someone buried those bodies?"

Lesley looked at him, waiting for an answer.

"Sorry, ladies," he said. "Can't remember anything." He looked at Tina. "If them bodies have been up there six years, you'll never catch whoever killed 'em."

"Thanks for your time," Lesley said as she stood up.

He coughed, spittle landing on the table. "Yeah. Course."

"If you do think of anything, anything from six years ago or maybe more, please contact the local police station."

She had a feeling he'd be more likely to talk to a local.

"OK," he said. "But I can't remember anything. Sorry."

CHAPTER TWENTY-THREE

Lesley and Tina were leaving Samuel Waller's house when Lesley's phone rang. She glanced at the screen and nodded at Tina.

"You get in the car," she said. "I'll be right with you."

Tina gave her a puzzled look then walked towards the car. Lesley turned her back on the DC and took the call. It was Matt Crippins.

"Matt," she said, "have you reconsidered?"

"DCI Clarke," he replied. "I'm very well, thank you. How are you?"

Lesley ground her foot into the mud. Matt Crippins frustrated her.

"Is she back?" she asked.

"She is."

"When?"

"Late last night. Well, she got back to her flat late last night. She called me, came into the office early morning."

"And you're only telling me now?"

"You're not her mum."

"I was the senior investigating officer into her disappearance."

"The case that was closed, if I remember right," he said. "After she came back and told us to stop worrying about her."

82

Lesley ground her foot further into the mud. "Why has she suddenly turned up now?"

"She's got a story she wants me to run."

Lesley pulled back her shoulders, glancing at the car and Tina, who was looking back at her. "What kind of story?"

"We're working that out now. You know I don't reveal that kind of thing until I'm ready."

Lesley straightened. "Matt, if this is a story involving the police, then it's protocol to contact us first for comment. We can confirm whether what Sadie has is true or not."

"In theory."

"Not in theory. I know how you work, I know how Sadie works."

Matt laughed. "Not Sadie. Not always, anyway."

"Look," she told him. "I thought you and I were cooperating on this. I've given you sensitive information, the least you can do is share your story before you run it."

He cleared his throat and muttered something.

"Matt?"

"Sorry," he said. "Just talking to someone."

"Put her on," Lesley said. "Is it Sadie?"

"She's gone out. It's somebody else."

Lesley didn't believe him. "Matt," she said. "Please, before you run that story, I want to know about it."

The line went dead.

CHAPTER TWENTY-FOUR

The office was empty when Elsa arrived the next morning.

Her chest felt tight, her breathing thin. She knew what she was about to do could land her into a lot of trouble.

She hurried up the stairs to the first-floor offices, aware that her gaze was darting from side to side, like some kind of hunted animal. *Stop behaving so suspiciously*, she told herself.

She put a hand on the door to the main office and hesitated, her eyes closed. She drew the hand down the wood and smoothed it through her hair before opening the door.

Trying to keep her movements even, she scanned the office. The more she tried to look innocent, the more guilty she would appear. But there was nobody here. Half past seven in the morning: even lawyers didn't start that early in Dorset. In London, she'd have had to arrive at 4am to be sure of beating everybody else.

The file she wanted was in the filing room at the far end of the office, two doors from her own office. She crossed to it, aware that once she committed to this action, she had to get it over with quickly.

The set of keys on her keyring included a key to the filing room. She opened it swiftly and closed the door behind her.

She slipped off her shoes and walked further into the room. Nobody would know she was here.

She scanned the shelves. Some files were boxed up, others in hanging folders. It depended how old they were, and how active the client was. This client was active, but most members of the firm knew little about him, which meant boxes, not folders.

Gritting her teeth, she searched for the box she needed. She pulled it out and placed it on the floor, rifling through the contents. There were two files in here that hadn't been sent to the CPS yet. Kelvin expected them to conveniently go missing.

She pulled out the first of the files and stared at it a moment, her eyes prickling.

Could she do this?

Yes, she told herself, *just get a move on.*

She took the file out and laid it on the floor beside the box, followed by the second file. She placed the lid back on the box, and shoved it under the shelf, checking that it was straight, just as she'd found it. There was a shredder in the far corner of the room. She grabbed the files and made for it.

Elsa switched the shredder on and stood next to it, shifting from foot to foot, waiting for it to power up. She tapped her fingernails on the file, muttering under her breath.

A sound from behind her made her jump. She stiffened.

Somebody was in the main office. Elsa looked towards the door, hardly daring to breathe.

"Hurry up," she muttered, still waiting for the shredder to come to life.

At last, the screen lit up. She tapped a couple of buttons then took the first sheet out of the file.

"Ms Short?"

She looked up.

A woman stood in the doorway, watching her.

"Is everything alright, Ms Short? Is there something I can help you with?"

Elsa shoved the sheet of paper back into the folder.

"It's fine," she said. "Just something I forgot from yesterday."

The woman frowned. It was Sam, Ameena Khan's former PA. She was working for Elsa part-time since Ameena died, but Elsa was struggling to find work for her given that she already had her own PA.

"Elsa," Sam said, "please let me help."

She stepped forward, her arm outstretched.

"It's fine," Elsa replied. "I'm finished."

Sam looked down at the paper bin below the shredder. It was empty. Elsa let out a nervous laugh.

"Wrong files," she said. "I'll just take these to my office."

Sam looked at her. "You sure I can't help?"

"No." Elsa gave the younger woman her most reassuring smile. "Thanks anyway. I need you to do some photocopying for me later. I know it's grunt work, but is that OK?"

Sam shrugged. "Of course."

"Thanks. I'll speak to you later."

Pushing past Sam, Elsa stumbled out into the main office, aware of the other woman's eyes on her back.

Shit, she thought to herself. *Did she see the file?*

This had been a bad idea all along.

CHAPTER TWENTY-FIVE

Lesley parked in the shadow of Exeter Cathedral. The gothic building loomed over her, dominating the street. She got out of her car and paused to check her phone for directions. The pathologist had said that once she found the cathedral, she'd be in the right place. Roughly.

"Got it," she muttered. The morgue was just two streets away. She paid for her parking and grabbed a coat from her boot, wishing she'd brought some city clothes with her. In her wardrobe at Elsa's flat – her flat, she reminded herself – she kept the suits and smart shoes she'd worn in her old job in Birmingham. But after eight months of tramping around fields and getting splattered with mud, she'd resigned herself to boots and fleeces. Today she felt scruffy.

She arrived at the morgue to find a woman already in the pathologist's office. She was young, with long, dark hair. She wore a green suit that made Lesley feel even worse about her ill-fitting waterproof coat. The woman turned as she saw Lesley come in and stood up, holding out her hand.

"You must be DCI Clarke."

"I am, and you are?"

"Bea Steadman. Beatrice really, but everybody calls me Bea. I'm the forensic anthropologist."

"You got here quickly."

A smile. "I got the first train down from London after Gareth called me."

"Well, thank you. Have you had a chance to look at our evidence yet?"

"The bodies arrived here this morning. We were waiting for you to arrive."

"OK." Lesley wasn't sure if she was flattered or irritated; she'd rather they got on with their jobs.

Dr Bamford entered, bringing in a blast of cold air. "Lesley. You've met Bea?"

"She told me you were waiting for me."

He smiled at her. "I knew you wouldn't be long. Kyle has got the first body ready, let's go in."

Lesley stood up. "What were your conclusions from examining the bodies at the crime scene yesterday?"

He beckoned for her to walk with him. They passed along a corridor that smelled of bleach and formaldehyde.

"They'd been there a fair while," he said. "It didn't look like they'd been moved, not deliberately anyway." He opened a set of doors and waited for Lesley to go ahead. "My hypothesis is that they were buried at the top of those cliffs and then the first time they moved was when the land shifted yesterday morning."

"So whoever buried them knew the local terrain," Lesley suggested. "They'd have known that that was a spot that was unlikely to shift."

Bea turned to her. "How much do you know about the geology along that stretch of coast?"

"My colleague DC Abbott grew up in Lyme Regis. She's told me a bit. Subject to landslips, something to do with the structure of the soil."

They were in the space outside the post-mortem room. The pathologist indicated hooks with overalls for them to put on.

Bea shrugged hers on and turned to Lesley.

"OK," she said. "I'll give you the brief version. The ground along this stretch of coast is mainly blue lias and mudstone. Over in the east, where you are, it's older, from the paleogene."

Lesley knew she'd never remember any of this. "And?"

"Sorry. I can get a bit…" Bea glanced at the pathologist, who was smiling at her. "I studied geology before I switched to anthropology. Basically, the ground here is loose. When it gets sufficiently wet, it behaves like a liquid. Which is how you get landslips. The section of cliff where the bodies were buried is further back, with more greensand. It's just that little bit more stable, which is why it took so long for the bodies to move."

"So whoever buried them might well have an understanding of geology."

Bea wrinkled her nose. "Either that, or they know the history of landslips around here."

"People have long memories along this stretch of coast," Dr Bamford added.

Lesley nodded.

"But here's the thing," said Bea. "Normally, you wouldn't expect that section to move, not for hundreds of years, but—"

"Don't tell me, climate change," Lesley interrupted. "It's always climate change."

"It *is* partly climate change," Bea replied. "But there are other factors in play. To be honest, the fact that they keep moving the coastal path and doing engineering works, it tends to send reverberations through the ground."

"But there was a storm the other night," Lesley said.

"That was what would have finished it off," Bea replied. "When the ground gets wet enough, it hurtles down the cliffs, faster than anybody can run, incredibly dangerous. Imagine an avalanche of mud. We were lucky nobody was there at the time."

Lesley eyed the anthropologist. The woman's eyes gleamed; she was in her element. But they were all suited up, and there were more pressing matters at hand. "So, are we going to take a look at these bodies then?"

Dr Bamford opened the door to the post-mortem room. "After you."

CHAPTER TWENTY-SIX

"Hello, if it's not the prodigal daughter!"

Tina batted away Dougie's jokes as she descended the steps towards the beach.

"Why aren't you up there already?" she asked him, nodding towards the Spittles.

"I could ask the same of you," he replied. "I heard you came to see Naomi last night?"

She felt her jaw clench. Her sister had been welcoming, but there'd been an unspoken question in the air. *Why haven't you visited sooner?*

"I did. Your little girl's gorgeous."

His expression softened. "Thanks. I think so too." He stifled a yawn. "Mind you, sometimes in the mornings, I think she's the spawn of Satan."

"That makes sense," Tina replied. "She's your kid after all."

He gave her a mock punch. "Just because you're a fancy DC now, doesn't mean I can't take you down."

She laughed.

They followed the concrete walkway leading towards the base of the cliffs where the bodies had been found. The CSIs were already up there, white suits moving around in the distance.

"Seriously," she said to him. "I'm sorry it's taken me so long. Things have been hectic."

"How so?" he asked.

"Well," she said. "I've got myself a fella, for one."

"I heard, another fancy DC. Mike Legg."

Tina frowned and stopped walking. "Did Naomi tell you?"

He stood back for her to descend the concrete steps to the beach. "Tina, I work for Dorset Police just like you. Don't you think gossip can make it all the way over here?"

She pursed her lips. "I suppose not."

She didn't like the idea of bobbies across Dorset talking about her relationship with Mike.

They reached the bottom of the steps. The tide was out, fossil-hunters wandering around on the beach. A group of people stood at the bottom of the cliff, watching the CSIs. Lyme Regis folk, Tina knew, always wanted to know what was happening.

She didn't blame them. Lyme Regis was the sort of place where everybody knew everybody else's business. After the tourists went home at the end of the season, it changed in character. It became a small town, one where people looked out for each other. You could sense the place taking a collective sigh of relief every autumn. But in the summer, they all knew the money the holidaymakers brought in would keep the town going for the rest of the year.

As they approached the bottom of the cliffs, two young men, little more than boys, turned to them.

"Tina Abbott," one of them called out. "What are you doing here?"

She cocked her head at him. Andrew Cooper. The younger brother of one of her old mates.

"My job, Andrew," she said. "What d'you think I'm doing?"

"Come on, boys," said Dougie. "Surely you should be at school?"

"Doesn't start for another fifteen minutes."

Dougie looked at his watch.

"There's no way you're getting to school in fifteen minutes." He jerked a thumb backwards. "Now, make yourselves scarce before I tell Mr Plurton that you're skiving off."

The two boys looked at each other, shrugged, then ran past them and up the steps. The school was up the hill, going out of town. The speed the two boys were going, Tina reckoned they might just make it in fifteen minutes.

"Are you going to stay down here?" she asked Dougie. "Make sure nobody comes up?"

"I'll wait for Wendy," he told her. "She's on sentry duty today, then I need to go off and do some paperwork."

"Lucky you."

He smiled. "We can't all be fancy members of the Major Crime Investigations Team." He waggled his fingers in air quotes.

Tina turned away, ignoring the comment. She was over the moon that she'd passed the detective's exam and been made a permanent member of the team. But she knew people back at home found it difficult to understand why she'd moved away, and in particular, why she rarely visited.

She rolled her shoulders as she scrambled up the cliffs, trying to clear her head. She needed to focus on the case. Gail was up there with two of her team, Brett and Sunil. Tina wondered where the fourth CSI, Gavin, was. Maybe in Exeter with the pathologist?

"Morning, Gail," she called as she approached them.

"Hi, Tina," came the response. "Lesley not with you?"

"She's gone to Exeter to see the pathologist."

"Good. Hopefully we'll get a firm date on those bodies."

Tina nodded. "You've not found any more forensics up here?"

"Nothing yet," Gail replied. "But we've got a wide area to comb." She pointed to the top of the cliffs. "We need to cover the entire sweep of the slope from the top there down to the sea. We're going to start at the bottom and work our way up. That way the chances of the sea washing anything away are minimised."

"What can I do?" Tina asked.

"You got eagle eyes today?"

"Always."

"Good. You go down there, right to the water's edge." Gail pointed and Tina turned to look.

"Anything that looks out of place," Gail continued. "Anything that could have been left, particularly if it's old."

"Old?" Tina asked.

"Not *ichthyosaur* old," Gail said. "You know what I mean."

"I do. How shall I let you know if I find anything?"

"Use the radio," Gail said. "No point trudging up and down the beach."

"No problem," Tina told her.

"Sunil will come with you." Gail clicked her fingers and the youngest member of her team looked up.

He smiled at Tina. "You want someone to show you how it's done?"

"I know how it's done," Tina replied. "I spent four years in Uniform, remember?"

He scoffed. "Yeah, I'll show you how it's done."

CHAPTER TWENTY-SEVEN

The pathology technician stood back as Lesley entered the room with the pathologist and anthropologist. The first of the two bodies, the man, was already prepped. He lay on the metal table, the Y incision already cut into his flesh. Lesley swallowed as they approached.

"Anything of note?" Bamford asked the technician.

He nodded. "This one's got a pacemaker, a Nevono."

Bamford raised an eyebrow and looked at Lesley. "Well, that tells us one thing."

"What's that?" Lesley said.

"Hang on a moment," Bamford replied. "Let me check it."

Lesley tapped her foot on the floor. She needed to get back to the crime scene, see how Gail and her team had progressed in their search for forensics. Her phone was inside her jacket pocket, hanging on a peg outside the room. She felt cut off in here.

"What is it?" she asked Bamford.

He raised a finger and leaned over the body.

"We'll need to remove this," he said. "Disposing of a body with a pacemaker makes things a bit trickier."

"How so?" Lesley asked.

He looked up at her. "I'm not sure what instructions this chap will have made for disposal of his body, but you can't cremate a pacemaker."

"No," Lesley said. There was a risk of the thing exploding in the crematorium, setting the whole place on fire.

She sighed. "So how long will we have to wait?"

"To be honest, I wouldn't be too worried about that," the doctor said. "Until we've got an ID on him, we can't decide whether he needs to be cremated or interred anyway."

"So what is it about the pacemaker," she asked, "that tells you something?"

He straightened. "It's a Nevono. American manufacturer. The devices are always engraved with the manufacturer's details, as well as individual identifying information, of course."

"And what's the significance?"

"Nevono stopped trading under that name in 2009." He pointed at the body. "This thing's been inside him for over twelve years."

Lesley frowned. "How long were pacemakers left inside people back then, before they had to be replaced?"

He shrugged. "Batteries weren't as good back then. I'd have to check but I'd hazard a guess at no more than three years."

"So he's been dead for somewhere between nine and fifteen years."

The pathologist nodded. "Like I say, I'd need to check." He turned to his assistant. "Ash?"

The technician nodded and made a note on a whiteboard.

"Anything else helpful?" Lesley asked.

The pathologist leaned over the body. The anthropologist, Bea, followed his lead, standing on the other side of the table. Lesley watched as their eyes roamed over the man in silence, Dr Bamford's fingers edging over the skin.

Lesley had seen plenty of post-mortems over the span of her career and was no longer affected, but this body was different. It was desiccated, the skin dry and yellow. There were holes in the cheeks, either where animal or insect activity had damaged the flesh, or where it had rotted away.

"The fact that the body's so dry," she asked. "Does that tell us anything?"

"It tells us that whoever buried these bodies chose their spot wisely," Bea said. "They knew where it wouldn't get too wet."

The pathologist nodded. "It's impressive, for a cadaver that's been in the ground so long. There's little sign of putrefaction. Not much rot, not much insect activity." He stood up, looking at Bea, then at Lesley. "Bea's right," he continued. "It'll help you find where he was originally buried."

The other body was in the same condition. "That one too," the pathologist added, looking at it.

Bamford turned to the tech. "Make sure the CSIs know about it, and we might need to get a geologist out."

Lesley folded her arms across her chest. "So we have a body that's been in the ground at least nine years, and a killer who knew the terrain."

Bea smiled at her. "Looks like it. I can do more work on the tissue samples we'll be taking, ascertain a more precise time of death."

"And we can access pacemaker surgery records from local hospitals," Dr Bamford said. "That might narrow it down."

Lesley surveyed the bodies. How had they been in the ground so long without anybody finding them or reporting them missing?

"It's not David and Carmela Stubbs, then."

"Who are they?" Bea asked.

Lesley sighed. "A couple who went missing six years ago." She shook her head, glad they hadn't contacted the Stubbs's relatives.

"They've definitely been dead longer than that," Bea told her. "It'll take me a day or so to work out exactly how long. But you're looking at an older case."

CHAPTER TWENTY-EIGHT

"Yes, boss," said Tina. "I'll make sure Gail knows."

She hung up and turned to Sunil, who was still on the beach with her.

"That was the DCI," she said. "They've got a date on the bodies."

"And?"

"At least nine years, less than fifteen."

"How do they know that?"

"The man had a pacemaker, old model. Apparently there was a window within which it would have been replaced."

"Good," he said. "You going to tell Gail, or shall I?"

"I'll do it." She grabbed her radio.

Gail's voice crackled through the receiver. "Tina," she said, "you found something?"

"I've had a call from the DCI. She says the bodies are between nine and fifteen years old."

"OK," replied Gail.

"Have you found anything up there?" Tina asked.

"No, but we're about to work our way further up the cliff. There's a geologist on his way, too."

Tina looked back towards the steps that led from the car park. Sure enough, a man was walking down them carrying a rucksack. He arrived at the bottom, peered around, and spotted Tina and Sunil on the beach. Tina pointed up towards Gail, who waved. The man started along the beach and upwards towards Gail.

"I'm heading up there, Sunil." Tina wanted to know what was happening so she could relay it to the boss.

He shrugged. "Fair enough. Send PC Sharman over to help me, will you?"

"Will do."

She trudged up the cliffs, grabbing her phone to call Wendy Sharman. Wendy was three years younger than her, not someone she remembered from school. But, like Tina, she was born and bred Lyme.

"Hang on." The ground was loose, and Tina had to concentrate to keep her balance. "Can you give Sunil a hand? On the beach," she panted, then put her phone in her pocket. She needed both arms for this.

At last she was standing next to Gail and the newcomer, presumably the geologist. He was young, with messy blond hair and a grey duffel coat. The rucksack was propped against his legs.

Tina took a few breaths. She wasn't as fit as she should be. She heard a shout from behind and saw Wendy join Sunil on the beach. She waved in return.

"I've told Andy here about the time window," Gail said. "He says that means we need to be further up the hill if we're going to find where the bodies were buried."

"Fair enough," Tina replied, aware that she was panting.

She glanced at the geologist, who gave her a quizzical look in return.

"Lead the way," she told him.

Gail put her hand on Tina's arm. "Slow down," she said. "We haven't finished in this area yet."

"I'll head up there," Andy said. "See if there's any evidence."

Gail gestured towards the other white-suited CSI. "Brett," she called, "you accompany Andy here."

"I'll be fine on my own," Andy told her.

"You need a CSI with you." Gail eyed him. "This is a crime scene, we need to protect it."

"I know what I'm doing."

"Look, mate. I'm sure you'll be careful, but you aren't a trained forensic technician. Brett will show you what you can do without disturbing the scene."

Andy shrugged and looked at Tina. "You're coming too? Who are you, anyway?"

"Tina," she said, holding out a hand. "DC Tina Abbott, Major Crime Investigations Team."

He whistled. "Fancy. All the way from Winfrith?"

She tried not to show her irritation. "Well, it's not every day you get a double murder."

"Indeed it's not," he said, "and this one was ten years ago. At least."

Tina plunged her hands in her pockets. She didn't like the man's tone. But he was an expert on the layout of these cliffs, so she'd have to work with him.

"Come on, then," she told him. "Let's take a look."

He looked at Gail who nodded.

Brett was with them. "Where are we headed, Andy?" he asked the geologist.

The geologist pointed up the hill. "To be honest, we might be better off approaching from the road."

"OK." Brett looked at Gail. "Alright if I take the van?"

"Hang on," Tina said. "So we're going to walk all the way up the steps, drive around, and get up to the point up there that you're indicating?"

"Safest route," the geologist said.

"He's right," Gail told her. "And it might give us an idea of the route the killer took when they buried the bodies."

"There's hardly going to be anything evidential now," said Tina. "Not after so many years."

"You'd be surprised," the geologist told her.

"OK." Tina sighed. "Lead the way."

CHAPTER TWENTY-NINE

As Lesley was leaving the pathologist's office, a woman jumped out of a blue Ford Focus and hurried towards her.

"DCI Clarke?" she asked.

"That's me," Lesley replied. *A journalist?* "Can I help you?"

"I'm DI Hannah Patterson, Exeter Police."

"Dennis told me to expect you."

The woman walked backwards in front of Lesley, matching her stride. "Can we sit somewhere?"

"My car's as good as anywhere," Lesley replied.

She led the woman over to it and got into the driver's seat. The woman took the passenger seat and turned to her.

"You do realise you're on my patch?"

Lesley closed her eyes momentarily. "Gareth Bamford is the closest pathologist to the crime scene, it made sense to bring the bodies here."

"Yes," DI Patterson replied. "To Devon."

"Really? We're going to play interforce politics with a cold case that's ten years old?"

The woman cocked her head. "I thought it was six years? That's what DS Frampton told me. The Stubbses, it's the most likel—"

"No," Lesley replied. "Dr Bamford found evidence that the bodies had been there for at least nine years, possibly fifteen, no longer."

"What evidence?"

"A pacemaker. Don't ask me the details, I'm sure he'll be able to fill you in. The two of you have worked together, I imagine?"

"Yes," Hannah replied, her voice hard. "But even if it's not the Stubbs case, you need to bring me in on this investigation. You'll need to use our resources and you're less than two miles from the boundary."

"The bodies were found in Dorset," Lesley told her. "Look, I'm as happy as the next person to reduce my workload. But I know my bosses won't be pleased if I cede control of this case to a different force."

She stared out of the front window. The area around the cathedral was busier than it had been when she'd arrived, shoppers and people out for a stroll.

"I'll tell you what," she said. "Let's work on it together and when we discover who the victims are, we'll allocate roles accordingly."

DI Patterson pursed her lips. "You still don't know who the bodies are?"

"Maybe you can shed some light. Any cold cases ten to fifteen years old?"

"I was in Uniform nine years ago."

"I thought you might have been."

Lesley looked her up and down. The woman was young, in her mid-thirties. She had probably been a trainee when those people had died.

Lesley started at a knock on the window behind her. It was Gareth Bamford. She opened her door.

"Dr Bamford," she said. "Everything alright?"

He nodded, his face animated. "I've got news."

"OK." She glanced back at the DI and got out of the car. The DI followed. Lesley was relieved the woman hadn't remained in the passenger seat. It was one thing encroaching on her case, but encroaching on her space…

"What is it?" she asked the pathologist, leaning against the car.

"Dental records," he said. "My technician made a few calls. We've managed to get an ID."

CHAPTER THIRTY

"Who?" Lesley asked, looking at the pathologist.

He looked around them. "Why don't we go into my office?"

"Why? Is this sensitive?"

He shrugged. "No, but we can go over this in more detail inside."

"OK." Lesley looked at DI Patterson. "You coming?"

"You bet."

The two women followed the pathologist back into the hospital and along corridors until they reached the morgue. Finally, they were back in his office. Bea Steadman was nowhere to be seen.

Lesley leaned against the door, while DI Patterson took a chair.

Lesley folded her arms. "You've made me wait long enough. Tell me who they are. We know it's not this cold case of DI Patterson's, so who is it?"

The pathologist looked at the DI.

"Who were your victims?"

"David and Carmela Stubbs," Patterson told him. "They went missing six years ago. I'm told the time window doesn't fit."

He shook his head. "No. And those aren't the names I've been given."

He turned on the laptop on his desk, pressed a couple of keys, and turned it towards them.

"We found a dentist in Dorchester, he had records for both of them. Their names are – were – Kenneth Fogarty and Catherine Lawson."

Dorchester, Lesley thought. So it was a Dorset case.

Dr Bamford looked between Lesley and the DI. "Mean anything to you?"

"Nothing," Lesley said.

DI Patterson shrugged. "Where are they from?" she asked. "Dorchester?"

"All I know is where their dentist was based. He's sending over more records, but apparently, it's been ten years since he last treated them."

Lesley whistled. "Fits."

DI Patterson leaned forward and pulled the laptop towards her. "Are you sure these are the right people?"

"Dental records match," said the pathologist. "Like I say, their files will be coming in soon, and then hopefully you'll have an address."

"I'm calling my DS." Lesley grabbed her phone.

Dennis answered after two rings. "Boss. Any developments?"

"A significant one," she told him. "We've got a potential ID for our victims, last treated by their dentist ten years ago."

"That's good. Who are they?"

"Kenneth Fogarty and Catherine Lawson, both based in Dorchester."

"Not necessarily," interrupted DI Patterson.

"They had a Dorchester dentist at least," Lesley said, eyeing the DI. "Dennis, can you get onto it? Find out what you can about those two people. Where did they live? Who are their next of kin? When were they last seen alive?"

"No problem, boss," he said. "I don't suppose you've got photos?"

"Only the crime scene photos," she replied. "I don't imagine a dentist would keep photos of their clients after ten years."

"Only X-rays," the pathologist said.

Lesley nodded.

"Have a look on HOLMES, see if they've ever been involved with the police, and check the electoral register for Dorchester. We'll find them, and once we know who they were, we'll be a step closer to finding out who killed them."

CHAPTER THIRTY-ONE

Tina was at the top of Timber Hill with Brett. They were combing the land, trying to find anything that might have been left behind when the land slipped and the bodies were sent down the cliffs. Andy, the snippy geologist, was further up, using some sort of instrument to take measurements.

The coastal path wound along here, almost a mile inland from the coast itself. When Tina had been a girl, the path had been half a mile south of here, closer to the beach. But over the years, each time the land had slipped, the path had been shifted further back. It was wrecked in places now, and the land was barely stable. She had a feeling the council would be rerouting even more of the coastal path to follow the Charmouth Road.

She stood up and put a hand over her eyes to shield them from the low sun. Their search had been fruitless so far, nothing left behind. No clothing, no artefacts. Nothing had conveniently fallen out of the two victims' pockets. And of course there would be no trace of whoever had brought them here and buried them in the first place, not when it had happened ten or more years ago.

She looked across at Brett.

"I'm going back up to the van, get some water," she said. "D'you want some?"

"Let's take a break. Is there anywhere we can get a cup of tea?"

"I can go and get a flask from my mum's. If you don't mind me using your van."

Brett laughed. "It's not often a DC tells me that, but I won't say no. I'll walk up with you to the van, make some notes. It's less exposed up there."

Tina nodded and turned along the path towards where Brett had parked the CSIs' van. It was right at the edge of town.

As she walked her phone rang: the DCI.

"Boss," Tina said, "We've been searching the top of the cliffs, haven't found anything yet."

"I've got news," said the DCI. "An ID on our victims."

Tina pumped a fist. She looked at Brett.

"An ID. Who?"

Brett's eyes widened.

"Kenneth Fogarty and Catherine Lawson," the DCI said. "We've got dental records. They were last seen by their dentist in Dorchester ten years ago."

"Dorchester," Tina said, "so it's not Devon's cold case?"

"Nope," replied the DCI. "Hopefully that means we can get DI Patterson out of our hair."

Tina nodded. She hadn't come into contact with the DI yet, but she knew the uniformed officers at Lyme Regis police station often had dealings with their counterparts over the border. Crime didn't know the difference between one county and another.

"So what do you need me to do, boss?" she asked.

"Carry on with what you're doing, but be aware that you might be looking for evidence of a man and a woman being left ten years ago."

"I'll let Gail know," Tina said.

"Thanks." The DCI hung up.

"We'll need to tell the geologist," Brett said. "I'll go back."

"Cheers." Tina watched as he turned back along the path.

"Brett! Wait!"

He turned.

"The keys?"

He grinned then fished the van keys out of his pocket. He threw them to her. "Get us that flask of tea, will you?"

"Of course."

As she was starting the van, her phone rang. She turned off the ignition; the van didn't have hands-free.

"Tina, it's Gail. Lesley has just told me you've got a confirmed ID, and a date."

"An approximate date."

"You're local. Were you living here ten years ago?"

"Yes."

"Do you remember anything suspicious?"

"Gail, I was fourteen. All I can remember was the name of the guy I had a crush on."

Gail laughed. "OK."

"But if there's anything to remember, my mum'll know about it. I'm heading back there now."

"Why?"

Tina felt her face heat up. She wasn't sure if Gail would approve of her using the van to go and get a flask of tea for her and Brett. "Just needed some equipment."

"OK. But let's not go talking about this to all the locals."

The passenger door opened: Brett, a blast of cold air coming into the van with him. "I've told Andy," he said. "He seemed nonplussed."

Tina nodded. "I wish this van had hands-free."

"Is that Brett?" Gail asked. "Put him on."

Tina handed the phone over. Brett gestured towards the steering wheel. Did he want her to drive them to her mum's, or back to the crime scene?

She sniffed as she turned in the road. She'd have a hard time keeping the details from her mum. They would be all around the town by tonight. But if they were looking for local knowledge, the best place to start was at the police station.

CHAPTER THIRTY-TWO

Lesley yawned as she drove back towards Lyme Regis. The single bed she'd been allocated in Annie Abbott's house had been comfortable enough, but she'd been woken at 5am by seagulls landing on the roof. She'd thumped the ceiling a couple of times, as quietly as she could, but it seemed the seagulls liked it there.

She was suppressing another yawn as her phone rang.

"DCI Clarke, it's Gareth Bamford."

"Doctor Bamford, any news for me?"

"Er, yes. News and an apology."

"What have you done?"

"You do get to the point, don't you? I feel a little embarrassed that I didn't identify the cause of death earlier. With the bodies in the state they were in…"

"You have a cause of death?"

"For the man, Kenneth Fogarty."

"And it is?"

"Well, this isn't something you see very often in Exeter, even less so in Lyme Re—"

"Just tell me what it is." Lesley suppressed another yawn. She swerved to avoid a car coming at her along the narrow road, its horn blaring.

"Fogarty has a gunshot wound in the side of his neck. It was obscured by animal damage, and not immediately apparent, bu—"

"A gunshot wound?"

"Yes."

Lesley whistled. She imagined the pathologist was right: not exactly common round here. "Can you give me any more information?"

"We're conducting further examinations for residue, but with the bodies so old... Am I right in thinking your CSIs found a metal object near the bodies?"

Lesley shook her head. "It was a drinks container. Three years old, according to the manufacturer."

"So not connected," Bamford said.

"No. What about Catherine Lawson? Does she have a similar wound?"

"I haven't been able to find one. Yet."

"Yet?"

"It's not straightforward, examining bodies that have been in the ground so long. They're remarkably well preserved, but still there are challenges."

Lesley braked as she rounded a bend and found a tractor lumbering along in front of her. "Damn."

"Everything OK?"

"Just rural traffic. OK, let me know if you find anything else."

"Of course."

CHAPTER THIRTY-THREE

The office was quiet, each of the three men head down in their search for Kenneth Fogarty and Catherine Lawson. Dennis was trawling through HOLMES, Mike was on Google, and Stanley was working through the electoral register.

Dennis had found nothing so far on HOLMES. Fogarty and Lawson hadn't been reported missing, and neither of them had been in trouble with the law. He leaned back in his chair and raised his arms above his head, stretching and yawning.

"Who wants a cuppa?" he asked.

Mike and Stanley looked up in unison.

"Coffee, no sugar, please," said Mike. "If you don't mind, Sarge?"

"I don't mind," Dennis said. "I need to stretch my legs."

Pam had been nagging him about spending too much time at his desk. He needed to be out and about, working the case with the DCI. Interviewing suspects, exploring crime scenes. Instead, he was stuck here. His back was ageing by the day.

"Stanley," he asked, "what can I get you?"

"Tea, please. Two sugars."

Dennis frowned. "You don't normally take sugar, do you?"

"It's an experiment, Sarge."

"OK," Dennis replied, wondering what kind of experiment involved adding sugar to tea when you didn't normally take it.

Still, he wasn't going to argue. He heaved himself out of his chair and made for the kitchen.

Five minutes later he was back. He placed Stanley's tea in front of him.

"If you don't mind me asking, Stanley. I'm puzzled by an experiment where you *add* sugar to your tea. Isn't it more normal for people to stop taking sugar?"

"It's a theory my girlfriend's got, Sarge. She reckons if you have sugar in your tea, it will feed your sugar cravings and stop you from eating things like chocolate and biscuits the rest of the day. Do you know how many teaspoons of sugar there are in a Hobnob?"

Dennis laughed. "No idea, and I don't want you to tell me."

He placed Mike's coffee in front of him. Mike was leaning into his screen, his eyes inches from it.

"Have you got something?" Dennis asked.

Mike nodded absently. "I might have, Sarge. I've got something on Kenneth Fogarty, anyway."

Dennis leaned over the desk. "Go on."

"Society pages of the Bournemouth Echo. This is a photo of him at some do twelve years ago."

"That fits," Dennis said. "If he went missing ten years ago."

Mike nodded. "Do you recognise that bloke he's standing next to?"

Dennis cocked his head to one side. "Zoom out. See if there's a caption."

The photo depicted four men, all of them white and middle-aged. One was slightly younger than the others, a full head of hair. He was familiar.

"I do know him," Dennis said. "That's Harry Nevin."

"The one whose girlfriend killed him?" Stanley asked.

"That's the chap," Dennis replied. "Formerly of Nevin, Cross and Short."

Mike sucked in a breath. He pointed at the screen. "And that's Fogarty standing next to him. He's got his arm around him."

"These society types," said Stanley. "All very pally."

Dennis grunted.

"Keep looking," he told Mike. "Find out what the link is between Fogarty and Nevin."

"I'll do a search with both their names," Mike said.

He typed into his computer. Another page came up, the *Way Back When* site.

"What's that?" asked Dennis.

"It's like a snapshot of the internet through time," Mike told him. "Shows you what a website would have looked like on a given date."

"OK. In that case, go back ten years. See if you can find anything with Fogarty."

"It doesn't work like that," Mike said. "You can't do a search on a date and expect to find the website, you need to know the site first."

"What about Harry Nevin?" Stanley suggested. "Try looking at the Nevin, Cross and Short website on *Way Back When*."

Mike looked across the desks. "Good idea."

He clicked his mouse and tapped in some search terms.

"Shit."

"DS Legg," Dennis reprimanded him.

"Sorry, Sarge," Mike said.

He glanced towards the filing cabinet where Dennis's swear box had been hidden since the DCI had arrived last summer, then pointed at the screen.

"That's the Nevin, Cross and Short website from ten years ago."

Dennis peered at it. "But it doesn't say Nevin, Cross and Short."

"No," said Mike. "It explains the photo, though."

"My goodness," Dennis said. "That firm gets everywhere, doesn't it?"

Mike nodded.

Stanley looked over the desks. "What is it? What firm?"

Dennis looked at him.

"Nevin, Cross and Short," he said, "It seems that ten years ago, they had a different name. Nevin, Fogarty and Lawson."

CHAPTER THIRTY-FOUR

Lesley was in the Lyme Regis police station car park, contemplating whether she could get away with a brief nap, when her phone rang again.

"DCI Clarke."

"Everything alright, boss?" Dennis asked.

She cleared her throat. "Sorry, Dennis. Woken up early by a seagull."

"That's the first time I've heard that."

She laughed. "It's a pretty poor excuse for not concentrating. What have you got for me?"

"We're piecing together a profile for the two victims," he replied. "We now know where they worked."

"And?"

"They were both lawyers based in Bournemouth."

"Don't tell me…" Lesley said.

"They were partners at Nevin, Cross and Short. Or to be precise, Nevin, Fogarty and Lawson."

"Shit," Lesley breathed. She heard Dennis cough at the other end of the line.

"OK," she said, ignoring it. "I'll let Tina know, get her to ask local police if there's any connection between them and Lyme Regis. I need you to go and see Aurelia Cross."

"Just Aurelia Cross?"

"This was ten years ago?" she asked.

"Yes."

"Aurelia Cross might have been employed by that firm then," she told him. "Elsa only started there a year ago."

"Very well," Dennis replied, his voice terse.

"Dennis," she said, shifting in her seat to pull herself upright. "If this has got anything to do with my girl–friend, you can rest assured that I will be professional and objective."

"Of course, boss. Like you say, she wasn't at the firm then."

"No."

Elsa couldn't have anything to do with this case. Fogarty and Lawson had died long before she'd even moved to the area.

It was fine.

Was it?

A thought pricked at her. Elsa might not be connected directly. She may not have met the victims. But there could be an indirect connection.

"Dennis," she said, "see if you can find out who Fogarty and Lawson's clients were, ask Aurelia Cross if she's got records."

"After ten years?"

"Ask anyway. And watch her reaction when you do so."

CHAPTER THIRTY-FIVE

Tina was leaning against the front desk of the Lyme Regis police station, sipping a cup of tea, when the boss hurried in. She flinched, almost dropping her drink.

"Boss," she said, placing the tea on the counter and glancing down at it. "How did it go with the post mortem?"

"We've got a cause of death." The DCI eyed Dougie, standing on the other side of the front desk. "Let's go to that cell again."

Tina frowned.

The boss put a hand on the counter, her gaze on Dougie. "Where's your sergeant?"

Dougie gave the DCI a confused look. "I'll just get him."

As he left the room, Tina stepped closer to her boss.

"What is it?" she asked. "Is there something you don't want Dougie knowing?"

The DCI shook her head. "Gareth Bamford's found a cause of death for Fogarty. And we've got more information about the two victims."

Tina nodded. "What kind of information?"

The boss drew in a breath, shaking her head. "We'll wait until Sergeant Connor's here. Come on." She brushed past Tina and through the door into the main part of the station. The sergeant was walking towards them, looking puzzled.

"Everything alright?" he asked. "You look like you've seen a—"

"Everything's fine," the DCI replied. "I need to talk to you."

She beckoned for Tina to follow them, and headed towards the cell where they'd spoken to Dougie and Wendy yesterday. The boss entered the room and slammed herself into a chair. Tina followed, standing to one side. Sergeant Connor took the seat opposite the DCI, placing his elbows on the table and twisting his fingers together.

"What's happened?" he asked her. "Is it something sensitive?"

The DCI eyed him for a moment. "We have two new pieces of information." She looked at Tina. "I don't suppose you've got anything more from the scene?"

Tina shook her head. "Gail and Brett are still up there. But sorry, no. It's been too long."

The DCI slumped in her chair. "It has, but we're looking for evidence of a gun. Bullets, maybe the weapon itself."

The sergeant scratched his head. "A gun?"

The DCI chewed her bottom lip. "Kenneth Fogarty's cause of death is a gunshot wound to the neck."

Connor winced. "Poor fella."

"Poor fella indeed. Do you know of any local gangs that might have had access to guns at around the time the murders took place?"

"This is Lyme Regis, Ma'am."

"I thought you'd say that. No gangs at all? Drugs activity?"

"Yes, but very low level. Anything bigger is in Exeter."

"Not Bournemouth or Dorchester?"

"People here tend to orientate towards Devon. More direct roads."

The DCI grunted. "And I don't hold out much hope of finding anything at the scene."

"There won't be anything after ten years," he said. "Bullet fragments could have scattered anywhere by now. Birds could have had 'em."

The DCI looked at him. "There's a chance the gun might have been abandoned at the scene."

He crossed his legs. "Any criminal with access to a gun is surely going to be sensible enough, or nasty enough, to take it with them afterwards."

"Even so," said the DCI, "that's what I want the CSIs looking for."

He shrugged. "Your investigation."

"I need your help, though."

"Of course."

"I don't want talk of gunshots getting out to the local population any sooner than it has to. I get the feeling this is a tight-knit community, and I'd rather not tell your PCs for now."

"I trust those officers implicitly."

Tina scratched the skin on her arm, uneasy. She'd known Dougie and Wendy since she was a girl. But she knew what people could be like here.

The sergeant looked at Tina. She nodded.

"Fair enough," he said. "Don't blame me if it gets out some other way, though."

"I won't," the DCI said. "Tina, can you give Gail a call, update her?"

The boss put a hand on the table.

"There's another thing," she said, her gaze on the sergeant. "Have you heard of a law firm called Nevin, Cross and Short?"

Tina held her breath. She knew that firm. Harry Nevin, the lead partner, had been murdered. Elsa Short, the newest partner, was the boss's girlfriend.

Sergeant Connor shook his head.

"Never heard of them. Who are they?"

"Kenneth Fogarty and Catherine Lawson were partners in that firm," the DCI told him. "Its name ten years ago was Nevin, Fogarty and Lawson."

Tina didn't realise she'd gasped until she noticed the DCI had turned to her and was frowning at her.

"Sorry, boss," she muttered.

What did this mean? She knew there was something going on between Lesley and Elsa, but was it related to this case?

The DCI balled her fist on the table. "I've already spoken to Dennis. He's going to pay a visit to Aurelia Cross, find out what she knows about Fogarty and Lawson's client list before they died."

Tina nodded. "What about their families?"

"Dennis is still piecing it together, Stanley and Mike too."

Tina hadn't called Mike since she'd got here. She wondered if he'd even noticed.

"What do you need me to do, boss?" she asked.

"Come with me to the crime scene."

CHAPTER THIRTY-SIX

Lesley checked her watch as she and Tina left Lyme Regis police station. She was in two minds. Should she stay here, keep an eye on the local investigation and the forensic search, or should she go back to base so she could be closer to the investigation into the victims?

"Boss," Tina said, jerking her head sideways. "Your car's over here."

Lesley shook her head to release the fog that had swept over her. "Sorry, Tina. Miles away."

She made for the car. She'd go to the crime scene with Tina, tell Gail what they were looking for, and then she'd decide what to do.

"You drive," she told Tina. She was in no state to navigate the narrow and hilly lanes of Lyme Regis. Yesterday they'd waited ten minutes while two buses tried to pass each other in an impossibly narrow lane. If it had been up to her, she'd have had a word with the drivers, and not a very patient one, or at least tried to squeeze past herself. But Tina had simply turned off the ignition and waited, along with a group of nearby pedestrians who seemed to consider it their entertainment for the day.

Lesley's phone rang as she got into the passenger seat. When she saw who it was, she pushed the car door open.

"Hang on a moment, Tina." She got out and leaned against the car, one arm on the roof of the vehicle.

"Hi, love," she said. "Everything OK?"

"Any reason it shouldn't be?" Elsa asked.

Lesley clenched her fist on the roof of the car. "Your firm's going to be getting a visit from Dennis. Two former partners, they're the bodies we found in Lyme Regis."

Elsa whistled. "Ouch. What are their names?"

"Kenneth Fogarty and Catherine Lawson."

"I've heard of them. Never met them, though."

"That makes sense," Lesley replied. "They died at least ten years ago, long before your time."

"Should I warn Aurelia?"

"No. In fact, I haven't told you."

"No," Elsa agreed. "You probably shouldn't have. I'll give Dennis an hour, if he's not here by then…"

"He'll be there," Lesley told her. "Anyway, why were you calling me?"

"I wanted to say sorry."

"What for?"

"Last night on the phone. I was distracted, stuff going on at work. I shouldn't take it out on you."

"It's OK," Lesley told her. "That's what I'm here for. Is there anything you want to talk about?"

She held her breath. Elsa had been in contact with DCI Mackie before he'd died. It had been on Lesley's mind and she was pretty sure it had been on Elsa's too.

"Nothing you want to tell me about?" she repeated.

"No," Elsa said. "Not today, anyway. I might be able to tell you at the weekend."

Lesley thumped the roof of the car. "Elsa, is this relevant to the case?"

"What case?"

"Fogarty and Lawson, your former partners."

"No." Elsa sounded puzzled. "Should it be?"

"I don't know," Lesley replied.

She wasn't lying. The two murders could well be related to whatever Elsa had been talking to Mackie about. Or it could be a coincidence.

"Elsa," she said, "are you sure you don't want to tell me what's been bothering you?"

"I'll tell you at the weekend," Elsa replied. "Promise."

CHAPTER THIRTY-SEVEN

Dennis scraped his fingernails along the arm of the chair as he waited in the reception area of Nevin, Cross and Short. Mike was in the chair opposite him, looking down at the floor. Dennis gritted his teeth and started drumming his fingers on the chair.

Mike looked up. "You alright, Sarge?"

"Fine." Dennis flicked his wrist to check his watch.

"How long has it been?"

Dennis let out a slow breath. "Fifteen minutes."

He wondered why Aurelia Cross was keeping them waiting. Did she know what they were here about? Was there something she'd be trying to cover up?

He stood and turned towards the door separating them from the offices. Was she in there right now, destroying evidence?

He'd just placed a hand on the door handle, about to push it open, when somebody pulled it from inside. Dennis stumbled, slamming a hand into the doorframe to keep his balance. A young woman stood in front of him, her eyes wide.

"Are you alright, Detective? Has something happened?"

"How long will Miss Cross keep us waiting?"

The woman smiled. "She's ready for you now."

Dennis raised an eyebrow. "It's been fifteen minutes."

"She was busy with a client call."

Dennis watched the woman's face. She seemed to be telling the truth, but then, who was to say Aurelia Cross hadn't lied to her in the first place?

"Very well," he said. "Take us through."

The woman smiled again and turned away. Dennis gestured for Mike to follow.

They were led to a corner office, the one Harry Nevin had occupied before his death. Aurelia Cross was inside, the desk in front of her empty, her hands palm-down on its surface. She looked up as they entered the room, offering a supercilious smile. She held out a hand and Dennis shook it.

"Detectives," she said, "how can I help you?"

Dennis caught movement out of the corner of his eye. He glanced back to see Elsa Short ducking into another door.

He narrowed his eyes. Surely the DCI hadn't warned her?

He cleared his throat, and sat down opposite Aurelia Cross. Mike closed the door and took the seat next to him.

"We have some bad news," Dennis told her.

She slid her palms towards her, across the desk. "What kind of bad news?"

"Are you aware that we're investigating the deaths of two people found on the cliffs above Lyme Regis?"

She shook her head. "No. Should I be?"

"It involves two former partners at your firm."

A frown. "You suspect them?"

Dennis noted that her first instinct hadn't been to ask him who the bodies were.

"No," he replied, wondering why she'd jumped to that conclusion. "I'm sorry to tell you this, but we've identified the two bodies. Their names are Kenneth Fogarty and Catherine Lawson. I believe they were previously partners at this firm."

Miss Cross's hand shifted across the desk, her movements stiff. Her face had paled. Dennis was confident she hadn't been warned.

"Kenneth and Catherine?" she asked.

Dennis nodded, not taking his eyes off her face. "Did you work with them? Did you know them?"

"I knew of them. They left the firm a year before I started here. Harry was sole partner for a while, until I was promoted. Well, until I managed to prove myself."

"So did you ever meet Mr Fogarty and Ms Lawson?"

"Sorry, never. I knew of them by reputation only."

"What kind of reputation?"

"I don't mean anything by that. All I knew about them was that they were old friends of Harry, good lawyers. They retired."

Dennis nodded. Once they were out of here, he'd be asking Mike to check Aurelia Cross's story.

"Is there anybody still at the firm who would have worked alongside them?" he asked.

She chewed her bottom lip. "I'm not sure, I'd have to check the personnel files." She picked up the phone on her desk.

Dennis put out a hand. "What are you doing?"

"Calling through to my PA. She can check the files, find anybody who was working here at that time. I presume you want to talk to them?"

He sat back. "We do."

"Good." She stared at him as she spoke into the phone.

"Carol, it's Aurelia. Can you do something for me? Find out if we have anybody working here who was with the firm…" She raised an eyebrow at Dennis, "ten, twelve years ago?"

"Ten," Dennis muttered.

"Ten years," she repeated. "And let me have their names. Don't speak to them, just give me the names."

She put the phone down. "It'll take a while. Can I offer you a coffee in the meantime?"

This wasn't a social call. Dennis shook his head. "Please, tell me what you know about Mr Fogarty and Ms Lawson."

She shrugged. "Not much, I'm afraid. They were friends of Harry's, good friends I think. The three of them were partners when the firm was first established. They retired, they were a couple. Moving abroad, I think? They died ten years ago, you say?"

"We're not sure of an exact date," Dennis said. "But it would have been at least ten years ago."

Miss Cross pushed back a lock of hair that had fallen in front of her eyes. "That tallies. If they left a year before I started, that would be ten years."

"Can you give me the date on which they left the firm?"

"It'll be in our records. Changes to the partners have to be formally recorded in the partnership deeds. Harry would have bought them out, I imagine."

"Good," Dennis said. "Find me that date, will you? And while you're at it, can you access client records for them? It would be useful to know who they were working with."

Her face darkened. "That might take a little longer."

Beside Dennis, Mike cleared his throat. He scribbled a note in his pad and showed it to Dennis.

It had one word: *Kelvin?*

Dennis reached out to cover the word with his hand. They both knew this firm represented Arthur Kelvin, an organised criminal masquerading as a respectable businessman. But he didn't know how long they'd been doing so.

If Fogarty and Lawson had represented Kelvin, and something had gone wrong in that relationship, could it explain their deaths?

"A client list would be most useful," he said to Miss Cross. "As soon as you can."

CHAPTER THIRTY-EIGHT

As Lesley and Tina drove up the steep hill away from the police station, a car appeared coming the other way. Tina stopped in front of a parked car, waiting for it to pass.

Instead, it stopped next to them and the driver's window opened. Lesley looked past Tina to see DI Hannah Patterson in the other car.

She sighed. "Shit. Open the window, would you Tina?"

Tina glanced at Lesley then opened the window, leaning back to give Lesley a view across the cars.

"Hannah," Lesley said. "We don't need you anymore."

Hannah smiled. "Oh, I wouldn't say that."

Lesley shook her head. "The victims were from Bournemouth. Two lawyers, worked in a firm we've had dealings with before. They were found in Lyme Regis *in Dorset*, they came from Bournemouth *in Dorset*."

Hannah pursed her lips. "Do you know where they lived?"

"Not yet, but we will." Lesley looked away. The sea was just visible from up here, between the houses.

"Well, then," Hannah replied. "In that case, let's decide who is and isn't needed on this case when we know that for sure. Just because they were found in Dorset, doesn't mean they were killed in Dorset."

Lesley shared a look with Tina, who was still leaning back, trying not to block the conversation between the two women. "Haven't you got other cases to be working on?" she asked Hannah. "I mean, if it was me, I'd be only too glad to be relieved of responsibility for an ancient murder case so that I could get on with the rest of my job."

Hannah gave her another one of those smiles. "Ma'am, I'm sure you understand that it isn't my decision to pursue this."

Lesley gritted her teeth. She knew full well what Superintendent Carpenter would be like if the boot was on the other foot.

"Fair enough," she replied. "For now, we don't need you. But if things change, I'll be in touch."

Hannah's arm rested on the windowsill. She tapped her fingers against the car door. "I'll keep my eye on what's going on, if you don't mind. Keep in touch with Dr Bamford."

"That's your prerogative. If you want to waste your time…"

"We'll see about that. Thanks for your help, DCI Clarke."

"Thank you for yours," Lesley replied, hoping the sarcasm in her voice wasn't too apparent.

She gestured for Tina to close the window. Hannah did the same and drove off.

Lesley stretched out her fingers, forcing the tension from her body as Tina rounded the parked car and headed up towards the road into Lyme Regis.

"Everything OK, boss?" Tina asked.

"Fine," Lesley told her. "I just don't need interforce politics on top of everything."

"Are you worried about this involving Nevin, Cross and Short?"

"No," Lesley replied. "I'm not. It's just a case. We deal with it like every other case."

"Sorry, boss," Tina's voice was low. "I didn't mean to…"

Lesley leaned back in the seat and closed her eyes. "It's fine, Tina. I'm sorry, I shouldn't take it out on you."

She was worried about Elsa. What was it that Elsa was planning to tell her this weekend? Was it related to the case, or to Mackie's death? Or maybe both?

She didn't like being so far away. She'd told Dennis to watch Aurelia Cross's reaction when he broke the news, but she'd rather have been there herself.

"Let's just get to the crime scene," she said. "I'll have a quick chat with Gail, drop you off, and then I'm going back to the office."

CHAPTER THIRTY-NINE

Gail stooped over and frowned.

"Is that what I...?" she muttered.

She looked up, getting her bearings. She was maybe a hundred metres further up the hill from where the bodies had been found. The landslip hadn't affected this patch of ground, maybe diverted by the scrubby bushes she'd been searching in.

She crouched down, anxious to get a better angle.

It was.

She'd seen a dark object half-hidden by soil beneath a bush. It was well hidden, and had probably only recently been partially uncovered. There was no shine on it; it had been here a while.

Holding her breath, she fired off a couple of photos, wanting to capture it where she'd found it. Then she reached in and pulled it out, gritting her teeth as she did so.

She placed a marker where she'd found it and took more photos. Then she stood up.

Gail held the object up in front of her. She turned it over in her hand, then placed it on the ground. She placed a measure next to it and took some more photos.

Shit.

Well, this fit.

She pulled an evidence bag from her pocket and slid the object inside.

Gail straightened again, scanning the cliffs for her colleagues. She could see figures a way off; Lesley and Tina.

Perfect timing.

Lesley would certainly be glad to have arrived just after Gail had found a gun.

CHAPTER FORTY

Elsa looked up as the door to her office opened and Aurelia slid inside, closing the door behind her.

"What's happened?" Elsa asked.

"Don't you already know?"

"I saw DS Frampton and his colleague."

Aurelia threw herself into the chair opposite Elsa. "They're investigating a double murder. Two bodies found in Lyme Regis. They used to work here."

"When?"

"Ten years ago."

"Well before my time. Who?"

"Kenneth Fogarty and Catherine Lawson. They were Harry's partners before I started here." Aurelia leaned forwards and placed her elbows on the desk. "The two of them set this firm up with him."

Elsa looked at Aurelia, who had turned pale. "And they've been found dead?"

Aurelia gave Elsa a long, slow nod. "They died ten years ago. We – Harry – thought they'd retired."

"And nobody reported them missing?"

"They were emigrating. Canada, according to the minutes of their final partner meeting. The pair of them sold their interest to Harry. He was retiring from the law, she was considering retraining in something else. He'd just finalised a divorce. Harry must have just assumed they'd lost touch."

Elsa leaned back. "Fogarty's ex-wife didn't report him missing?"

"It seems not," Aurelia replied. "Ten years and nobody noticed they were gone. What does that say about a person?"

Elsa pursed her lips. If she went missing, Lesley would raise hell till she was found.

She felt a chill run through her chest. Harry had died, murdered by his girlfriend. Ameena Khan, a junior partner, she'd been killed, too.

Now these two former partners. And here was she, working for their most notorious client.

She swallowed. "Do the police know how they died?"

"If they do, they're not telling me about it. They're talking to Kate Jingwell and Justin Osman now, they're the only people who were here ten years ago. I imagine they're trying to piece together a picture of their lives. Who they worked with, who they might have pissed off."

"Their clients?" Elsa asked.

Aurelia looked her in the eye. "Kenneth had one main client."

Elsa knew what was coming next. "Do I want to know who this was?"

"I don't think you need me to tell you."

Another shiver ran across Elsa's skin. "Do you think that's why they died?"

"It could be unrelated. Up on the cliffs, it *could* have been an accident." She stood up and eyed Elsa. "Keep him happy, won't you? Don't piss him off."

Elsa dug her fingernails into the desk.

"Do as he tells you," Aurelia said.

Easy for you to say. Elsa nodded, mute.

"I'd best be going," Aurelia told her. "They'll want to talk to me again."

"Let me know if there's anything I can do."

"You weren't here ten years ago."

"Nor were you."

"Yes, but…"

Elsa nodded.

Aurelia had started in the firm not long after Fogarty and Lawson would have left. She knew Harry better than Elsa did. She was connected to this, like it or not.

"I'll let you know if anything else happens," Aurelia told her.

"Thanks," Elsa replied, aware that her voice was thin.

As Aurelia opened the door, Elsa spotted Sam passing outside. She drew in a breath. "Aurelia, can you grab Sam for me please?"

Aurelia frowned. "Why?"

"Something I need her to do for me."

"OK." Aurelia left the room.

Elsa waited for Sam to return. She had to do this, and she had to do it now.

CHAPTER FORTY-ONE

"Where did you find this?" Lesley asked Gail, turning the bag over in her hand.

Gail pointed up the cliffs. "Higher up. Not far from the road."

"How come it hadn't been found already?"

Gail shook her head. "It was buried under some bushes. If we hadn't been trying to work out where the bodies started out, we never would have spotted it."

"The chances of it being a different gun to the one that shot Kenneth Fogarty are infinitesimally small."

"This is Lyme Regis."

"Exactly. But still, we need to match it. Any ideas?"

"Not yet," Gail replied. "You'd have to speak to the pathologist, find out if there are bullet fragments inside the bodies."

"He's working on that."

"Good," Gail said. "I'll talk to him, see what we can find."

Lesley looked up at the cliffs, towards the spot where the gun had been hidden for so long.

"Was there anything else up there? Anything belonging to the victims, or the killer?"

Gail smiled. "Yes, actually…"

Lesley knew that look on Gail's face. "Go on…"

"Well, I found a driver's licence with a name on it. A receipt for that gun from the shop where it was bought, and also two credit cards in a wallet."

"Really?" asked Tina.

Lesley turned to her. "Gail does this. When she can't find anything, she likes to make up stuff. Normally you're a bit more subtle."

Gail wrinkled her nose. "Not in the mood for subtle today. I'm bloody freezing. I don't suppose either of you have brought a flask of tea with you?"

"Sorry," said Tina. "I should have thought of it."

"It's fine," Gail told her. "It's not your job to keep the CSIs fed and watered. We'll take a break, go up to the van."

"Where is your van?" Lesley asked. "I didn't see it in the car park."

"We're parked up on Charmouth Road, closest spot to where we found that." She indicated the gun.

"Are there any distinguishing marks on it?" Lesley asked her. "A serial number, by any chance?"

"Not by the looks of it," Gail told her. "The rust and dirt are disfiguring it. We'll have to clean it up, but I wouldn't hold out much hope after this long."

"This has definitely been here for ten years?" Lesley asked.

Another shrug. "No idea, but I might be able to get a botanist in to check the vegetation that's stuck to it."

"They can do that?"

"You'd be amazed."

Gail held out a hand and took the gun from Lesley. She placed it in the pilot case and snapped the lid shut.

"I want to get this into the van, safe from prying eyes."

Lesley nodded. "Let me know when you've done a full analysis. And the results of your conversation with Dr Bamford."

"Of course," said Gail. "I'll have it for you first thing in the morning."

CHAPTER FORTY-TWO

Dennis shook himself out as they arrived back at the office. He wasn't a big fan of lawyers, and the lawyers of Nevin, Cross and Short were worse than most. On top of that, he didn't enjoy dealing with the firm that Lesley's girlfriend worked for, it made him worry that he might find himself in the middle of something he'd rather not be involved in.

He stood behind his chair and yawned. "Anybody want a coffee?"

Stanley, still at his desk, looked up. "That'd be smashing, Sarge. I haven't moved since you and Mike left."

Dennis raised an eyebrow. "Have you found anything?"

"Tracked down Kenneth Fogarty's ex-wife."

"Good." Dennis nodded at Mike. "Do you mind getting the coffees?"

Mike frowned. "Do I have to?"

"I need one," Dennis told him. "It won't take you five minutes, the evidence will still be here when you get back."

Mike clenched his jaw, shrugged his coat off, and hung it on the door before pushing it open to head for the kitchen.

"So," Dennis asked Stanley, "tell me about our widow."

"Her name's Eleanor, Eleanor Fogarty."

"She kept her married name?"

"According to the records I've found, yes. Divorce hadn't long been finalised when Fogarty disappeared."

"And she didn't report him missing?"

"No record of any report on file. She's not on the system, and nor is he."

"OK," said Dennis. "Let's have a look at her, then."

Stanley brought up a web page. It showed a group of people dressed in suits, standing in an office posing for the camera.

He pointed at the woman in the middle. "That's her," he said. "Works for a stationery supplies business in…"

Dennis looked at the caption. "Exeter?"

"Exeter," Stanley confirmed.

"Does she live in Exeter?"

"I haven't got to that yet, Sarge. I'm checking the electoral register."

"It's OK," said Dennis as the door opened and Mike appeared holding two mugs. "Mike can do that, can't you?"

"Mike can do what?" Mike asked, his voice tight.

"Check the electoral register for Kenneth Fogarty's widow."

"We've got a name?"

"We certainly have," replied Stanley.

"OK," said Mike. "She's not on the system anywhere?"

"She isn't," Dennis told him.

"She didn't report him missing?"

"Probably happy he'd gone."

Mike nodded. "Where have we last got a record of her?"

"Exeter," Stanley told him. "She works for a stationery supplies firm."

"Glamorous." Mike placed a mug on Dennis's desk and another on his own. "Sorry, Stanley. I couldn't remember how you take it."

"It's OK," Stanley said. "I could do with moving around, I'll get my own."

Mike smiled. "Thanks, mate." He sat down at his desk and pulled his chair in.

"Good," Dennis said. "We'll find this woman and then we can go and see her."

Mike looked up. "Surely that's the Devon force's job if she's in Exeter?"

"You're right." Dennis sniffed. "The boss is not going to be happy with this."

CHAPTER FORTY-THREE

"That's good," Lesley said, in a tone that suggested it was anything but, as she put down her phone.

Gail gave her a questioning look. "What's up?"

"Dennis and the team have managed to track down Kenneth Fogarty's wife. Ex-wife."

Gail's eyes narrowed. "She never reported him missing?"

"They'd just completed the divorce process, I guess she was glad to see the back of him. He and Catherine Lawson were supposed to be emigrating to Canada."

"Which would explain why nobody realised they were gone," said Tina.

"Bingo," Lesley replied.

"So what's the problem?" Gail asked.

"Guess where she lives?"

"Don't tell me. Somewhere in Devon."

Lesley raised a finger and made a tick shape in the air.

"Exactly. So I'll need to speak to our friend DI Hannah Patterson, and get her back on board."

"It's not that bad, is it?" asked Tina. "I mean, when I was in Uniform in Lyme Regis, we often worked with the Devon force."

Lesley sighed. "I know, I'm being petty. I'm just not used to inter-force cooperation, it wasn't something that came up very often in Force CID."

"Looks like you're going to have to get used to it now," said Gail. "You'll be fine."

Lesley nodded. "Tina, can you get yourself a lift back to the station? I might as well head over to do this interview now."

Tina looked at her watch. "It's half past five, boss. By the time you get to Exeter at this time of day it'll be seven o'clock. You think Hannah Patterson's gonna be OK with that?"

"Well, if she's not OK, I can do the interview on my own."

"Don't do that," Gail said.

"What?" Lesley asked, spreading her arms out.

"Don't trick her into not being involved. You know what Carpenter'll say, you know how he likes to play politics."

"You're right," Lesley said. "I'll give her a call, arrange to visit Mrs Fogarty tomorrow. Tina, is there any chance your mum could put us up again?"

CHAPTER FORTY-FOUR

The office was emptying out, staff leaving in dribs and drabs. Elsa kept checking the clock on the wall of her office.

Quarter past six now. Aurelia had left ten minutes ago, and there was just one man left in the open office.

She stood and stretched her arms above her head. They were shaking. She opened her office door and went to stand just outside it.

"Chris," she said.

The man turned to her. He was a junior associate, with the firm for just eight months.

"Everything alright, Ms Short?"

"You can call me Elsa. Is there a reason you're working late?"

"My wife's away, she's a chef. Sometimes travels when she's in charge of private dining experiences." He waggled his fingers in air-quotes.

"Nice. Anyway, why don't you get home now, make *yourself* a private dinner?"

He scoffed. "Yeah, it'll be a Maccie's for me."

"No point sitting around in the office all night, though. I'll see you in the morning."

He shrugged and started tidying the paperwork on his desk. Elsa retreated into her office, watching him through the glazed door. When at last he'd left, she looked up at the clock again. Twenty-five past six. She'd give it five minutes, just in case.

At half past six, her heart was racing and her eyes hadn't left the clock.

She rose from her chair as smoothly as she could and left her office. The filing room was at the far end of the office and she had the key in her pocket.

She opened it smoothly and ducked inside, just as she had this morning. Her throat was tight.

She went to the file, quickly this time, knowing exactly what she was looking for, and drew out the folder containing the documents she needed to shred.

She stepped towards the shredder.

Once again, it had been turned off, but it was still warm.

She switched it on and stood over it, tapping her foot in impatience. At last, it came to life.

Swallowing deeply, Elsa drew out a document from the folder. She held it above the shredder, staring at it for a moment before she let it fall.

The paper went through the machine, fine strips emerging and sliding into the plastic bin beneath. The bin had been emptied. She'd have to empty it again.

Elsa watched as the strips curled into the bottom of the bin. She took another sheet from the file. She held it over the shredder, paused again, then dropped it.

The door to the filing room opened.

The office had been empty. She'd checked.

She pulled the folder close to her chest and looked at the person who'd entered.

Sam Chaston.

"Sam," she said, trying to sound calm.

"Elsa." Sam eyed the shredder and the bin beneath it. "Everything alright?"

"Yes," Elsa replied. "Everything's fine. You can go home."

CHAPTER FORTY-FIVE

Tina sat on her old single bed in her mum's house, the door closed.

The DCI had spent most of the evening in her own room, descending briefly to eat dinner with them around the kitchen table. It had been an awkward affair, the DCI in an odd mood. The DCI was often in an odd mood lately.

Tina's mum had tried to make small talk, asking the DCI how long she'd been in her job, where she'd lived before. The boss had responded with curt answers, little more than a word each time. Eventually, Tina had taken over the conversation, steering her mum towards gossip about Mrs Jukes over the road, who'd had a hysterectomy a month earlier.

Glad to be alone, Tina lay back on her bed, pillows bunched behind her, and brought her phone out of her pocket. It was picked up on the second ring.

"Hey, T."

"Mike," she said, feeling warmth flood through her. "How's things back at the ranch?"

"Boring, without you."

She smiled. "Sorry I didn't return your call last night. It's a bit weird being here with my mum."

Her stomach grumbled. She put a hand over it.

"I'd like to meet your mum sometime," Mike said.

Tina dug her thumbnail into the palm of her hand. "Really?"

"If we're talking about living together, then we need to meet each other's parents."

"I haven't met *your* mum."

"Yes you did," he replied. "You saw her that time when she was at my flat and you came to pick me up."

"That was five minutes," Tina told him. "She was leaving, I was arriving. We said hello and that was it."

"Well," he said. "Maybe I can organise something more formal? We can take her out for dinner."

"I'd like that. She seemed nice."

"She is. What about your mum?"

Tina glanced towards the door. "My mum's lovely in her own way. She's over the moon having the DCI here to cluck over."

"So she's that kind of mum."

"What do you mean, *that* kind of mum?"

"The type who likes to make a fuss. You think she'll embarrass you by fussing over the new boyfriend."

"She probably will," Tina said. "But I can deal with it. It's not like I'm going to get any ideas from her."

Mike laughed. "I don't see you as the clucky type."

"Dear God, no. So what have you been working on with the DS?"

"Looking into the victims," Mike told her. "We found a wife for Kenneth Fogarty. Did you know?"

"Yeah," she said. "The DCI's going to see her tomorrow morning, taking DI Patterson with her from the Devon and Cornwall force."

"I heard about that," Mike said. "DCI's not happy?"

Tina lowered her voice. "She's not happy about a lot of stuff."

"What d'you mean?"

"I don't know." Tina glanced at the door again. "There's just an edge to her at the moment. It's like she's about to say something, and then she doesn't. I'm wondering if it's something to do with the fact that the two murder victims worked for the same firm her girlfriend does."

There was silence at the end of the line.

"Mike?" Tina asked. "Did you go and see Aurelia Cross today?"

"The sarge took me."

"What was she like?"

"Evasive," he replied. "She made out like she didn't know anything about Fogarty and Lawson, but we'll get to the bottom of it."

Tina licked her lips. "I miss you."

Her stomach rumbled again. She winced.

"You too," he replied. "When are you coming home?"

"Hopefully tomorrow," she said. "Now they've found the gun at the crime scene, I can't see how they need us here anymore."

"Good," he replied. "I'll buy a nice bottle of wine and we'll have an evening in."

CHAPTER FORTY-SIX

The office was quiet when Elsa arrived. It was ten to seven, well before most people got in for the day.

She eased the door to the outer reception area shut and walked towards her office. She was trying to inject confidence into her stride, but her eyes darted from side to side.

Was Sam in yet?

Aurelia wouldn't be, not for another half hour or so. She had less than an hour to work out what she was going to do.

Elsa glanced at Aurelia's office as she passed it, pulling her own office key out of her bag. As she did so, the door to Aurelia's office opened.

Aurelia stood in the doorway.

Elsa dropped her keys.

"Elsa," Aurelia said, "I was hoping that was you."

Elsa dropped to the ground to pick up her keys, avoiding eye contact. "Aurelia, you're in early. D'you have a court appearance?" She stood up and risked looking her partner in the eye.

Aurelia shook her head. "Come into my office, will you?"

"Give me a moment, I'll just dump my things."

"I'd prefer to see you straight away."

Elsa put her keys back in her bag and slung it over her shoulder. She followed Aurelia, trying not to feel like a naughty girl who'd been summoned to the headmistress.

Aurelia strode through her office door and let it close behind her, not holding it for Elsa. Elsa put a hand on it, her fingers trembling.

This was bad.

She pushed the door open to see Aurelia sitting behind her desk. She leaned back in her chair, her hands in her lap, her posture stiff.

She wasn't alone.

Beside her, standing to the side of the desk, blinking rapidly and looking between Elsa and Aurelia, was Sam.

CHAPTER FORTY-SEVEN

Eleanor Fogarty lived in a grand Victorian house on the outskirts of Exeter. Lesley pulled up and took a moment to check herself in the mirror. It had been early when she'd left Annie Abbott's house, and she hadn't wanted to spend too long in the bathroom. She was developing dark circles under her eyes; those damn seagulls had woken her again.

She just wanted her own bed. Not to mention Elsa.

She'd tried calling Elsa last night, but got no answer. It wasn't like Elsa not to return her messages.

A car pulled up on the other side of the road and DI Patterson got out. She strode to Lesley's car and stood by the driver's door, waiting.

Lesley wound down her window. "Morning."

Hannah smiled. "I can only apologise."

"What for?"

"The fact that you've got to put up with me again."

Lesley leaned her head back. "It probably doesn't need two of us to do this interview, but at least it meant I could leave Tina back at Lyme Regis with the CSIs."

"Tina?"

"DC Abbott."

"You've only got a team of one?"

"The rest of my team is back at headquarters, looking into the two victims' pasts."

"*And* the fact that they were once partners in your girlfriend's law firm," Hannah replied, an eyebrow arched.

Lesley felt her stomach clench. "How did you know that?"

Hannah gave her a wink. "I'm a detective, Ma'am. It's my job to know things like that."

"Well," Lesley replied, "my connection to the firm has no bearing on my handling of this case."

Hannah straightened. "No, Ma'am. I didn't say it would."

"Good."

Lesley got out of the car and smoothed down her skirt. She was still wearing the same one she'd had on two days ago when she'd first set off for Lyme Regis. If she was going to stay here any longer, she'd need to send someone back to get some things from Bournemouth.

Or maybe she could go back herself, find out why Elsa wasn't returning her calls…

"Right," she said. *Focus.* "Let's see what Mrs Fogarty has to say."

She looked up and down the quiet street, then walked to the house whose number Dennis had given her. The front curtains were closed but the garden was neat and tidy. Early daffodils in beds that had been recently weeded. At the first-floor windows, the curtains were also drawn. There was no bell at the front door, just an old-fashioned knocker, freshly polished by the look of it. Lesley gave it two sharp raps.

"Maybe she's not in?" Hannah suggested.

Lesley shook her head. "The garden's immaculate, and the curtains are drawn. The kind of person who plants spring bulbs and weeds their garden at this time of year isn't the kind of person who leaves the house in the morning without opening the curtains."

Hannah shrugged.

The door opened and Lesley resisted an *I told you so*.

Inside was a woman in her late sixties with grey hair scraped back from her face. She wore a battered red fleece and a freshly washed pair of jeans with a rip in one knee.

Lesley held up her ID. "Mrs Fogarty?"

"That's me. How can I help you?"

"I'm Detective Chief Inspector Clarke, this is Detective Inspector Patterson. Can we come in, please?"

Mrs Fogarty frowned. "What is it? Is it Henry?"

"Who's Henry?" Hannah asked.

"My stepson. Has he got into trouble again?"

"No," Lesley told the woman. "Please, if we can just come in?"

"OK." The woman turned and led them into the house. "Where do you want to sit?"

"Wherever you feel most comfortable," Lesley replied.

"Come into the kitchen."

The kitchen was at the back of the house, a long narrow room jutting out into the back garden. Something bubbled on the stove and a newspaper lay open on the table. Eleanor Fogarty gestured towards the table and Lesley took a seat, waiting for Hannah to do the same.

"Cup of tea?" Mrs Fogarty asked.

"No thanks," Lesley told her.

"Fair enough. There's a pot ready if you change your mind." She gestured towards a brown teapot that sat in the centre of the table, covered by a blue cosy.

Lesley smiled. This kitchen was almost as homely as Annie Abbott's.

"If you don't mind," she said. "We'd like to talk to you. Do you want to sit down?"

Mrs Fogarty looked at her for a moment, as if deciding whether she might sit down or make a run for it. Lesley wondered just what her stepson had been up to. Eventually, Mrs Fogarty sniffed and took the chair opposite Lesley.

"If it's not Henry, what is it?"

"It's about your ex-husband, Kenneth."

Mrs Fogarty's shoulders slumped and the breath seemed to leave her body.

"That bastard. What does he want?"

"I'm sorry to tell you we found his body in Lyme Regis two days ago."

"Lyme Regis?"

"He'd been buried at the top of the cliffs. A storm created a landslip and his body was uncovered."

"What was he doing in Lyme Regis?"

"I was hoping you could tell me that."

Mrs Fogarty shook her head. "Canada. That's where he was, not Lyme Regis."

Lesley nodded. "I gather he had plans to emigrate after retiring?"

A snort. "With that bitch Catherine."

Lesley exchanged glances with Hannah.

"Are you referring to Catherine Lawson?"

"Yes. Is she in Canada?"

"No," Lesley replied. "She was with Mr Fogarty in Lyme Regis."

"She killed him?"

"She was dead as well."

"Catherine Lawson?"

Lesley nodded. "We found the two of them in the same spot. Their bodies were buried above the cliffs east of Lyme Regis ten years ago."

Mrs Fogarty frowned. "Ten years?"

"I know this is hard," Lesley said.

"It's not hard at all. He was out of my life by then, about to leave the country. But you're saying he was killed ten years ago and nobody missed him?"

Lesley shifted in her chair "Did you notice any lack of communication from him?"

The woman shook her head. "I didn't expect any. We didn't exactly split in amicable circumstances. The divorce had been finalised, the finances sorted. As far as I was concerned, the less communication I got from him the better."

"So nobody got in touch with you asking where he might be?"

"Nobody. We sort of, well, we each got custody of a different group of friends after the divorce. To be honest, he didn't have any friends. Just work colleagues. And her."

Lesley sat back in her chair. "Were you aware of anyone who might have wanted your husband dead? Someone he'd annoyed in the course of his work, or come across personally?"

Mrs Fogarty stared at her. "I'm not sure."

"What do you mean, you're not sure?" Hannah asked.

Mrs Fogarty flinched and looked at the DI. It was as if she'd forgotten the other woman was there.

"He had some clients who were… unsavoury. Or at least he seemed to. He didn't like talking about work."

"Did he say anything to you about these clients?" Lesley asked.

"Of course not, he didn't tell me anything. For six years he was having an affair with that Lawson woman and he never told me that. Why should he tell me about his *clients*?"

"But you said he had unsavoury clients?" Hannah said.

A shrug. "There were phone calls late at night, he had a second phone. There was always something different about him after he'd answered it. He was scared, I think."

"Do you know who these clients might have been?" Lesley asked. "Were they definitely clients?"

"That's what he told me. He could have been lying though. Kenneth lied about everything."

Lesley exchanged glances with DI Patterson.

"Thank you, Mrs Fogarty. You've been very helpful."

CHAPTER FORTY-EIGHT

"Sam," Elsa said. "What are you doing here?"

Sam said nothing but looked at Aurelia instead.

"Take a seat," Aurelia said to the younger woman.

Sam shuffled backwards and slid into a chair, her gaze not meeting Elsa's.

Elsa moved towards the other chair, the more comfortable one immediately opposite Aurelia's desk.

"Not you," Aurelia said.

Elsa's head flicked up, looking at Aurelia. "Sorry?"

"You can remain standing."

Elsa put a hand on the desk. "Is there a problem?"

"You could say that."

Aurelia stood up. She bent down and lifted something from behind her desk. A plastic box. In it were shards of paper, the output of the shredding machine.

Elsa felt her stomach lurch. "I can explain."

Aurelia raised a finger, shaking her head. "Sam has told me everything."

Elsa glanced at Sam, who was looking down at her lap. Sam was scared for her job. She was desperate, Elsa knew that.

Elsa lifted her chin, looking Aurelia in the eye. "You're the one who made me work for him. You know the kind of thing it entails."

Aurelia gripped the edge of the plastic box. "Destroying evidence is a criminal offence."

Elsa slammed a hand onto the desk. "Come on, Aurelia, don't be so naive. When you work for men like Arthur Kelvin you know that sometimes you have to cross a line."

Aurelia leaned forwards. Her gaze flicked to Sam. "No."

"Don't tell me Harry never did anything like this."

"Harry managed to represent that man while keeping everything above board."

Elsa scoffed. "Well, if you believe that—"

"If I believe that, what?" Aurelia interrupted.

"You're fucking naive."

Elsa knew she was burning bridges now.

Aurelia sat down, slamming herself into the chair.

"I expect you out of here by the time everybody else arrives."

"Really? I'm a named partner. You can't just kick me out."

"Check the partnership agreement. I think you'll find I can. And I think that compared to the alternative, which is informing the Law Society, you'll be quite pleased when I do."

Elsa forced her muscles to relax. She blinked a few times at Aurelia, then looked at Sam. Sam's legs were crossed beneath her, her eyes almost closed.

"Very well," said Elsa. "But who's going to represent him now?"

CHAPTER FORTY-NINE

Gail stared into her screen, at the magnified images of the gun they'd found at the Spittles. She'd examined it in the flesh, or rather in the metal. But she could make out more detail by zooming into these photographs.

She moved her mouse around, dragging the picture across the screen and zooming in.

She leaned back in her chair.

"Gav," she said.

Gavin looked up from the desk opposite. "What's up?"

"Come and have a look at this."

He pushed his chair back, yawned, and rounded the desks to stand behind her.

"The gun," he said.

"The gun."

It wasn't often they found a gun at a crime scene. Particularly a crime scene as old as this one. This gun had been buried in the ground, or hidden in the undergrowth, for ten years. Gail found it impossible to believe nobody would have come across it in all that time.

Or maybe they had, and had chosen to ignore it?

She pointed at the screen. "It's been filed."

"No surprise there. If you're going to use a gun to kill a couple of people, you don't want to leave any identifying marks."

Gail nodded.

"The gun had no prints on it," Gavin said. "No fibres, no DNA."

"After ten years…" Gail turned her head to one side, frowning at the screen.

"Even after ten years, there would have been something," Gavin said. "It was thoroughly cleaned before it was dumped."

"Let's X-ray it. There's a rusty patch there and part of the serial number might still be intact beneath it."

Gavin sniffed. "We can give it a go, I guess."

"Where is it?" she asked.

"It hasn't gone to Winfrith yet. It's still in our evidence store."

"Good," she told him. "Let's get it out, run it through the X-ray machine. See what we get."

CHAPTER FIFTY

Lesley resisted the urge to look back as she and Hannah Patterson left Eleanor Fogarty's house.

"What did you think?" Hannah asked.

"Worth following up these 'unsavoury' clients," Lesley replied. "I'll get my team on it."

Hannah cocked her head. "A Dorset lead, that'll make you happy."

Lesley clenched a fist inside her pocket. "That's just how it is, Hannah. If the lead is in Dorset, my team can work on it. If you want to look into Eleanor Fogarty's background, or the circumstances of her divorce, be my guest."

Hannah screwed up her mouth.

"Not that I think it'll get you anywhere," Lesley continued.

"Maybe," Hannah said.

"Come on," Lesley replied. "She didn't do it."

Hannah raised a finger. "We both know how many murders are domestic. The unfaithful husband and the mistress, in one fell swoop."

"Where would she have got a gun?"

"She hated him."

"You didn't answer my question."

Hannah licked her lips. "The gun is tricky, I'll admit. But she had motive. And I find it hard to believe she wouldn't have noticed he hadn't made contact and mentioned it to someone, at least."

Lesley shook her head. "They were estranged."

"To the extent that he disappeared and not one mutual friend missed him or said anything to her?"

Lesley sighed. "OK. You look into Eleanor, if you want. I'll stick with the forensics."

"Good luck with that."

Lesley grunted.

Hannah eyed Lesley. "This dodgy client story might be a smokescreen. Maybe my team should check his professional dealings, given that you have a connection to—"

Lesley stopped walking. "DI Patterson, are you questioning my integrity?"

"No. But I think—"

"Stick to your side of the border, Inspector, and I'll stick to mine. Let me know if you uncover anything suspicious about the widow."

"I will."

"You won't."

Hannah said nothing.

They were at Lesley's car. She put a hand on the door. "Thank you for your help with the interview."

"Any time." Hannah walked away, without making eye contact.

Lesley watched her. The woman was desperate to bring the Devon and Cornwall force into this, but she'd find nothing on Eleanor Fogarty. And Lesley knew more about Kenneth Fogarty's former firm than Hannah did. In particular, about its 'unsavoury' clients.

CHAPTER FIFTY-ONE

"It's ready," Gavin said.

"Good." Gail dragged her chair around to his side of the desk. "Show me."

He pulled up an image on his screen, the first X-ray image of the gun. He'd taken them from various angles and there were twelve in all.

"Where's the one that most closely corresponds to the photo I showed you before?" asked Gail.

"Hang on a minute."

He clicked his mouse a few times and brought up an image.

Gail had been about to speak. She stopped, her mouth open.

"It's still there," she said after a moment's silence.

"And the serial number."

She nodded. "Zoom in."

She could sense that Gavin was holding his breath too. They'd both seen the same thing, but they wanted to check it.

He zoomed in, licking his lips. He looked at her. "It is, isn't it?" he said.

She nodded, holding her breath.

"Shit." She put a hand on Gavin's shoulder. "This blows the case wide open."

CHAPTER FIFTY-TWO

It was a relief to be driving back towards Winfrith. Lesley rolled her shoulders as she left Lyme Regis behind her and skirted the coast towards the east.

Sure, Lyme Regis was pretty enough. She could see the charm. But she'd felt like she was on the edge of the world.

Sometimes Swanage made her feel like that. But in Swanage, there was the knowledge that a ten minute ride on a ferry took you to Poole and civilisation. Lesley liked civilisation. Much as she was loving living in Dorset, especially living with Elsa, it would take a long time to knock that out of her.

She hit hands-free on her phone as she approached Bridport. It rang out a few times, then Elsa's voicemail kicked in. Lesley hung up; she'd left enough messages.

She'd try Elsa's work.

Again, it rang out a couple of times. Then a woman's voice answered, Elsa's PA.

"Hi, Amanda," Lesley said, "is Elsa about?"

"This isn't Amanda."

"Sorry. I need to speak to Elsa."

"This is Brienne."

Brienne was Aurelia's PA.

"OK," Lesley said. "Where's Amanda?"

"She went home for the day."

Why so curt?

"Can you put me through to Elsa please? It's Lesley."

"I know your voice."

Lesley glanced in her rear-view mirror to see the car behind flashing its lights. She'd waited too long at the roundabout. She squinted at the road signs, trying to get her bearings. West Bay off to the right, Dorchester to the left.

She drove off and took the Dorchester turn.

"Brienne?" she said. The line had gone quiet.

"Sorry, DCI Clarke."

Lesley frowned. "Lesley."

"Sorry, *Lesley*. Elsa's not here, either."

"I've been trying her mobile but there's no answer."

"No."

"What do you mean, no? Why is she not picking up her phone?"

"She doesn't have it anymore."

"Why?" Lesley asked. "What's going on? Has she left it in the office?"

"I think you should ask her that."

"So where is she if she's left her phone behind?"

Lesley wrinkled her nose.

Elsa didn't go anywhere without her phone. Lawyers were like coppers. Always contactable, never truly off-duty.

"Is Elsa OK?"

"I think you need to speak to her yourself."

The line went dead.

Lesley looked at the phone in its holder.

"*Shit*. Where are you, Els?"

What was going on? And was this related to whatever Elsa was planning to talk to her about at the weekend?

CHAPTER FIFTY-THREE

Lesley threw her car into a space when she reached Winfrith and hurried up the stairs towards her first-floor office.

She'd tried Elsa's mobile twice more. She'd also tried the phone that Elsa had used to contact DCI Mackie when he'd still been alive. That was dead. Finally, she'd left another message on Elsa's official phone.

Should she go back to the flat, or maybe to Elsa's office?

No. Given that they were investigating the death of two former partners, it wouldn't be wise to turn up there on personal business.

A woman was standing at the top of the stairs, waiting for her. It was Carpenter's PA. Lesley felt her body sink. *What now?*

"Carla," she said. "Can I help you with something?"

Carla smiled, her eyes hard. "He wants to speak to you."

"I'm on my way into the office, we're in the middle of a murder enquiry."

"Now," Carla said.

"OK. I just need to let Dennis know where I am."

"No. It won't take long."

Lesley gritted her teeth. "Fine."

She followed the woman to Carpenter's office. Carla stopped outside the door, pushed it open and gestured for Lesley to go inside. She did so, bracing herself as she entered. What was Carpenter going to give her a bollocking for this time?

The door closed behind her.

Two men sat in the comfortable chairs by the window.

One of them was Carpenter: silver hair, ironed shirt, neatly done tie, the usual.

The other was less well turned out. Uncombed hair flopped over his left eye and his blue jacket had a stain running down the sleeve. He wore jeans that had seen better days and a pair of trainers that were probably designed to look trendy, but failing.

Lesley leaned against the door and stared at him.

"Matt Crippins," she said, glancing at Carpenter. "What's happened?"

CHAPTER FIFTY-FOUR

Dennis peered out of the window. He could see the DCI's car in the car park, straddling two spaces. But there was no sign of her. He'd watched her approach the building, her brow furrowed, footsteps hurried, and wondered what mood she'd be in when she got up here.

But now, fifteen minutes later, there was no sign of her.

He turned back to the team. His mobile was buzzing on his desk. He grabbed it.

"DS Frampton."

"Dennis, it's Gail. I'm trying to get hold of Lesley, d'you know where she is?"

He glanced towards the window.

"She's back. She hasn't made it into the office yet, though."

"OK, I need to speak to her when she gets back. It's urgent."

"Anything I can help with?"

A pause.

"Gail," Dennis said. "If the boss has been waylaid, the team and I can be working on whatever it is you're calling about while we wait."

Gail sighed. "You're right. This is sensitive, though. Are you alone?"

Dennis looked at Stanley and Mike, both heads down in front of their computers.

"I'm with Mike and Stanley. It's fine."

"OK. Just be careful how you react."

Dennis rolled his eyes. "Tell me what it is, please."

"The gun, we've managed to use X-ray to identify the serial number."

"And you know whose it was?"

"We don't know whose it was, but we know which organisation it belongs to, or rather used to belong to."

"Go on," Dennis said. This would be organised crime, he was sure.

Gail cleared her throat. "OK, Dennis, like I say, this is sensitive. As soon as you see the DCI, you tell her. Get her to call me, I'll give her the details, and then she can decide how to take it from there."

"Gail," Dennis said, "just tell me, please."

Another pause.

"It's a police issue gun, Dennis. Ten years ago, somebody used a police gun to kill Kenneth Fogarty and Catherine Lawson."

CHAPTER FIFTY-FIVE

"What's happened?" Lesley asked, looking at Matt. "Is it Sadie?"

Matt stared back at her, his expression impassive.

"I suggest you take a seat," Carpenter told her.

Lesley hurried to sit next to him on the sofa.

"Is Sadie OK?" she asked, looking at Matt.

He nodded, then glanced at Carpenter.

"What's happening, Sir?" she asked. "Are we reopening the investigation into Sadie's disappearance?"

"It's not quite like that," Superintendent Carpenter said.

"What is it, then?"

The super picked up his cup, took a sip, and then placed it back on the saucer.

Lesley realised that two cups of coffee sat on the table between him and Matt Crippins. She wondered how well these two men knew each other.

"Matt," she said, "will you please tell me what's going on?"

He leaned back, crossing an ankle over his knee. "Sadie's back. She's got information that I've had no choice but to tell your superintendent about."

Lesley moved her hand under her leg and sat on it, hard.

Typical that this had happened while she'd been away in Lyme Regis. If she'd been here, she'd have been able to head Matt Crippins off at the pass and avoid the super getting involved.

"What information?" she asked, keeping her voice level.

Matt looked at the super.

Carpenter hunched forward, leaning over his knees. He swivelled his head to look at Lesley. "Sadie has managed to get hold of a copy of DCI Mackie's suicide note."

Lesley frowned at him. "How?"

"She spoke to his wife," Matt said.

"But Gwen didn't have the note. It was in the evidence store."

"How do you know that?" the super asked.

"Well, of course it was in the evidence store. It was part of the evidence in the case that led the coroner to declare it suicide. It would have been retained by the police."

"It seems that Gwen Mackie had a copy," Matt said.

Lesley slumped in her seat. Why hadn't Gwen told her or Zoe this?

"So Sadie got a copy of DCI Mackie's suicide note from his widow?"

"Yes," Superintendent Carpenter said.

Lesley thought of the conversations that she'd had with Petra McBride, the psychologist she'd asked to take a look at Mackie's note.

Gail had confirmed that the note was written by Mackie. But Petra had examined the style of writing and concluded that while it might have been Mackie's writing, they weren't his words.

She swallowed. "What has Sadie discovered from the note?" she asked Matt.

"I'm not in a position to say right now, but we will be running a story on it. I've given your superintendent enough information for him to reopen the enquiry."

Carpenter nodded.

Lesley wondered why he wasn't standing up to Matt. What was going on?

"Sir," she said. "We're reopening the investigation into DCI Mackie's death?"

"Yes." He smoothed his hands on his knees. "And there'll be an internal investigation into certain officers' conduct in relation to the case."

Lesley stiffened. "Which officers?"

He turned to her.

"You don't need to worry about that. But watch yourself, Lesley. You need to make sure you stick to procedure from now on."

CHAPTER FIFTY-SIX

Lesley crashed into the office, her mind racing. There were questions she wanted to ask Superintendent Carpenter, but not while Matt Crippins was there. There were also questions she wanted to ask Matt Crippins, but not while the super was there.

She gritted her teeth as she opened the door, and pulled on a smile.

"I'm back, guys," she said. "How are we getting along?"

Dennis looked up. "A significant new piece of evidence has come in from the CSIs."

"That's promising."

Her heart was racing. She tried to push away thoughts of what the super had told her. Was her job at stake? Was Zoe's?

But then, this case... was Elsa in danger?

"Go on then," she said to Dennis.

He looked at the door. "You're going to need to tell Carpenter about this."

Lesley raised her face to the ceiling. The last thing she needed was another chat with the super.

"What is it, Dennis? Just bloody well tell me."

He bristled. She raised a palm.

"I don't want to hear it, Dennis. I'm not having a good day. Just tell me what Gail's found."

He approached her and lowered his voice. "The gun that was used to kill Catherine Lawson and Kenneth Fogarty, it was police issue."

Lesley felt her mouth drop open.

"My office."

He followed her inside. She glanced back to see that Mike and Stanley were both trying very hard not to look at them.

"Seriously?" she asked Dennis. "A police gun?"

With Fogarty and Lawson having been partners in Elsa's firm, she was expecting it to be organised crime.

Did this mean police were involved in the murders? Was it yet another case of corruption to add to an ever-growing list?

"Whose gun?" she asked. "Which unit?"

"We're trying to determine that right now. It was ten years ago, the records aren't what they should be. It hasn't all been digitised."

Lesley dragged her hand through her hair. "OK. That's our first priority, we need to find out which unit that gun belonged to and which officer was authorised to use it."

Dennis cocked his head. "What do you think we're doing?"

"Sorry, Dennis. I don't need to tell you how to do your job. But just get on with it, OK?"

Lesley looked down at the carpet and took a few breaths. *Elsa, where are you?*

She forced herself to look up. "I need to tell the super."

CHAPTER FIFTY-SEVEN

Elsa pulled her car onto the driveway of a generously-proportioned house in Sandbanks. She almost skidded on the gravel in her haste, then jumped out and slammed the door. Hurrying towards the house's entrance, she caught herself. *Slow down.*

She had to keep her composure. She had to handle this properly.

A tug on the chain, and a bell rang deep inside the building. Elsa pulled her shoulders back and smoothed down her jacket. She rubbed beneath her eyes, where she imagined her mascara had run. She took deep breaths as she waited.

A woman in a black dress and white apron opened the door. "Can I help you?"

"My name is Elsa Short, I'm Mr Kelvin's lawyer. I need to speak to him."

"Do you have an appointment?"

"He'll see me."

"Wait one moment."

The door closed in Elsa's face. She stared at it, her teeth gritted. *Come on.*

A moment later, the door opened again. A large, middle-aged man stared back at her, a lock of hair bobbing over his right eye.

"What do you want?"

"Arthur, let me in. I have something I need to inform you about."

He grunted. "*Inform* me about?"

She looked back towards her car, and past it onto the street. This house had heavy wrought-iron gates. But still, anybody could see her from the street. She had to be more careful.

Another grunt. "Come on then."

He led her through to the back of the building, into his wide office with views of Poole Harbour. Elsa took a seat, not waiting to be asked.

"Feeling confident today then, are we?" He stood over her, his arms folded against a substantial chest.

"You're not going to like this," she told him. "But I'm afraid it's out of my control."

"What is?"

He walked over to a bookcase and took out a decanter. He poured whisky into a glass and sipped at it. He didn't offer her a glass.

"Go on then," he said. "What the fuck's happened?"

Elsa swallowed. Her mouth was dry. She looked towards the door. She was pretty sure he hadn't locked it. But then, this was Arthur Kelvin.

"I did what you asked me to," she said. "Those documents."

She looked around the room, her eyes snagging on the corners where the walls met the ceiling. She imagined he had CCTV. She also imagined there would be people eager to hack that CCTV.

"Good," Kelvin said.

He leaned against the desk, drumming his fingers against his glass. It was cut crystal, expensive.

"It didn't go quite according to plan," she told him.

He raised an eyebrow. "And that's my problem?"

"It could be."

"Just fucking tell me what happened, woman."

She stood up. She wanted to be eye to eye with him for this, but she also wanted to have quick access to that door. She took a step sideways, bringing herself a little bit closer to it. She had no idea who might be on the other side.

"I was seen," she told him, looking into his eyes.

He didn't flinch. "Seen?"

"By a colleague."

"Who?"

"Nobody you need worry about."

He stepped forward.

"Who?"

Elsa forced herself not to blink. "Aurelia Cross." She wasn't about to give him Sam's name. "She came to the filing room while I was shredding the documents. She was walking past, she must have seen me in there."

He gave her a wry smile. "Aurelia Cross just *happened* to be walking past the filing room when you were doing that? I thought you said you were going to be careful."

"Aurelia was working late."

He spat. "Bollocks. I don't believe you."

"It's true. You can ask her."

Her voice was becoming breathy. *Calm down.*

"Anyway," she said, feeling the bile rise in her throat. "Destroying evidence in a criminal case is a criminal offence in itself."

"I knew that," he said. "Since when is it my problem?"

"I'm your lawyer," she told him. "Or I was. But now I've committed a crime…"

He shook his head. He eyed her for a moment, then took another swig of the whisky. She watched his Adam's apple bob.

"No way that bitch is going to rat you out," he said. "You're a partner in her firm, you're all in it together."

"She's fired me."

He laughed. A low, growling laugh. "Bollocks, she has."

Elsa glanced at the door again. "It's on my file, black and white. Aurelia said firing me was the only way to avoid having to report me to the Law Society. Or worse."

He grunted. "Hang on a fucking minute. Aurelia Cross isn't going to bloody fire you. You're representing her firm's biggest client. If she fires you, who's going to look after me?"

"That's not my problem anymore," Elsa told him. "The fact is, I no longer work for Nevin, Cross and Short."

She wondered how long it would be before the name on the door changed to Nevin and Cross. Or maybe just Cross and Associates. The firm had a habit of haemorrhaging partners.

A chill ran across Elsa's skin. Kenneth Fogarty and Catherine Lawson. They'd been partners.

She felt her skin shrivel. Had she done the right thing? *Yes.* She had to be shot of him.

"So I can't act as your lawyer any more," she told him, trying to sound confident. "I'm very sorry."

He grunted.

"Shysters, the lot of you. I'll speak to Aurelia, she'll see me right. Now fuck off."

CHAPTER FIFTY-EIGHT

Superintendent Carpenter was standing by his window when Lesley entered. He gazed out, hands in pockets, face blank.

She cleared her throat. "Sir, you'll want to know the latest development on the Fogarty and Lawson case."

He turned to her. A moment's confusion ran across his face before he recovered himself.

"They're reconfiguring the car park out there. Did you know that? It's going to be a bloody nightmare. There'll be half as much parking for the next four weeks."

She frowned. "I don't think it'll take them that long, Sir."

He sniffed. "You'd be surprised. So, what's this development?"

"We've discovered the owner of the gun. Well, not the individual who owned it, but the organisation."

He raised an eyebrow. "Organised crime?"

She shook her head and stepped closer to him, checking the door to make sure it was closed.

"It was a police issue gun, Sir."

His eyes narrowed. "You're sure?"

"Gail has examined it under X-ray. She verified the police inscription. She also got the serial number from it, and Dennis has run that through the system. It's a police-issue gun, Sir."

"Which unit?"

"We're working on that now. It was ten years ago. The information isn't readily available."

"Get a move on," he said. "I want to know whose it was."

"Of course. Is that all?"

"No," he said. "We need Professional Standards in on this."

Lesley's shoulders fell. She'd been expecting this.

"Can we at least wait until we know exactly whose gun it was?"

"No, DCI Clarke. We have to do this by the book. I'll make a call, you can expect involvement from PSD."

"When, Sir?"

"How am I supposed to know that? It depends on their level of resourcing, doesn't it?"

"Of course. Do you need anything else from me?"

"No," he said. "But tell me as soon as you've got an ID on the owner of that gun."

CHAPTER FIFTY-NINE

"Got it, Sarge." Mike pumped his fist in the air.

Dennis stood up from his chair and rounded the desks. Stanley did the same.

"The gun owner?" Dennis asked.

"The officer it was signed out to."

"Good work. What's the name?"

"Authorised Firearms Officer Christian Davison." Mike looked up. "Heard of him?"

Dennis shook his head. Ten years ago he'd been a DC in Dorchester. He'd have had no cause to fraternise with AFOs.

"Bring up his record," he said. "Is he still on the force?"

"He's still working as an AFO."

"Wow," breathed Stanley. "*Shit.*"

"Stanley," Dennis muttered. "I'll thank you not to—"

"Sorry, Sarge." Mike saw Stanley shoot a glance towards the filing cabinet where Dennis had hidden his swear jar after the DCI had joined the team. Who'd told him about that?

Dennis took a deep breath. "Print it off," he told Mike. "I'll need to tell the boss about this."

CHAPTER SIXTY

Christian Davison walked to his sofa, balancing a plate and a cup of coffee in one hand, and the latest copy of *Top Gear* magazine in the other.

He tossed the magazine onto the sofa and placed the coffee mug on the side table. The plate held a sandwich: ham and mustard on white bread, his favourite.

He took a large bite then sat down, shuffling to settle himself into the dent in the sofa that had formed over years of use.

He picked up the remote control from the arm of the sofa and pointed it at the TV.

It was five o'clock in the afternoon. He'd been on an early shift, home at three.

Christian was a man of habit. He'd walked through the door, taken a shower, blow-dried his hair, gone downstairs, checked his emails, opened his post, then made himself a sandwich. Now, he was looking forward to *Pointless*, followed by a takeaway Chinese and an evening in front of the box.

He took another bite of the sandwich, swallowing half of it. His job made him hungry. *Pointless* was starting, Alexander Armstrong opening with his usual banter.

Christian reached out to the coffee table where he kept his notepad and pencil. It was easier to get fewer points if he wrote down all the potential answers to a question.

Christian wondered what his colleagues would think if they knew that he came home and sat in front of a TV show that was primarily watched by pensioners. But it kept his mind active in different ways than his job did. This calmed him, prepared him for twelve hours of inactivity, allowed him to switch off from the high stress levels of the job.

He picked up the plate again, about to devour the second half of the sandwich, when there was a loud knock on the door.

He flinched. The sandwich jolted off the plate and fell on the carpet.

Damn. He picked it up and checked both sides. It was OK. No carpet fluff, he'd hoovered yesterday.

He placed the sandwich back on the plate and the plate on the table. He dusted off his hands and stood up, flicking the remote control to pause the TV. He might be watching live TV, but he wasn't so old-school that he didn't have Sky and couldn't pause it.

The door hammered again. Christian frowned. There was only one reason a door got hammered like that, and he was all too familiar with it from his job.

"It's OK, I'm coming!" he shouted, loud as he could.

He had to make sure they knew he was in here and that he was cooperating. If they didn't, the enforcer would be out, and that door would be down. He'd spent two days painting it last month, and he didn't want to see it wrecked.

He hurried out of the living room and into the hallway. The hallway was narrow and dark. The door had a small pane of glass at the top, but not enough for him to see who was outside.

"I'm coming!" he shouted. "Don't bust the door down!"

"Police!" came a voice. "Open up!"

Christian felt his chest clench. He stared at the door for a moment, then slammed a fist into the wall.

He stared at it. He shouldn't have done that. He'd painted that wall, it had taken him a week.

Still, he knew what was coming. He'd been waiting for it long enough.

He walked to the door, focusing on his breathing, and pulled on a blank expression as he opened it.

Four men stood in front of him, bulky in their uniforms. Force Response. His vision was hazy, he realised. A panic attack?

Christian looked between the faces. They all wore helmets and he couldn't identify them. He wondered if they were men that he'd worked with. He wondered if he'd stood with these men and done exactly the same to others as was being done to him right now.

He raised his hands in supplication.

"OK, OK," he said. "I'm cooperating. You don't need to bust the door down, you don't need to hurt me."

"We're not going to hurt you, Sir," came a voice. A man at the back. "Just as long as you cooperate."

"I'm cooperating," he said, his voice loose.

Was this how it felt to be on the other side of the fence?

The four men parted, and another walked through. He wore a long dark coat, and a grey suit beneath it. His orange tie clashed with the sombre outfit and the uniforms of his colleagues.

Christian didn't recognise him. But then, CID were a blur to him.

The man looked at Christian for a moment, and then brought his ID out of his pocket. Christian didn't bother to look at it. He knew enough to have no doubt that this was what he'd been waiting for all these years.

"Christian Davison?" the man said.

"That's me." Christian stood almost to attention.

"You're under arrest for the murders of Kenneth Fogarty and Catherine Lawson. You do not have to say anything, but anything you do say may be used against you at trial."

CHAPTER SIXTY-ONE

Tina stood behind the CSI van, shuffling her feet and slapping her hands together to try to get warm.

"So is that everything?" she asked the CSI.

Brett was loading pilot cases into the back of the van. He stood back to survey it and then closed the doors, turning to Tina.

"All done. We ain't gonna find anything else here. You've got that gun, that's your main piece of evidence."

"You didn't find any spent bullets?" Tina asked.

"Not after ten years, mate. That would have been a minor miracle."

Brett yawned. "I'm not looking forward to the drive back to Dorchester," he said. "I'm knackered."

Tina smiled. Was he flirting with her?

Sorry, I'm taken.

"So what about you?" Brett asked her. "Are you staying here a bit longer or heading back?"

Tina shook her head. "No reason to stay. The investigation's moving back to the office, there are no witnesses in Lyme Regis. We've spoken to everyone who could be of use to us."

"You gonna miss your mum?"

"How did you know...?"

"Sorry. Gail told me. Shouldn't be so nosy. Comes with the job, dunnit?"

Tina shrugged. "Maybe."

It had been nice seeing her mum for a few days. Sleeping in her old bed, being waited on. But it was beginning to tire, and she was missing Mike. They needed to talk.

"I'll see you back at the office," Tina told Brett.

"Most likely," Brett replied. "Go easy, Tina. Look after yerself."

Tina frowned. "Of course I will."

Brett gave her a smile and a slap on the shoulder. "See you later."

CHAPTER SIXTY-TWO

Lesley and Dennis pulled up outside Christian Davison's house. She'd told Carpenter that they were heading over there, and he'd grudgingly given his authorisation on the proviso that all she would do was question Davison and not arrest him.

She needed to know whether that gun had fallen into anybody else's hands.

Maybe it had been stolen, maybe Christian Davison had let somebody else have it? God only knew why he might do that, but she had to give the man the benefit of the doubt. He had a clean service record, Stanley had checked him out on the system and there were no blemishes against his name.

So here they were, just intending to ask questions. No warrant required, no arrest planned.

She looked past Dennis at the house. It was a squat semi just outside Poole.

"Think he'll be expecting us?" she asked.

Dennis bit his lip. "That depends."

"On what?"

He smiled at her. "The answers to your questions."

"*Our* questions." She grunted. "If he tells the truth."

"All we have is that it was his gun found at the crime scene. We don't know for certain it was fired, we don't have bullets. And if it *was* fired, we don't know by whom.

Even if it hadn't been ten years, an AFO would know how to clean off gunshot residue."

"It's still worth a try."

Lesley peered up at the house. It was quiet, no movement.

"I know," she sighed. "It's all pretty circumstantial right now. But I want to know what he has to say for himself."

She opened her door and rounded the car, waiting for Dennis. She straightened her jacket and marched up the path, rapping loudly on the front door.

Dennis joined her and they waited. No answer. Dennis leaned in and rapped the knocker again.

"I already did that," Lesley told him.

"He didn't answer."

"You think he'll hear it again a couple of minutes later?"

"Sorry, boss. Is everything alright?"

She closed her eyes. "Sorry, Dennis. Can we get around the back, take a look if he's there?"

"There's a gate," Dennis said. "But we have no reason to go through it. No warrant, no reason to think he's in danger."

Lesley eyed her colleague. "If his gun was stolen, and we've just found it, and it was used to kill two lawyers, then he *could* be in danger."

"No, boss. I'm talking about immediate danger. We need to have seen something."

"You're right."

She walked along the narrow pathway leading to the side gate and rattled it. It was locked.

"Damn," she muttered under her breath, glancing back to check that Dennis hadn't heard her.

She returned to the front of the house and went to the front window, raising her hands against it to peer inside. A half-eaten sandwich was on a side table, and a mug. A notepad and pen were on the coffee table and the TV was on.

She straightened up and shook her head at Dennis. "If he left here, it was in a hurry."

"Why?"

She gestured towards the window. "Take a look."

Dennis peered in. "He could have popped out to the shops."

"And left the TV on?"

"Boss. We have no concrete grounds to think he's in danger."

"He's left his sandwich half-eaten and the TV on. Don't you think someone might have forced him to leave?"

"With respect, boss, there's no sign of forced entry. We've received no 999 call. We don't have grounds—"

She punched her thigh. "I know. Grasping at straws." And she knew as well as Dennis did that if they veered from correct procedure in a case involving a serving police officer, it would severely damage any case against him. And worse.

"We'll come back another time," Dennis said.

"He finished his shift four hours ago. If he's not at home, where is he?"

"Gone to the pub? Visiting his girlfriend?"

"There's a half-finished sandwich on the table."

"Maybe he doesn't tidy up."

"Uh-uh. House is immaculate."

Dennis looked back at her. "You're right. The only thing out of place is that sandwich and mug."

"Which means he was disturbed," Lesley said.

"Possibly."

"Question is, who by?"

CHAPTER SIXTY-THREE

Stanley leaned back in his chair as the phone was answered.

"Donna Turnberry speaking."

"Donna," he said, "it's Stanley."

"Stanley Brown." She whistled. "What happened to you?"

"I'm based out of Winfrith now," he told her. "Major Crime Investigations Team."

"Playing with the big boys. What can I help you with?"

Donna Turnberry was an AFO based out of Dorchester. She was also a former girlfriend of Stanley's, one of the few he'd managed to remain on decent terms with.

"I'm working on that double murder in Lyme Regis," he told her.

"That historical one. Two lawyers?"

"That's the one. Anyway, this is between you and me, but we've got the cause of death. Gunshot wounds."

"OK. And why are you calling me?"

Stanley lowered his voice. "We also found a gun."

"OK."

"I didn't tell you this, right?"

She made a zipping sound. "Lips are sealed, mate. Tell me more."

"It belonged to one of your guys."

"One of our guys? Really?"

"The serial number was corroded, but the CSIs X-rayed it. It's unmistakable, Don."

"Blimey. Who?"

Stanley paused. Mike was on the other side of the desks, also on the phone.

"Christian Davison," Stanley muttered. "You know him, don't you?"

There was coughing on the other end of the line.

"Don?" Stanley said. "You alright?"

"Yeah," she spluttered. "But, Christian? You're kidding me, right?"

"It was his gun," Stanley told her.

"Surely PSD should be investigating, in that case?"

"I think they might be. But I wanted to have a chat with you first, find out if you knew anything. It was ten years ago. Were you working as an AFO then?"

"You know I was," she told him. "That was when you and me were going out."

Stanley smiled. "How could I forget that?"

"Stop it."

"Sorry, Don. Look, is there anything you can tell me about Christian? Anything odd that was going on with him at the time?"

"How'm I supposed to remember that?"

Stanley looked up to see the door to the office opening. It was the sarge. Stanley hunched in his chair.

"Look, Don, I know it's a while back, but can you remember him acting funny? Was there a report of a gun going missing? Anything unusual you can put your finger on?"

"Hang on a minute," she said. "He was a bit odd, that was around the time he split up with Sunika."

"Who's Sunika?"

"His wife. Ex-wife. He was, yeah, he was a bit away with the fairies then. But I guess he was just coping with the divorce."

"In what way was he 'away with the fairies', Don?"

"Distracted," she said. "Moody. He called in sick a few times."

"And you're sure this is ten years ago?"

"Something like that. I remember because he and Sunika split around the same time I was seeing you."

Stanley nodded. "And what about the gun?" he asked. "Anything reported missing?"

"I can't remember that," she told him. "That's the sort of thing that would have been between Christian and his sarge."

"Who was your sarge back then?"

"Adam McCory."

"Never heard of him."

"He retired not long after. Good guy, though."

"So he's the man I need to speak to, I suppose?" Stanley said.

"If you can find him. Him and his wife went off travelling, I think."

"OK," Stanley told her. "Adam McCory, you say?"

"That's the one."

"Thanks, Don. And if you remember anything else about Christian from around that time, you'll let me know, will you?"

"Of course I will, Stan. Nice to talk to you."

"You too, Donna."

CHAPTER SIXTY-FOUR

Lesley shoved her phone into her pocket as she pushed open the doors to Dorset Police HQ. Dennis had gone on ahead and she'd hung back to make a phone call. She was still trying to get hold of Elsa. There was no answer on her mobile phone, and she'd given up with the office. *What's going on, Els?*

She headed for the stairs, just as her phone rang again. It was Carpenter.

"Sir," she said. "I've just got back. Do you need me to come and see you?"

"Not just yet. How did you get on?"

"He wasn't in," she told him.

"You didn't wait around?"

"He looked like he'd been disturbed. We checked through the front window of the house, it was tidy, but there was a half-eaten sandwich on the table and a mug, and the TV was on in there, too. I think something might have happened to him, Sir."

"What kind of thing?"

"Well, if organised crime were involved in these killings and they knew his gun had been found…"

"DCI Clarke," the super said. "Do you have reason to believe there might be a leak in your team?"

Lesley was halfway up the stairs. She stopped in her tracks.

"No, Sir. Of course not."

"The CSIs?"

"No, Sir."

He grunted. "Leave it for now, I'll speak to PSD."

"What about the AFO team? I could always go to—"

"No, Lesley. Leave it with me."

Lesley gritted her teeth and shoved her phone back into her pocket. She hurried up the remainder of the stairs, pausing at the top and considering heading for the super's office, then thought better of it.

She pushed into the office, her footsteps heavy.

Stanley looked up as she entered. "Boss," he said. He exchanged glances with Dennis.

"What?" she asked him, irritable.

"I think I might have something."

"On what?"

"Christian Davison, our guy with the gun."

Lesley rolled her eyes. "You make it sound like a Bond film, Stanley."

He smirked. "Sorry, boss."

Dennis looked at her. "Do we need a briefing?"

She looked towards her office. She couldn't remember the last time the team had gathered in there. Most of them were here now, everyone except Tina.

"Have we heard anything from Tina?" she asked Dennis.

"She'll be on her way back later," Dennis told her. "Getting a lift from Uniform."

"Good. Call her, let's get her in on this."

CHAPTER SIXTY-FIVE

Lesley closed the door to her office and walked to her desk. She eased herself into the chair, glad to be back. Lyme Regis had been lovely, but she'd missed the office. She'd missed sitting here in briefings, bouncing ideas back and forth, combining the intuition and experience of the team.

Dennis placed his phone on the table. "I've got Tina on speakerphone, she'll be leaving Lyme Regis tonight."

"Boss," came Tina's voice through the phone.

"Tina," Lesley said, "can you hear me?"

"Yes, boss. What's up?"

"We just want to get our heads together on where we're at with this case. I wanted to make sure you were in on it."

"Thanks."

Lesley leaned back in her chair and nodded at Dennis. He walked to the board. They had the crime scene photos, plus snapshots of Fogarty and Lawson in life. There were also plans of Lyme Regis, maps showing the locations where they'd been found and where the gun had been discovered. A red line on a map showed the route their bodies would have taken down the cliff when the landslip kicked in. As well as that, there were pictures of Aurelia Cross and Eleanor Fogarty. Plus the logo of Elsa's firm, except it looked different. Instead of *Nevin, Cross and Short*, it said *Nevin, Fogarty and Lawson*.

"So," she said. "Where are we?"

Dennis looked at Stanley. "You just phoned your friend in the AFO unit?"

"I have, Sarge."

Lesley raised an eyebrow. "Does Carpenter know we're talking to the AFOs?"

Stanley shifted in his chair and looked warily at Dennis. "Er…"

"Stanley used to work with this woman," Dennis said. "He's just using his initiative."

Lesley smiled. "So what did you discover?"

Stanley smoothed his hands down his trousers. "So, Donna, that's my mate. She worked with this Christian guy ten years ago. She says there's nothing dodgy about him, he's got no blemishes on his record. She's not aware of him ever having been disciplined."

"We got all that from HOLMES," Lesley said. "What about the insider information? What's he like? Has he behaved suspiciously at any point?"

"She said he was a bit weird around that time, but he was getting divorced. So she figured that explained it."

"What kind of weird?" Lesley asked.

"Away with the fairies, was what she said. Distracted, irritable. She just assumed it was the relationship break-down."

"It might have been something else." Lesley looked at the board. "Why isn't his photo up there?"

Dennis looked at her. "I thought it might not be…"

"It's fine, Dennis. He was the owner of the gun that was found at the crime scene. If he wasn't police, his photo would be up there front and centre, wouldn't it?"

"Yes, boss."

"Let's find a mugshot of him, add it to the board. We need to find out everything we can about him. Can we speak to his ex-wife?"

"And it might be worth speaking to the man who was his sarge at the time," Stanley suggested. "Adam McCory. He's retired now, but he might have had a chat with Davison. Donna says if there was anything about a gun going missing, the sarge would have known, for a start."

Lesley nodded. "Retired, eh? As a private citizen, there's nothing to stop us having a chat with him."

"Are you sure, boss?" Dennis said. "I thought PSD were being brought in."

"Until I get official notice of who in PSD is heading up this case, it's still ours. Let's talk to his ex-wife and sergeant. Stanley?"

"I don't think I should do it," Stanley said. "I'm too close."

"Really?"

Stanley's neck flushed. "OK, boss. I'll do it."

"Good. You and Mike, track down the ex-wife. Dennis and I will deal with the sergeant."

"No problem," Mike said.

"Good. You've been very quiet, everything OK?"

"Fine, boss." Mike looked perturbed. "Just didn't have anything to add."

"Missing Tina?"

He stiffened, glancing at her phone on the desk. "Err…"

Lesley raised an eyebrow. "You should be." She shook her head. "Don't worry, Mike. I'm happy for the pair of you. I just don't want it affecting your work."

"It won't."

"Tina?"

"It won't, boss." Tina's voice came from the phone on the desk.

"Good. Is there anything else from the crime scene? No bullets, I suppose?"

"Nothing. Sorry."

No. Tina wouldn't have waited to tell her if they'd found bullets.

"OK," she said. "So, that's the gun. We still have Fogarty's ex-wife. I went to speak to her and she seemed legit, but I can't get past the fact that she didn't report him missing."

"She thought he'd emigrated, didn't she?" Mike said.

"He was leaving the country," Tina added. "Canada."

"He was," Lesley confirmed. "But even so, you'd expect some contact between them afterwards. Sorting out finances maybe? Even just a Christmas card."

She thought of Terry, her own ex-husband. The decree absolute had come through a week ago, but there would still be contact between them. Their lives were entwined through Sharon, their daughter, and through the fact that they'd lived together so long.

"I want to find out more about Eleanor Fogarty," she said. "Can we get the documentation from the divorce? Find out what was used as grounds? She knew about his affair with Lawson. Could it have been that?"

"No problem, boss," said Dennis.

"Good. So, that's the ex-wife and the gun. What about Catherine Lawson? What have we found out about her?"

"I did a bit of digging," said Mike. "She moved to Dorset from Yorkshire fifteen years ago. She'd been practising law up in Yorkshire and she got herself a junior partnership with the firm pretty quickly. I think that might be why she moved down. She was promoted to named partner within a year."

"And when did her relationship with Kenneth Fogarty start?"

"His wife said it had been going on for six years," Mike said.

"OK," she said. "I want to know more about Catherine Lawson."

"Do we need to consider who Fogarty and Lawson's clients were?" Dennis asked.

Lesley breathed out. "I thought we were already on that. Do we have a list?"

Dennis nodded at Mike, who pinned a sheet of paper to the board.

"There's a lot of them," he said.

Lesley walked to the board. She peered at the list, trying to place the names.

"Have you checked them all out?"

"I'm working through them on Companies House," Mike said. "Half of them don't exist anymore, the other half seem legit."

"Have you checked who the owners are? One of these could have been a front for something."

"But that doesn't fit with the AFO's gun, boss," Stanley said.

"It might do," she told him. "If Christian Davison was dodgy, a gang might have blackmailed him, forced him to let them have the gun. Even hired him to take out Fogarty and Lawson."

Dennis spluttered. "Take out?"

"You got a problem, Dennis?"

"This isn't 1930's Chicago, boss. This is Lyme Regis. People don't *take each other out*."

She cocked her head. "Somebody killed that couple, and it looks like they did it with a police gun. We need to know three things. Firstly, was it a police officer who shot them? Secondly, if so, why? Thirdly, if not, how did the shooter get hold of the gun? Follow up on those businesses, Mike, and leave Davison's ex-wife to Stanley. Include the businesses that don't exist anymore. Check historical records on Companies House. I want to know exactly who Fogarty and Lawson were representing, and if any of them might not have been best pleased that their lawyers were leaving the country."

"You're thinking it's Kelvin," Dennis said. "What with the firm representing him now…"

Lesley nodded. She didn't trust herself to say any more.

"I'm still worried, boss," Dennis said. "PSD will step in the minute we start sniffing around the AFO side of things."

"I'll take responsibility, Dennis." She turned to him. "As far as I'm concerned, Christian Davison is missing. And if he's tied up in these murders, then he could be in danger."

CHAPTER SIXTY-SIX

Dennis gestured for the other team members to leave the room. Lesley watched him as they began to shuffle out. She thought back to the conversation she'd had with Carpenter, to walking into the super's office and finding Matt Crippins there.

"Hang on a moment," she said.

Stanley was in the doorway, Mike already outside. Stanley turned. "Do you need us to do something else, boss?"

She shook her head. "Come back in, all of you."

Dennis gestured for Mike to come back. He walked back in, his brow furrowed, and closed the door.

Lesley licked her lips. "Take a seat, everybody."

Mike and Dennis took the two seats opposite her desk. Stanley hovered, looking anxious.

Lesley jerked her head towards her own chair. "You can sit there," she told him.

"You sure, boss?"

Lesley smiled. "The seat doesn't bite, it's just a chair. Sit down, Stanley."

Stanley shuffled around the desk, looking at Dennis as he did so. Dennis gave him a reassuring nod.

Lesley was still next to the board. She interlaced her fingers and pushed her arms out in front of her, cracking her knuckles. She took a couple of breaths.

"I've got something I need to tell you all about. I don't imagine it will affect everybody in the team, but it could affect me, and possibly the sarge, and I just want you to know about it."

Dennis pulled his phone out of his pocket. "Do we need Tina in on this as well?"

Lesley shook her head. "I'll bring Tina up to speed when she's back."

"OK." Dennis put his phone away.

Lesley looked at him. She thought for a moment then stepped forward.

"I need to talk to you about DCI Mackie's death."

Dennis stiffened. "What's happened?"

"Superintendent Carpenter is reopening the investigation."

Dennis stood up. "What? Into the DCI's death?"

"Sit down please, Dennis."

Mike, sitting next to Dennis, was looking puzzled. Stanley, behind the desk, had a blank expression. He'd never known DCI Mackie, he'd certainly never known about the controversy over his death. He was about to find out.

"OK," Lesley said. "So, the journalist Sadie Dawes. You might remember her from the Brownsea Island case. She's been sniffing around DCI Mackie's death. She reckons he didn't kill himself."

She looked at Stanley. "How much do you know about DCI Mackie?"

"I know that he was found at the base of the cliffs at Ballard Down," Stanley replied, his eyes on Dennis. "I also know that he left a note and it was recorded by the coroner as suicide."

"Good," Lesley said. "What you also need to know is that I sent that note to a psychologist and she doesn't think that Mackie wrote it."

Dennis shook his head. "Gail had a graphologist go over it at the time. I was there. The graphologist confirmed that it was the DCI's writing."

"And we've double checked that," Lesley said. "But even though it was his writing, Dr McBride thinks that somebody dictated it to him."

"Dr McBride?" Mike asked. "Isn't she the one who came in on the Globe case?"

"That's the one," Lesley said. "Dr Petra McBride, the profiler who helped us with that case. I've worked with her in the West Midlands as well. She's good, I trust her." She eyed Dennis. "If she says that Mackie didn't come up with those words, that means that Mackie didn't come up with those words."

"Which means what?" Dennis asked, his body language tight.

"Are you OK, Dennis?" Lesley asked. "I know this is hard for you. You and Mackie were close."

Mike blew out a breath. "But he threw himself off the cliffs. The coroner said it was suicide."

"I've talked to Gail," Lesley said. "She's run through the forensic evidence with me, it's inconclusive."

"Gail was doubtful at the time," Dennis said. "But then after she got the graphologist in…"

"I know," Lesley told him. "But anyway, Sadie Dawes, the journalist, she got hold of a copy of the suicide note."

"How?" Dennis asked.

"Dennis. You don't have to shout." Lesley looked at the glass wall that separated her office from the open plan office beyond. "We don't want people knowing about this, not just yet."

"Why not?" Stanley asked.

Lesley closed her eyes briefly. "Because I brought in a former colleague, a DI from the West Midlands, to help me investigate, and I'm sure you know that that's not exactly standard procedure."

"Does Carpenter know about this?" Dennis asked.

"He does."

"Why hasn't he disciplined you?"

"That's a good question, but it's probably only a matter of time."

"Does Carpenter know more than he's letting on?" Mike asked.

"He's the super to you," Lesley said. "And I don't think it's wise to start questioning his motives."

Mike shook his head.

"So, what does this mean?" Dennis said. "Are we going to be leading the reopened case?"

"Definitely not," Lesley told him.

"And where's Sadie Dawes now?" Stanley asked. "Wasn't she missing?"

"She's back," Lesley said. "She's working with her editor at the BBC and they're compiling a story."

"Shit," Mike said. Dennis flashed him a look.

"Exactly," Lesley added. "Look, I don't know any more than this right now, but I just wanted to warn you all. Keep this close to your chests, but at the same time, we're not keeping any secrets. Not from management, and not from the BBC."

"Surely the BBC—" Dennis began.

"No," Lesley interrupted. "If they ask us questions, we tell them what we know."

"But we don't know anything," said Stanley. "All you've got is a hunch about this suicide note based on what some shrink said."

"She's not a shrink," Lesley told him. "Her name's Dr Petra McBride. She's an esteemed psychologist and she's worked with me on profiling offenders."

Stanley sniffed.

"Just trust me on this, Stanley," she said, irritated.

Stanley was the newest member of the team. She appreciated the fact that he brought a fresh perspective to things, but at the same time, challenge wasn't what she was looking for right now.

"We need to pull together on this, folks," she continued. "I know I haven't been straight with you, and I know I haven't told you everything that's been going on. That's been to protect you as much as anything. But now this is going to become public, and I just want you to know that I'm here for you if you need me."

Dennis grunted.

Lesley looked at him. "I mean that, Dennis," she said. "This is going to be stressful. It'll bring back memories. If you need my support, you come to me."

CHAPTER SIXTY-SEVEN

Dennis walked behind the boss as they filed out of the office. Her body language was tighter than usual, her footsteps not much more than a shuffle.

As Stanley reached the desks, he turned and looked at Dennis.

"Sarge," he said, "can I have a word?"

Dennis glanced at the boss. "Of course you can, Stanley. Just give me a minute." He turned to the DCI. "What do you need us to do now?"

She shook her head and looked at the clock above the door.

"It's gone seven o'clock. Send everybody home, we'll return with fresh heads in the morning."

"You sure?" he asked.

"I think we all need a bit of downtime."

He watched as she went back into her office, picked up her bag, then emerged, giving him a tight smile before leaving through the main door.

Dennis felt his muscles relax as she left.

"Sarge?" Stanley said.

"Yes, Stanley," Dennis said, irritated.

"Can we talk somewhere private please, Sarge?"

Dennis pursed his lips. He looked at the door, wondering if the DCI might return. No. Once she'd made her mind up to do something, she generally did it.

"Let's go into the DCI's office," he told Stanley.

He walked into the room, waited for Stanley to enter, then closed the door. Back at the desks, Mike was trying not to let them see he was watching them. Dennis gave him a dismissive wave and Mike looked away.

"What can I do for you, Stanley?" Dennis asked.

Stanley looked down at the floor. He had his hands in front of him, twisting them together.

"Stanley?" Dennis asked. "If it's alright with you, I'd quite like to be home before midnight."

"Sorry, Sarge." Stanley looked up. "I don't like this, Sarge."

"What don't you like?"

"The boss. She brought in a DI from another force to help work on an investigation. How come she wasn't disciplined for it?"

Dennis folded his arms across his chest. "I don't see how that's your business, Stanley."

"It is, Sarge, I'm new to this team. I thought you're all above board. I've seen police corruption before and I don't want any part of it."

Dennis took a step forward. "The DCI is not corrupt, Constable."

"She broke the rules, Sarge." Stanley blinked back at him. "She investigated the death of DCI Mackie, a case that was already closed." He leaned forward "Why? She wasn't even here when the old DCI died, why does she care so much?"

"Because she's a good copper," Dennis replied. "Because she cares about getting things right."

Stanley shook his head. "So why didn't Carpenter pull her up on it?"

Dennis realised his fists were clenched beside him. "How am I supposed to know the answer to that, Stanley? And it sounds like he is pulling her up on it. Then there's the fact that he's reopened the case, and the BBC are getting involved. Looks like whatever the DCI's done, she's shedding light on things, not hiding them."

Stanley shrugged. "It smells off to me, Sarge."

"You just get on with your job, Stanley," Dennis said. "Focus on the Lyme Regis case. I'll keep you out of all this stuff about DCI Mackie if you prefer."

Stanley eyed him. "You think we have a choice in who gets drawn into this, now that there's an investigation going on and the case has been reopened?"

"Stanley," Dennis said, "you're sailing very close to the wind here. Now I suggest you go out to your desk, pick up your stuff and go home. In the morning I expect an apology."

Stanley looked back at him, his mouth open. He stared for a moment then looked down.

"Yes, Sarge. Sorry, Sarge."

CHAPTER SIXTY-EIGHT

Elsa sat at the pub table, her hands wrapped around her glass of tonic water. She'd chosen a pub in Blandford Forum, miles away from where she lived, miles away from where Lesley worked. Miles away from Lyme Regis, and miles away from Arthur Kelvin's Sandbanks mansion.

"Hello?"

She looked up to see a young woman standing next to the table. It was Sam Chaston.

Elsa tensed. "Can I get you a drink?"

"A glass of wine would be nice."

Elsa raised an eyebrow. "You're not driving?"

"I got an Uber."

"They have Ubers out here?"

Sam smiled. "You'd be surprised."

"Fair enough." Elsa stood up, went to the bar, and ordered the glass of wine, realising she hadn't asked what kind of wine. She took a guess, the house red, and brought it back to the table.

"Sorry," she said. "I got you the house red. Is this OK?"

"Perfect." Sam picked up the glass and took a sip, licking her lips afterwards. "About what happened this morning," she continued. "I'm sorry about that. It must have been—"

Elsa put up a hand. "It was fine, it was inevitable. Aurelia was going to be pissed off, what did you expect?"

Sam shrugged. "I know, but—"

"You did the right thing." Elsa looked around the pub, checking nobody she knew was here. She turned back to Sam. "You did exactly what I needed you to."

Sam leaned back in her chair, her fingers on the base of the glass. "Did I get it right?"

"You got it perfect," Elsa said. "I'm free now, I don't have to work for Arthur Kelvin, and I don't have to look behind me every time I walk down a dark alley."

"Was it that bad?"

"Do you know about the Fogarty and Lawson case?"

Sam looked up. "I heard about it."

"They were partners," Elsa said. "Partners in the firm with Harry. Before Aurelia and I started here, they represented Kelvin and his businesses. They ended up dead on the cliffs at Lyme Regis."

She looked at Sam for a moment. "I was starting to worry I might end up like that."

Sam nodded. "So, what are you going to do now?"

Elsa shrugged. "Well, if Aurelia had a better sense of ethics, she'd be reporting me to the Law Society, and I'd get struck off. I'd be looking for a job in another sector."

"But?"

"But Aurelia doesn't have that sense of ethics," Elsa told her. "So all she's done is fire me, as you know."

Sam nodded. "You're going to find a job somewhere else then? Go back to London, maybe?"

Elsa considered. If Sam had asked her six months ago, she'd have been back in London before the question had left the woman's lips. As far away from Arthur Kelvin as she could get.

But now, she had Lesley.

"No," she said. "I'm going to set up my own firm. Probably in Christchurch, take on clients in Hampshire. Hopefully avoid crossing paths with Arthur Kelvin too often."

Sam took a sip of her wine. "D'you think that'll be possible?"

"I'll certainly give it a good go." Elsa surveyed Sam. "You did me a huge favour, I appreciate it. And I'll need a PA."

Sam's eyes brightened. "Yes, please."

Elsa grinned. She held out her glass and Sam chinked hers to it.

"You're on," Elsa told her.

CHAPTER SIXTY-NINE

Lesley opened the front door to the flat and threw her bag onto the floor.

She was tired. Sleeping in that pokey spare room in Lyme Regis, listening to the seagulls, had been bad enough, but now she had Sadie Dawes's reappearance to contend with. Not to mention the reopening of the Mackie investigation.

Carpenter had been unhappy about her bringing Zoe in, but he hadn't disciplined her, for reasons he hadn't chosen to share. She had a feeling that now things were out in the open, he might not be so circumspect.

She walked through to the living room, rolling up her sleeves.

"Els," she called out. "I'm back."

The living room was dark. She flicked on the light and looked around. The room was empty, no sign of habitation. The kitchen was clean, a couple of glasses sitting next to the sink, draining.

"Els," she repeated.

She left the living room and went into the bedroom. Sometimes Elsa sat on the bed, propped up against the pillows with her laptop.

The bedroom too was in darkness.

"Where are you?" Lesley muttered.

She grabbed her phone and dialled Elsa's number: voicemail. She dialled the second number. Dead. She sat down on the bed then lay back, staring up at the ceiling. She had no idea what the reopening of the investigation into DCI Mackie's death would mean for her. Could she be in trouble, or was this about to be her finest hour?

She grabbed her phone again.

"Hi, boss."

"Zoe," Lesley said. "Not boss."

"Sorry, *Lesley*. How's things?"

"They're reopening the investigation into DCI Mackie's death."

Lesley sat up, pulling her hand through her hair. She knew Zoe couldn't see what a state she was in, but still…

"Why?" Zoe asked.

"Sadie Dawes has turned up again. Apparently, she's managed to get hold of a copy of his suicide note."

A whistle came down the line. "Shit."

"Exactly," Lesley said.

Neither of them wanted the press to publicise this before the police got to grips with it, but it looked like it was too late for that.

"Anything I can help with?" Zoe asked.

"You need to keep well away from this," Lesley told her. "I'm worried that I might have got you into trouble."

"Sorry."

"Not your fault, it was me who asked you."

"I could have said no."

"Would you have?"

A pause.

"No," Lesley said. "I don't think you would."

"No," Zoe agreed.

"I've just got one question for you," Lesley told her.

"Go on."

"Sadie Dawes, I don't suppose you've heard from her again have you?"

"I'd have called you straight away if I had."

"OK, thanks. Take care."

"I will," Zoe said. "Carl and I are buying a house, come visit next time you're in Brum."

Lesley smiled. "Congratulations. That would be nice."

She hung up and stared at her phone for a moment. Should she try calling Sadie? Find out what it was the woman had?

That would just get her into more trouble.

She threw her phone across the bed. It bounced a couple of times before it toppled off the other side. She lay down again.

Elsa, where the hell are you?

CHAPTER SEVENTY

Lesley had been sitting on the sofa, hands wedged between her thighs, staring at the blank TV for fifteen minutes now. Every couple of minutes she looked at her watch.

She'd given up trying to call Elsa. If her girlfriend didn't want to speak to her, then she didn't want to speak to her. Was there any point sitting here waiting, or was she just going to drive herself mad?

She stood up, brushed herself down, and grabbed her keys from the table in the hall. She hurried out of the flat and to her car, starting the ignition before she had time to stop herself. Thirty minutes later, she pulled up outside Superintendent Carpenter's house in Christchurch.

She looked in the rear-view mirror, rubbed at her bleary eyes, took a deep breath and got out of the car. She surveyed the super's house. The lights were on, no sign of movement. She marched up to the front door and pressed the bell heavily.

She was surprised when Carpenter himself answered.

"Lesley," he said, wiping his hands on a tea towel. "What's happened?"

"I'd like to ask you some questions, Sir."

He frowned. "I'm having dinner with my family."

She peered past him. A woman was in the kitchen beyond, clearing plates into a dishwasher. She could hear music from upstairs.

"It looks like you've finished, Sir."

He glared at her. "You've got a fucking nerve, interrupting me at home like this after everything you've done."

"I just want to know what's going on, Sir."

He sighed. "Come in, then."

He turned away from her and went into the kitchen. He murmured something to his wife, who looked past him at Lesley, her eyes wary.

Lesley gave her a smile, which wasn't returned.

Carpenter turned back to her. "Come into my study."

She followed him into a small room with a desk taking up one wall and a row of bookshelves on the other. There was only one chair, positioned behind the desk. Carpenter took it and swivelled to face her. Lesley stood with her back to the door.

"Go on, then," he said. "What is it you want to ask me?"

"If you're reopening the investigation into DCI Mackie's death, does this mean you believe he didn't commit suicide?"

A shrug. "I'm not going to make any decisions until we've reviewed the evidence."

"You wouldn't be reopening the case if you thought he killed himself. Surely the whole point—"

He raised a hand. "The coroner declared it a suicide. Reopening a case like this is a pain in the arse as I'm quite sure you already know, but because of your meddling and talking to journalists and bringing in people from outside forces, I don't seem to have much choice."

"Sadie Dawes approached me, Sir," she said. "I never would have gone to her."

He raised an eyebrow. "Really? Not even after Gail Hansford told you her doubts about the crime scene?"

Lesley swallowed. "How did you know about that?"

"I'm not stupid, DCI Clarke. I keep an eye on what's going on in my team."

"But Gail doesn't work for you."

"She does indirectly. She's been chatting to people, not just you." His voice was harsh.

"Don't blame Gail for any of this," Lesley told him. "This is my fault."

"Oh, I know that," he replied. "Don't worry, the blame for this almighty cockup is going to rest squarely on you."

"I don't understand," she said to him. "Why are you so worried? Do you think that somebody in the force was involved?"

He stood up. "DCI Clarke, given the years you spent working in Force CID in West Midlands, and also given the cases you were dealing with as you left that team, you're coming across as very naive."

She met his gaze. "What has Sadie Dawes said about the suicide note?"

"I don't know," he told her. "That's the fucking problem, isn't it? What do *you* think she knows?"

"They're not Mackie's words."

"No?"

She shook her head. She hadn't planned on telling him about Petra, but she needed to come clean to Carpenter, just as she had to the rest of the team.

"I spoke to Dr McBride, the profiler that we brought in on the Brownsea Island case."

"I know who you mean."

"She took a look at the suicide note, compared it to some diary entries that he'd written."

"And where did you get those?"

"Gwen Mackie."

He took a step towards her. "What were you doing bothering Gwen Mackie?"

"Gwen was happy to talk to us. She doesn't believe her husband killed himself. As far as she's concerned, he knew full well what a suicide meant for the people dealing with it afterwards, and he would never have done that to his colleagues."

"You think I don't know that?"

"With all respect, Sir—"

He shook his head. "Just get out, Lesley. Leave me alone to my evening."

"Sir," she said. "Who will be leading the new investigation?"

"I don't know," he told her. "People higher up than me will be determining that. It'll probably be somebody from an outside force."

"Why? Is there suspicion of corruption?"

"A DCI was potentially murdered, DCI Clarke. The possibility that he was corrupt has to come into play, don't you think?"

Lesley swallowed. She still didn't think DCI Mackie had been corrupt. He'd exchanged text messages with Elsa, but those had been about a case. He'd helped Dennis on a case after retiring, but he'd been the sergeant's mentor. None of these things were suspicious.

But his death?

"I'm sorry to disturb you, Sir."

"I should think so, too. Now leave, before I decide to sack you."

CHAPTER SEVENTY-ONE

Tina didn't have much in the way of luggage with her. After all, she hadn't been expecting to stay over in Lyme Regis. But her mum had given her a shopping bag for the few things she wanted to take back with her.

"When are you going to be back?" Annie asked.

Tina shook her head. "Mum…"

"Look, your sister needs some help with that baby, and we never see you. I know you're busy at work, but…"

Tina turned to her mum. "It's OK. I'll come back in a couple of weeks, with Mike."

Her mum's face brightened. "Finally I get to meet the infamous Mike."

Tina smiled. "You'll like him."

"Of course I'll like him, love." Annie pulled her daughter in and kissed her on the forehead. "You like him, so I will."

Tina laughed. "It doesn't always work like that mum. Remember Adam, who I went out with in sixth form?"

Annie scoffed. "You were sixteen, you didn't have the best of judgement."

Tina thought back to Adam. She'd heard he'd been arrested a couple of years ago, possession of drugs. No, she hadn't had the best judgement in those days.

"Anyway," she said, picking up the shopping bag and putting a hand on her mum's arm, "I'll call you. We'll set a date."

"No, we'll do it now."

Tina sighed. Her mum was right. She knew that if she didn't agree to something now, time would pass, life would get in the way, and it would never happen, or at least not for a few months, by which time…

She pulled a phone out of her pocket. "OK. Assuming this case is concluded, how about a week on Saturday?"

"Lovely," Annie said.

"You're not going to put it in your diary?"

Her mum laughed. "I'm not exactly a social whirl, love. I'll be here. You're going to come to the house?"

"I thought we could go out in Lyme, find a pub or something?"

Annie nodded. "Let's go to the Cobb Arms."

The Cobb Arms was nice. Mike would enjoy the view.

Annie pulled her in for another hug. "Is there something you're not telling me, love? I'm surprised you haven't been back more to see Naomi. The day before yesterday was the first time you met the baby, and she's already four months old."

Tina pulled back, gripping her mum's arms. She took a breath. Was she ready to tell her mum? She hadn't even told Mike yet.

"OK, Mum," she said. "I've been hoping this would go away but, well, it's not."

Annie cocked her head. "You can tell me, whatever it is."

Tina licked her lips. "I'm pregnant, Mum."

Annie pulled away, all but jumping into the air. She clapped her hands together. "Oh Tina, that's wonderful!"

"You're sure?" Tina asked.

"Of course it is! Come here, give me a hug."

Tina let herself be bundled into Annie's arms.

"I've not been with Mike that long, we're not even living together."

"You'll work it out. I'm sure he's a lovely boy."

"Man," Tina said.

"Man," Annie repeated. "Who are his mum and dad?"

"His mum lives in Bournemouth, his dad… His dad was from Jamaica, but he hasn't seen him for a few years."

"That's a shame. Do you reckon now he's having a baby he might be able to make it up with him?"

Tina stiffened. Mike had refused to talk about his dad whenever she'd attempted to broach the subject. She wasn't about to poke that beast now. Not when she was about to tell him he was going to become a father himself.

Christ, how will he react?

CHAPTER SEVENTY-TWO

Lesley grabbed the wine bottle on the kitchen counter. About to pour a glass, she paused. She put it down, replaced the glass in the cupboard, and grabbed a whisky tumbler. She needed something stronger.

As she was rummaging in the cupboard for a bottle of Talisker, she heard the front door close. She felt her muscles unclench. *Thank God.*

She stood up, the bottle still in her hand.

"Els?"

Elsa appeared at the doorway to the living room.

"Sorry. You've been trying to get hold of me, haven't you?"

"Is everything OK?"

Elsa shook her head and wiped her cheek. Lesley put the bottle down and went to her girlfriend.

"What is it, sweetie?"

Elsa buried her head in Lesley's chest. "I think I'm rid of him."

"Rid of who?"

Elsa pulled away. She looked into Lesley's eyes, her own red-rimmed.

"I need to tell you about something."

"OK." Lesley glanced towards the kitchen. "Would a drop of whisky make it any easier?"

Elsa smiled. "It bloody would."

"Good."

Lesley pushed Elsa towards the sofa and returned to the kitchen, pouring two generous glasses. She sat next to Elsa on the sofa, their knees touching, and placed the glasses on the coffee table. After a moment, she picked them up and handed one to Elsa. Elsa drank it greedily, then wiped her mouth.

"That's better."

Lesley sipped at her own, then placed it on the table. "What is it you need to tell me?"

She could feel her heartbeat picking up. Was this to do with the case?

Elsa drank again. She let the empty glass fall into her lap.

"I've done something…" she hesitated, closing her eyes then reopening them. "I've done something illegal, love."

Lesley gritted her teeth. "OK."

"I destroyed a document for a client."

"What kind of document?"

"See, I can hear it in your voice. You're judging me."

"I'm not judging you," Lesley said. "Just tell me."

"You know I work for Arthur Kelvin, right? I represent his business interests."

Lesley nodded.

"Well, there's more to it than that. He's brought me in on the occasional, let's say shady deal."

"Does this have anything to do with DCI Mackie's death?" Lesley asked, watching Elsa's reaction.

Elsa frowned. "No. Why would it have anything to do with that?"

"The phone calls," Lesley said. "You were in contact with Tim Mackie before he died."

Elsa shook her head. "That was a case I was working on. He was a witness."

"Why were you talking to a witness for the prosecution in a criminal case?"

"He wasn't a witness for the prosecution. He was a witness for the defence."

"Whose defence?"

Elsa looked down, noticing the glass in her lap. She picked it up and put it on the table.

"There was a young guy called Ajit Malhotra, he was accused of drug smuggling. Mackie, as it turned out, had seen the kid at the same time that the smuggling was alleged to have taken place."

"In what capacity?" Lesley asked.

"When he was still on the force. He'd stopped him in the street, he and some other lads were causing trouble in Swanage town centre."

"OK."

Lesley's mind was racing. So Elsa had a legitimate reason to be in contact with DCI Mackie. But why had she used Harry Nevin's phone?

"The phone you used," she said. "It was the phone that you used for business with Arthur Kelvin?"

Elsa nodded. "DCI Mackie preferred that I keep our conversations anonymous. I'm a lawyer, Lesley, not a copper. If a witness asks for anonymity, I give it to them."

"Why did he want that?"

Elsa sighed. "I don't know, but I just wanted to keep him sweet as a witness. His statement was going to get my client off. But he didn't feel comfortable being a defence witness on a case involving organised crime."

"I can imagine."

Elsa looked at Lesley. "This isn't what I wanted to tell you about."

"No." Lesley scratched her cheek. "The document you destroyed for Arthur Kelvin."

Elsa nodded. "I got caught. I set it up so that I would get caught, and it worked."

"What do you mean, it worked?"

"Harry's PA, Sam Chaston. Do you remember her?"

"Vaguely," Lesley said. "What's it got to do with her?"

"I set it up so that she would see me destroying this document and report me to Aurelia Cross."

"And now you're being struck off?" Lesley asked.

Elsa shook her head. "Aurelia isn't reporting me to the Law Society, I knew she wouldn't want them looking too closely at the firm. But she did fire me."

Lesley put a hand on Elsa's knee. "Shit, Els. I'm so sorry."

Elsa smiled. "No, that's the whole point, don't you see? I wanted to be fired, because now I can't represent Kelvin. His contract is with the firm, not me."

"So you broke the law in order to extricate yourself from a client relationship?"

"I had to have a legitimate reason not to represent him any more. I couldn't just refuse to work for him, he'd never accept that, and nor would Aurelia. But now, I've got no choice in the matter. I can make out that I wanted to carry on working for him, but Aurelia's taken it out of my hands."

"So is Aurelia going to be representing him now?"

"Yes. What does that matter?" Elsa grabbed Lesley's hand. "The important thing is that I'm free of Arthur Kelvin. I'm going to set up my own practice, it's all going to be above board and legit. Sam's going to be my PA."

"Sam?"

"Sam Chaston, the one who caught me destroying the file."

Lesley looked at her girlfriend. Elsa had broken the law, but she'd done it to avoid having to represent a man who would surely make her break it in a far more serious way.

"Why did you do it now?" Lesley asked her.

"Surely that's obvious," Elsa said, dropping Lesley's hand. "Fogarty and Lawson."

"You were scared."

"They represented Kelvin," Elsa told her. "That's what Aurelia told me. They knew things about him, he wasn't going to let them retire. He had them killed. I – well, I haven't been working for him nearly as long as they did, or Harry did, for that matter. I don't know anything significant. I'm no risk to him. I've got out before it's too late."

CHAPTER SEVENTY-THREE

Lesley woke early the next morning. She lay still for a few moments, gazing up at the ceiling, until she realised there was no way she was getting back to sleep.

She turned to Elsa, fast asleep, her long dark hair splayed over the pillow. Lesley smiled, watching her girl-friend's chest rise and fall.

She lifted the duvet and slid out of bed, careful not to disturb Elsa. She went to the window and cracked open the blinds with her fingers. The dim light of dawn silhouetted the block separating them from the seafront. Lesley eased the blind shut and left the bedroom.

Heading into the hallway, she pulled on a fleece and a pair of boots and let herself out of the flat in silence.

The streets were quiet. She could hear bin lorries in the distance and the caw of seagulls towards the beach. She stretched her arms above her head then swung them by her sides, trying to pump energy into her body.

She'd lain awake half the night, mulling over the rami-fications of what Elsa had told her. Elsa might have come up with a legitimate reason not to work for Arthur Kelvin any more. But Kelvin wasn't the kind of man who would put up with an excuse like that. Whatever Elsa might say about her ignorance, Kelvin knew she would have information about him that he didn't want anybody else discovering.

Lesley was at the beach now. She stood on the prom, looking out over the sand. Elsa would wake and wonder where she was. But she needed to focus on the case. Maybe solving it could help keep Elsa safe?

She turned back towards the flat, pulling her phone out of her pocket. It was answered on the first ring.

"Dennis," she said, "I want you to meet me at Christian Davison's house."

"We're hoping he'll be in this time?"

"Yes, but let's be subtle."

"There's an Aldi around the corner," he said. "I'll meet you there, we can walk round."

"Good. I'll see you shortly."

CHAPTER SEVENTY-FOUR

Lesley and Dennis walked from the supermarket car park to Davison's house in silence. After a few minutes' awkwardness, Lesley decided to speak.

"How have you been, Dennis?" she asked.

"Fine, boss."

"You're not finding the fact that we're reopening the investigation into DCI Mackie's death difficult?"

He tensed, not breaking stride. "The shrink gave me techniques for coping with stress. I'll use them if I need to."

"Good." She eyed him. "Just let me know if it becomes a problem."

"It won't. DCI Mackie deserves justice."

Lesley nodded. Dennis was right, but she wasn't sure that Mackie was going to get justice.

As they neared the house, she put out a hand to stop Dennis. "Let's take it slow," she said. "Keep an eye on the house as we approach, he might be trying to avoid us."

"You think he was hiding in there when we came round yesterday?"

Lesley shook her head. "No, but there's something not right."

She approached the house and knocked on the front door. Dennis stood next to her where he couldn't be seen from the upstairs windows, watching the side gate. The curtains were still closed upstairs, but open downstairs.

She turned to him, shrugging. "No response."

"Maybe he's at work?"

"We'd have been told if he'd reported for duty. Perhaps PSD have arrested him."

"Surely the super would have told you?"

"I'm not sure the super wants to tell me very much at the moment."

Dennis raised an eyebrow. "No?"

"Don't worry about it, Dennis."

She walked to the front window and leaned in to look through the glass. The room was still in the same state it had been yesterday. The sandwich was curling at the edges.

"Excuse me," came a voice. "Can I help you?"

Lesley turned to see a man standing next to Dennis. He had a Jack Russell on a lead and looked puzzled.

She held up her ID. "Do you know if Mr Davison is in?"

The man frowned. "I'd have thought you'd know that, wouldn't you? He's one of your lot."

"Have you seen him over the last day or so?"

The man frowned. "Of course I have, I saw your lot arrest him."

Lesley exchanged glances with Dennis. "Arrest him? When?"

"Yesterday afternoon, it was about five o'clock. There was a whole bunch of them. Bundled him out, took him away in a car."

Lesley stepped closer to the man. "Are you sure it was the police?"

"Of course it was the police. Uniforms, radios, everything."

Lesley looked at Dennis. What wasn't the super telling her?

"Thanks for your help," she told the man. "I'll need your contact details in case we have more questions."

The man turned and pointed to a house three doors up. "I live there. When I finish walking Polly here, feel free to knock on my door."

"We will, Sir," she said.

CHAPTER SEVENTY-FIVE

Tina had spent the night at her own flat, not quite ready to talk to Mike yet. As she walked into the office, she steeled herself. He'd be annoyed that she'd come home and not told him. She was relieved to see that Stanley had arrived first and Mike wasn't in yet. Typical Mike to be late. She looked at the clock. Five minutes to nine. OK, so he wasn't late yet, not officially.

"Morning, Tina," Stanley said. "You back from Lyme Regis then?"

She shrugged off her jacket and draped it over the back of her chair.

"Yep, you'll have to put up with me again."

He smiled. "I'm glad you're back, the place doesn't seem the same without you."

"That's nice of you. Can I get you a cuppa?"

He laughed. "I wasn't angling for a favour, you know."

"I know you weren't, but I'm going to the kitchen anyway."

He nodded. "Coffee, two sugars please."

Tina smoothed down her jacket and headed for the door. As she did so, Mike came in. He stared at her as he opened the door, taken aback.

"T," he said.

She smiled, her heart racing. "Hi, Mike. I'm back."

"I can see that. Why didn't you tell me?"

"Sorry, I got back late last night, just wanted to sleep."

Mike looked at Stanley and then at her. He was holding something back, she knew. She didn't want to have this conversation in the office, with Stanley watching.

"I'm going to the kitchen," she said. "Can I get you one?"

He nodded. "Please."

Tina went out to the kitchen, her limbs heavy. She made three cups of coffee and brought them back to the office. When she arrived, they had company: Superintendent Carpenter.

"Sir," she said. "Is everything alright?"

She looked towards the DCI's office. It was empty, and where was the sarge?

"No," he said. "But you don't need to worry about that."

Stanley stood up. "Can we help you, Sir?"

The super looked towards the DCI's office. "Where's your boss?"

"She's not in yet," Tina said. "I assume she's out—"

"Tell me when she gets in," he said. "I need to speak to her urgently."

CHAPTER SEVENTY-SIX

Lesley stormed into the office. She all but ran to her own office, dumped herself on the chair, and then emerged, her breathing shallow. She needed to speak to the super. If PSD had arrested Davison and not told her...

"Boss," Tina said. "The super was looking for you."

"I bet he was," she replied.

Tina frowned. "Is everything alright?"

"Christian Davison has been arrested. Yesterday afternoon. A neighbour saw it. PSD, I'm assuming."

Tina frowned. "Are you sure, boss?"

"Why shouldn't I be?"

"I don't know."

Stanley looked up from his desk. "The super looked confused, boss."

"Confused, in what way?" Lesley asked.

Stanley shrugged. "Dunno. I suggest you go and see him pronto, though, he was mighty pissed off."

Lesley looked at him. "Keep digging into Christian Davison. Dennis is doing door-to-door on the rest of his neighbours."

She stormed out of the door and hurried towards the super's office. She knocked, holding her breath as she waited.

"Come," came his voice.

Lesley pushed the door open and slammed it shut behind her.

The super was behind his desk. He stood up. "Lesley."

"What's going on, Sir? We spoke to a neighbour of Christian Davison and he told us that our sole suspect was arrested yesterday afternoon."

Carpenter looked at her. "Arrested?"

She licked her lips. "Yes, Sir. I assume Professional Standards ordered it."

Carpenter shook his head. "Professional Standards went to see him yesterday evening, but he wasn't in."

Lesley put a hand on Carpenter's desk to steady herself. "Sorry, say that again?"

"Professional Standards went to his house and there was nobody in."

"What time was this?" she asked.

"Yesterday evening, about seven o'clock."

That was after she and Dennis had been there.

"Sir," she said, "are you sure PSD haven't arrested him?"

"Lesley," Carpenter leaned across the desk, "I know you think I'm an idiot. But I'd know if a suspect in a murder case had been arrested."

"In that case," she said, "who the hell *did* arrest him?"

CHAPTER SEVENTY-SEVEN

Christian Davison sat on the cold floor of the dingy space, his trousers wet. He'd held on as long as he could, but no matter how many times he'd shouted, nobody had come to let him go to the toilet.

He could smell himself. It was humiliating. He pulled – again – on the rope attaching him to a hook on the wall. What kind of person had a hook on a wall, ready to restrain someone?

He raised himself as best he could, attempting to straighten his legs. But there wasn't enough give on the rope. He crashed back down to the floor, wincing as he fell on his ankle. He needed to stop doing this, needed to conserve his strength. Where the hell was he?

Above his head was a high window. He could tell it was flimsy, wind whistling outside. The space he was in was made of brick, paint peeling and damp rising up the walls. There was a single door opposite him, solid, and he couldn't hear the sea. But then, his mind wasn't exactly working properly.

They'd put him in the back of a modern-looking saloon car that looked exactly like the kind of thing CID drove. He'd looked up and down the road and not seen any squad cars. For a moment, he'd wondered about that. If there were two uniformed constables, why wasn't there a squad car?

But he'd got into the back of the car regardless. The man in the front passenger seat had turned to him and told him to keep quiet. He'd been clean-shaven, well dressed. Wearing a suit. An expensive suit. Christian should have realised CID didn't wear good suits.

One of the men in uniform had climbed in beside him, and then the car had started. The man's uniform was convincing, Christian hadn't suspected a thing.

Why hadn't he noticed the caution? They'd used the wrong form of words. How had he not noticed that?

He'd been so prepared for this, almost anticipating it, that it hadn't occurred to him that when it came, it wouldn't be real.

And instead of taking him to HQ in Winfrith, or to a local police station, they'd driven south, towards Poole. They hadn't bothered to cover his head or use a blindfold. But about twenty minutes into the journey, the man next to him had thumped him on the side of the head with something hard, and he'd passed out.

And now he was here. Alone, locked up, and he didn't even know how long it had been.

Christian lived on his own. There was no girlfriend, no wife. His ex had long since forgotten about him and his parents lived in Scotland. Nobody would miss him. He wasn't expected at work for two days, tomorrow (or was it today?) was his day off. Would these people keep him alive for long enough for his absence to be noticed?

He heard footsteps outside the door and stiffened, pulling himself against the wall. He stared at the door, his eyes sore. He pulled his knees up against his chest for protection, and waited.

Nothing.

The door didn't open, and the footsteps had stopped. Christian could hear his own breathing in the cramped space. It was getting hot in here, despite the wind outside. The smell of his own dirt was overpowering now.

At last, the door opened. A dark figure entered, a man wearing a balaclava and bomber jacket.

That was good. If they didn't want him seeing faces, then they expected him to live.

But he'd seen faces at his house…

"Who are you?" he shouted. "I'm police, they'll notice I'm gone."

The man cocked his head, blinking at Christian. His eyes were small and dark.

His laughter was muffled beneath the balaclava. "No they won't, fuckwit. It's your day off."

Christian felt his heart still. So they knew.

"Look," he said. "Whatever it is you want—"

The man reached down and hit him across the face. Christian felt his head snap to the side. He suppressed a shout.

His nose was bleeding, he could feel it. But his hands were restrained, tied to the hook on the wall. He would just have to bleed.

The man laughed again. "Shut the fuck up, idiot, and maybe you'll live."

CHAPTER SEVENTY-EIGHT

Lesley hurried back into the office.

"We need to find Christian Davison, right now."

"What's happened?" Stanley asked.

"He's gone missing. PSD tried to arrest him last night and he wasn't there. They're not the ones who arrested him."

"Maybe he's in a station somewhere?" Tina suggested. "Maybe local Uniform have got him?"

Lesley shook her head. "There's something more sinister going on. Tina, check the system. I want to be completely sure he hasn't been arrested legitimately. I'm going back to his house. Mike, Stanley, get some background on him. Find out everything you can. Stanley, speak to your old mate in firearms. I want to know everything there is to know about Christian Davison, and who he hung out with."

"*Hung* out with, boss?" Tina asked.

"Hangs. Let's just hope he's still alive."

Tina's face paled. "D'you think whoever killed Fogarty and Lawson has got him?"

Lesley turned to the DC, a hand tugging at her hair.

"I don't know, Tina. But I think Christian Davison was involved in the deaths of Kenneth Fogarty and Catherine Lawson, and I think he's in serious danger."

CHAPTER SEVENTY-NINE

Lesley didn't bother parking in the Aldi car park this time, she just pulled up right outside the house. As she did so, a squad car arrived behind her and another one came from the opposite direction and parked in front of her. Two uniformed officers emerged from the squad car behind, and one of them hurried to her.

"PS Gates," he said. "I'm with Force Response, are you the officer in charge?"

Lesley nodded. "DCI Clarke, I'm the SIO on a double murder investigation and Christian Davison is a person of interest. He was witnessed being arrested yesterday at around five pm but he's not been arrested by any branch of police."

"It was faked?"

"He could still be in there, Sergeant. We have to consider—"

"I know what I'm doing, Ma'am. Did the neighbour see him being taken away?"

"Yes."

"So, what are we looking for?"

"Whoever took him will know we're coming. We have to check they haven't left us any surprises. While keeping the house clean for the CSIs."

"No problem." PS Gates spoke into his radio.

Lesley turned away, looking towards the house. "Do you have your enforcer?"

"Yes, Ma'am."

Two officers had left the other car. They approached the house, looking towards her and the sergeant for confirmation. Another vehicle drew up, a police van. Four firearms officers emerged.

Lesley frowned and approached the van. The sergeant in the front seat opened his window.

"We don't expect anyone inside," she said. "Let alone anyone armed."

"Orders from the super, Ma'am."

Lesley grunted. It couldn't do any harm going in mob-handed. She turned to the firearms sergeant.

"Are you AFO Davison's team?" she asked.

"No, Ma'am. I'm Sergeant Djalili, Davison's with Sergeant Weathers. There are two firearms teams."

"Good. You get behind Uniform, we'll open the door and go in first."

"Ma'am."

Dennis was standing by her car. Lesley walked over to him and they stood back as the uniformed officers approached the house. Within moments the front door was open and three of the firearms officers were inside. Another one went around the back, two Uniforms following.

Lesley heard voices and footsteps inside the house. She approached the front door.

"Safe to come in?" she called.

"Yes, Ma'am," came the voice of PS Gates.

Lesley stepped inside. The house felt cramped, full of bulky uniformed officers. But there was no sign of AFO Davison.

"Search anywhere someone might be hidden. Cupboards, wardrobes, under the stairs. Is there a shed or an outbuilding, a garage maybe?"

"Ma'am." Djalili was coming down the stairs. He indicated for his team to head off in different directions. One by one they came back.

"Nothing. No sign of him."

Lesley turned back to Dennis who was standing behind her in the doorway.

"He's not here."

"We never thought he would be, did we?"

Her shoulders slumped. "No, but… Well, for a moment. I had some hope."

"He's been taken, boss. We just need to work out where."

"You're telling me." She turned to the sergeant. "Get your team out of here as quickly as possible, they might be disturbing evidence."

"They know to be careful."

The officers hurried out, leaving Lesley and Dennis alone in the house. She peered up the stairs.

"Where do we start?"

"Where do we think he was when he was taken?" Dennis said.

"Living room," she said. "That sandwich."

"OK, we start there."

Lesley raised a hand to stop him entering. "Let's wait for Gail," she said. "We get a proper sweep, and determine if anything was left behind."

CHAPTER EIGHTY

Tina scrolled through the system, her eyes glazing over. There was nothing, no evidence of Christian Davison being arrested, no warrant for his arrest. No visits to his house, apart from the one made by the boss and the sarge. There would be one by PSD, but that wasn't on the system. If they'd had a warrant for his arrest, that would have been logged.

She leaned back in her chair, sighing.

"No joy?" asked Mike.

"Nothing. If he was taken, it wasn't by the police."

"What was the last job he did?" Mike asked.

"What do you mean?" she said.

"His firearms team, what was the last job they did?"

"Why does that matter?"

"Humour me," he said, looking at her across the desks.

She cocked her head. "Because it's you."

She bent to the system. "It's not on here," she said.

"OK," said Mike. "In that case, we need to go and talk to his colleagues."

Stanley stood up. "I'll go with you, I know one of them."

"Don't you think that means you should stay here?" Tina said.

Stanley shook his head. "It's fine, I can get her to open up. Come on, Mike, you come with me."

Tina looked at Stanley. Since when was he the one giving out the orders? He was the newest member of the team. But still, she was tired from the sleepless nights at Lyme Regis, the constant gnawing pressure to tell her mum about the pregnancy. She still hadn't told Mike. And then there was the nausea…

"OK," she said.

She didn't like this, she didn't like her pregnancy getting in the way of her being able to do her job.

"But tell me if you need me."

Mike gave her a grin. "Of course we will, T."

CHAPTER EIGHTY-ONE

The AFO unit that Christian Davison belonged to was based out of a low brick-built building in Poole.

Mike pulled up in the car park and got out, stretching his back.

"You alright there?" Stanley asked.

"Fine. Just pulled me back a bit the other week."

"Making an arrest?"

Mike shook his head. "Fell down the stairs."

Stanley spat out a laugh. "How old are you?"

"Yeah, yeah. Laugh all you want."

Stanley smirked at him. "I'd better look after you. Didn't realise I'd be on invalid duty today."

"Stop it," Mike said, wishing he hadn't said anything. "Let's go in. Who's the one you know?"

"Donna Turnbury. She's an old girlfriend."

"Of Christian's?"

"Of mine."

"Lucky lady."

"Hmpf."

Mike looked at him. "Why didn't you tell me this before?"

"It's not exactly something you brag about."

"Yeah, but…"

Stanley shook his head. "Don't be daft. It was years ago."

"How many years ago?"

"Ten, if you must ask."

"So you were going out with Christian Davison's colleague at the time that Davison may or may not have shot Fogarty and Lawson."

"Yes."

"Did you know Davison?"

"No," Stanley replied. "I met Donna at training college. I never worked with either of them."

Mike didn't feel comfortable with this. Should he speak to the sarge?

But the sarge was busy with the boss at Davison's house.

"It'll be fine. Come on, man," Stanley said.

"OK, but I'm staying with you. I want to make sure you don't get yourself into any trouble."

Stanley gave him a look but didn't object. They entered the office, both showing their ID.

"We need to speak to Christian Davison's sergeant," Mike said to the woman at the desk.

"Sergeant Weathers is off duty."

"OK," said Stanley, "in that case, is Donna here?"

The woman looked back at him. "Who wants to know?"

"I already showed you my ID. DC Stanley Brown, Major Crime Investigations Team. This is my colleague DC Legg. We're working on a murder inquiry."

She raised an eyebrow.

"Just get Donna for us, will you?" Stanley asked.

Mike shifted between his feet, not liking Stanley's tone.

The woman grunted and picked up her phone.

Two minutes later, a woman wearing a firearms uniform emerged from a back door.

"Stanley Brown." Her gaze flicked between him and Mike. "What are you doing here?"

"We need to know more about Christian," Stanley said. "Is there somewhere we can talk?"

Donna looked at the woman behind the desk. "We'll use the meeting room. Sal, can you lend me the key?"

The woman opened a drawer, her face hard.

"Don't worry about Sal," Donna said. "She just hates coppers."

Mike stifled a laugh. She was in the wrong job, then. He turned to Stanley and the laugh died in his throat. Stanley was looking at Donna in a way that made Mike uncomfortable.

"Come on, mate," Mike told him. "The meeting room."

Stanley nodded and gave Mike a grin.

They followed Donna along corridors that smelt of chip fat and sweat. At last they came to a door which she held open for them. Stanley walked in, giving the woman a punch on the arm as he did so.

Mike followed, making sure not to make physical contact with Stanley's friend.

The room was cramped and dimly lit, with a small table and four chairs. Stanley plonked himself down in one and Donna took the one next to him. Mike reluctantly sat opposite them.

"Thanks for this, Donna," said Stanley, smiling at her.

She smiled back. "What can I help you with?"

"We need to know what Christian's been doing lately," Mike said. "Anything out of the ordinary. Any days off sick, any incidents in the line of duty."

"What was your most recent op?" Stanley asked.

The woman looked between Stanley and Mike. "Drugs bust, Boscombe."

"They do drugs busts in Boscombe?" Stanley asked.

She raised an eyebrow. "You'd be surprised."

"It was a firearms op, and Christian was on it?" Mike asked.

"Yes. You're not PSD, are you?"

Mike felt himself stutter.

"Professional Standards?" Stanley looked shocked. "Definitely not."

"Good."

"Is there a reason you think we might be?" Mike asked.

She stared back at him, then at Stanley.

"It's OK," Stanley said. "You can tell us."

She twisted her lips together. "You're not PSD?"

Stanley put his hands to his chest. "Cross my heart, Don."

She shook her head. "Nah. I think you should talk to the sarge."

Stanley grabbed her hand. She flinched but let him keep hold of it. A flush crept up her neck.

"Christian's in trouble," Stanley said. "Someone's taken him."

"Who?"

"That's what we're trying to find out."

"Taken him?"

"We think they faked an arrest."

"It wasn't PSD?"

"Nope."

"OK." She looked at Mike. "There was an… incident. On the drugs op."

"What kind of incident?" Mike asked.

"Christian got… left behind."

"How do you mean?"

She sighed and slumped in her chair. "We swept the building for weapons, checked for suspects. Three arrests made. We did a cursory check for forensics but left that for the CSIs. Christian said he heard something in the garden, so he went back downstairs. When I left the house with the rest of the team, I thought he'd gone on ahead."

"But?" asked Mike.

"But he wasn't at the van."

"Was he in the garden?"

"There was no sign of him."

"Did you alert your sergeant?"

"I went looking for him first. I found him in the next door garden. He was…" She rubbed at the skin on the back of her hand.

"Go on," said Mike. "What was he doing?"

"He was talking to some bloke. I called out Christian's name, the bloke scarpered and Christian came back with me. That was all there was to it."

"Was this bloke a suspect?" Stanley asked.

"Not as far as I'm aware."

"Was he reprimanded afterwards?"

"I covered for him."

"Was that a good idea?" Mike asked. "It could be why he's been taken."

"I didn't know that, did I?"

"No." Mike looked at Stanley, who shrugged.

"Is there anything else we need to know, Donna?" he asked. "Where was the raid?"

"I can get the address."

"Who were the targets?"

"I don't know. We were just backup."

"OK. Thanks, Donna."

CHAPTER EIGHTY-TWO

"The cavalry's here!"

Lesley turned to see Gail walking up the front drive to Davison's house.

"What do you need?" she asked as she picked her way in through the damaged front door.

"I need anything that might have been left behind when the so-called arrest took place."

"OK, let's pull back. What's the case? Who's the suspect? Whose house is this?"

"You haven't been briefed?" Lesley asked.

"I got a call telling me to hurry over here. That's all I know."

"Who from?" Lesley asked.

"Mike. Sounded like he was in a hurry."

"OK." Lesley stepped towards Gail. "This house belongs to AFO Christian Davison. He's a potential suspect in the Fogarty and Lawson case. It was his gun you found."

"OK, that makes perfect sense now." Gail walked through the hallway onto the living room and scanned it.

"So what's this about a so-called arrest?"

"We came here to interview him last night," Lesley said. "He wasn't in. Turns out one of his neighbours saw him get *arrested*." She held up her fingers in air quotes.

"Earlier that day, except there's no record on the system of any arrest or arrest warrant."

"So somebody staged an arrest," Gail said.

"Bingo."

"And you need me and Gavin to look for anything that was left behind or evidence of who might have taken him or where they might have taken him to."

"That's exactly what I need."

"Fair enough. I'll look but I don't expect to find anything."

"No?"

"Anyone who staged an arrest convincing enough to take in a serving copper is going to have some forensic sense. I very much doubt that they've left anything useful behind." Gail paused, wrinkling her nose. It was the only part of her Lesley could make out under the forensic suit. "But you never know. Leave it with me."

"Good," said Lesley. "Start in the living room. He left a half-finished sandwich, that's where we think he was last."

Gail shook her head. "I'll start at the front door. They'd have knocked, he'd have answered, they might never have stepped inside."

Gail was right.

"You do what you need to do," Lesley told her friend.

"I take it you've been careful who's touched that front door?"

Lesley looked at it. The door was splintered around the lock, having been forced open by the enforcer.

"Sorry."

Gail laughed. "It's not the first time. I'll see what I can do."

CHAPTER EIGHTY-THREE

Tina sat back in her chair, staring vacantly at her screen. She'd trawled through HOLMES twice, not quite sure what she was looking for. She'd done a few Google searches, looking for Davison and other members of his team she'd found on the system. She'd worked through the case files from Fogarty and Lawson and looked at Davison's history. Where he lived, which units he'd worked in.

She'd found nothing useful. She wasn't contributing anything sitting here.

That last job that Davison had done, the drugs bust. Stanley had phoned, told her about it. Maybe there was something there.

She checked through the files on HOLMES, but there was nothing specifically about Davison.

Maybe going there might help. She might uncover something important.

She leaned forward, tapping her keyboard a few times and staring into the screen. No, this was useless.

She'd be more help to the rest of the team if she was out and about looking for evidence. Following up leads.

She grabbed her coat off the back of her chair and swung it over her shoulders. She needed to find a way to help with the case.

CHAPTER EIGHTY-FOUR

"Lesley, I've got something!"

Lesley turned in the direction of Gail's voice. "Where are you?"

"Upstairs, back bedroom."

She hurried up the stairs, hesitated at the top then entered the back bedroom. Gail was crouched on the floor, reaching under the bed.

"What is it?" Lesley asked.

"A laptop. It's been stashed under here." She looked up at Lesley, then reached her arm underneath and pulled the laptop out. She placed it on the bed.

"Maybe he wanted to hide it from burglars."

"Maybe," Gail replied. "But let's take a look at it."

She opened up the laptop.

"Damn," she muttered. "Password protected." She raised her head. "Gav, can you bring the code breaker?"

"I'll get it from the van," came Gav's voice.

"You have a device that'll break passwords?" Lesley asked.

"Doesn't always work, but it's better than me sitting here for twenty years trying to do it manually."

She prodded at keys.

"I wouldn't do that," Lesley said. "It might lock us out."

Gail smiled at her. "Don't worry, the gizmo Gav's bringing will override any cockup I make."

Gavin appeared in the doorway, holding out a USB stick.

"Is that it?" Lesley asked.

Gail plugged it into the laptop and characters appeared in the password field. They moved quickly, eventually slotting into place. The laptop came to life.

"Right," she said. "Let's take a look at what we've got."

She went to the file manager, scrolling through folders, then turned to the software history.

"Video app," she said. "Used yesterday."

She opened up the app and clicked on the most recent file. It was camera footage.

Gail cocked her head.

"That's the street," Lesley said.

"Yeah, but where's it from?"

Gail stood up, the laptop still in her hands. "Jesus, my knees. I'm not made for kneeling down like this."

There was a cough from the doorway. Lesley looked up to see Dennis watching them.

"Sorry, Dennis," Gail muttered. She turned to sit on the bed, placing it on her lap. Lesley sat next to her.

Gavin appeared behind Dennis. "There's a camera next to the front door. Well hidden, but it's there."

"Good," Gail said. "If we didn't spot it, chances are they won't have either."

She flicked through more files, eventually playing one whose timestamp correlated with what the neighbour had said about Davison being taken away.

Lesley watched in silence.

Five men hurried towards the door. Three of them wore police uniforms, or what looked like police uniforms. One was in civilian clothes. He was behind the men in the fake uniforms, face obscured.

After a moment, the fake officers moved to one side. The plain-clothed man, wearing a suit, turned briefly, towards the camera.

"Do you know him?" Lesley asked.

Gail screwed up her face. She shook her head.

"I might."

Lesley looked up to see Dennis's face was pale.

"Dennis? Who is it?"

"Let me see it again."

Gail turned the laptop to face him.

"Oh, my word," he said.

"What is it?" Lesley asked him. "*Who* is it?"

He licked his lips. "Darren Kelvin."

Lesley felt the blood drain out of her face. "Kelvin?"

Dennis nodded. "Not Arthur Kelvin. His nephew. Arthur Kelvin's nephew was the man who took Christian Davison."

CHAPTER EIGHTY-FIVE

Tina pulled up outside the house that Davison and his team had raided the previous week. It was a nondescript terraced house, the front garden full of litter and the wooden window frames rotting. She sat in her car for a moment, eyeing it. Should she knock on the door?

She watched it a little longer, scanning for signs of habitation. There was no movement inside, but that didn't mean that there couldn't be somebody at the back. She looked up and down the street. A woman was pushing a pushchair a few doors up, but that was all.

Tina got out of the car and edged towards the house, scanning the windows as she moved. Still nothing. There were no curtains drawn in the windows, it didn't look as if there were any curtains hanging. She hesitated at the front door, her hand raised. *Come on Tina*, she told herself. *No point in coming all the way here and then not knocking on the door.*

She gave it a firm rap. The kind of rap that only the police would use. No answer. She knocked again, still no answer.

It didn't mean there was no one inside, just that they didn't want to talk to her.

She waded through the rubbish in the front yard and headed for the front window, peering inside. The room beyond the glass was a tip, strewn with discarded cigarette wrappers, beer cans and takeaway cartons. She couldn't tell if it had been recently used or left like that some time ago. If Davison's team had raided the place just a week ago, it would have been in use then. According to the file, there'd been three arrests made.

She went to the side gate beyond the front door and gave it a push. It opened. She looked back at the street. Strictly speaking, this was trespass. But she was a police officer investigating a crime. If Christian Davison had done something here that would help them find him…

She pushed through the gate and walked along the rough tarmac leading to the back garden. A wheelie bin blocked her way, and she pushed it to one side.

The back garden was no better than the inside. The grass was almost up to her waist, and she couldn't see if there was rubbish hidden within its depths. A narrow path spanned the back of the house. She walked along it, avoiding litter and what looked like ash from an ancient fire, and peered in through the back windows.

The kitchen was filthy. Grime coated the oven, cupboards hung open, and dishes piled up in the sink. Tina rattled the back door. It was locked.

She sighed. There was nothing more she could do. Whoever lived here had scarpered after being raided by the police. If there was anyone left who hadn't been arrested.

Looking around the place gave her a feel for what Christian Davison had experienced on that raid, but brought her no closer to knowing why he had left his team. Had it been deliberate? Had there been something he was doing here? Someone he was meeting?

She looked back towards the garden. Maybe she'd find something there.

"Oi!" came a voice.

She snapped her head round, looking for its source. The alleyway was empty.

"You! What are you doin' over there?"

A man stared at her over the fence. He was bald, with narrow eyes and sweat beading on his forehead.

"Do you know if there's anybody in here?" she asked.

"Hasn't been for a week. Who are you?"

She swallowed. She wasn't here on official business, she didn't have a warrant.

"Nobody," she said.

The man grunted. "Bugger off then, or I'll call the police."

Tina suppressed a smile. "Sorry to disturb you, Sir," she said, and headed back along the alleyway.

CHAPTER EIGHTY-SIX

"You do it," said Stanley.

Mike frowned at his colleague, then knocked at the sergeant's door.

"Come in," came a voice.

Mike glanced at Stanley then pushed the door open.

"Sergeant Weathers," he said. It seemed she'd returned.

The firearms sergeant looked up from her desk. "That's me. DC Legg was it?"

"DC Legg and DC Brown," Mike said.

"What's up?" the sergeant asked.

"We were talking to one of your team," Mike replied, "about the drugs op you did last week."

Sergeant Weathers nodded. "You want to know about Christian going AWOL?"

"Surely in the kind of high-risk situations your team find themselves in," Mike said, "you take extra care to make sure you know where everyone is."

Weathers stood up from her chair, pushing it back. It hit the wall.

"Look," she said, "it wasn't my team's fault. They were all together, tight as usual. Christian was at the back, Donna thought she had him. He kept reassuring her he was with them, they peeled off, went into different rooms, searched the house, usual procedure."

"And then what?" Stanley asked.

Mike looked at Stanley. How well did Stanley know these people? He'd dated Donna Turnberry, hadn't he?

The sergeant had her hands in her pockets. "We finished the raid, left the building. I was on the doorstep watching the street. When the team came out, Christian wasn't with them."

"But wait," said Mike. "You were on the doorstep. If he'd left the building, you would have seen him."

"There was a back door."

"And you didn't have an officer on it?"

"We did, but he heard something in the garden and went to investigate. It must have been then that Christian left the building."

"Where did he turn up?" Stanley asked.

"Donna found him, talking to some bloke."

"Which bloke?"

"Just a passer-by, he said."

"You didn't think to check?" Mike asked.

She glared at him. "I trust my team."

"How long was he missing?"

"Ten minutes, no more."

"Did you question Davison afterwards?" Mike asked. "Find out why he went missing?"

"He said he'd heard something, neighbouring house."

"Did he have his body cam on?" Stanley asked.

Weathers looked at him. She took a few breaths. "DC Brown, DC Legg, I'd rather speak to your DCI."

"Hang on a minute," Mike said. "You're not under investigation, we're just trying to find out what Davison did. It could help us find him."

She shook her head. "I want to at least speak to your DS, preferably your DCI. I'm not answering any more questions."

CHAPTER EIGHTY-SEVEN

Tina's phone rang as she was driving along the A35 back to the office. She hit hands-free.

"DC Abbott," she said.

"Tina," came the boss's voice, "I need you to run something through the system for me."

Tina swallowed. She checked her rear-view mirror, seeing no cars behind her. She tapped the accelerator a moment, speeding up, then thought better of it and slowed back down.

"Sorry, boss. What is it you need me to run?"

"We've got CCTV from Christian Davison's. Dennis has identified one of the men in it, we want to ID the others. Can you run them through HOLMES, see if you can find a match?"

"Of course. I can't do it immediately though."

"Why not?"

"I… I'll be back in the office in five minutes."

"Tina," the DCI said. "Where are you?"

Tina swallowed. "I went to investigate the house where Christian Davison went on that drugs bust. I wanted to find out if there was anything there that might help us track him down."

"That's a crime scene," the boss said. "Please tell me you took back-up."

"Sorry, boss."

"Shit." The boss's voice was tight.

"Sorry, boss," Tina repeated.

"We haven't got time for this," the DCI said. "Just get back to the office as quick as you can and I'll send you these files. Call me as soon as you've got anything."

"Yes, boss. Sorry, boss."

"And stop bloody apologising."

CHAPTER EIGHTY-EIGHT

Lesley hung up, her nerves on fire. She turned to Dennis. "Tina's going to take a little while to get to those videos."

"Why?"

"It seems she took it upon herself to go and investigate the house where Christian Davison's team did the drugs bust last week."

Dennis's mouth widened. "She did *what*?"

Lesley gritted her teeth. "Don't be pissed off with her, Dennis. She's an inexperienced member of the team, she just wanted to help."

He shook his head. "Please don't tell me she went alone."

Lesley nodded.

Dennis's face reddened.

"Anyway," Lesley said, "we haven't got time. I'm annoyed with her too, but she was just being keen."

"There's keen and there's stupid."

"Look," she said, "this Darren Kelvin, what's he like? Tell me everything you know about him."

They were still in Christian Davison's bedroom. A CSI she didn't recognise entered and gestured to Gail, who stood up and followed him out, shrugging at Lesley.

"Let's go outside," Dennis suggested.

Lesley followed him down the stairs. Gail was in the front room; Lesley gave her a nod as she passed, then headed out after Dennis.

Dennis didn't stop walking until he reached her car. He turned to her, gesturing for her to open the door. She did so and slid into the driver's seat. Dennis got in the passenger side.

"Why all the cloak and dagger?" she asked.

He shook his head. "When it comes to the Kelvins, the fewer people involved, the better. You know how deeply unpleasant these people are."

Lesley smiled. "Deeply unpleasant? Is that the strongest description you've got for them?"

He looked at her. "Using profanities doesn't make it any stronger, boss. They are nasty people, dangerous people. If one of the Kelvins took Christian Davison, then he's in danger."

"We already know that."

"We can only assume that the Kelvins were involved in the murder of Fogarty and Lawson," he said. "They've taken Davison because he knows about it."

Lesley leaned back and gazed out the front window of the car.

"Davison was working for them," she said. "He either gave them his gun, or he did the job for them."

Dennis dragged his hands up and down his thighs, digging into his skin. "What would make a serving officer do that?"

"That's not the pertinent issue right now. We need to find him, then we can worry about motive."

"They'll know we're looking for them."

She looked at him. "They don't know about the CCTV."

He shook his head. "They stood outside his door in broad daylight, no disguise. What kind of confidence must they have, to do that?"

"There's confident, and there's reckless. We know they're involved with Fogarty and Lawson now. Once we find Davison—"

"Without a statement from him, we've got nothing."

Lesley looked at him. Her mouth was dry. "We need to find him."

"We do, boss. And not only because we need his evidence."

She gritted her teeth and nodded.

"So where will he be?" she asked. "Where might the Kelvins have taken him?"

"I don't know, boss. We need to access the system. Find out everything we can about Darren Kelvin's activities. Places he's used, business premises that he or his family own."

"It's a long list."

"We have to try," Dennis said. "They might have taken Davison to one of them."

"You're right." She grabbed her phone and called Mike.

"Mike, are you still with the AFOs?"

"Yes, boss."

"Tina's not able to access the system right now, but we need to get on HOLMES urgently. Can you get on it from the AFOs' base?"

"We should be able to, if Sergeant Weather lets us."

"There a problem with that?" Lesley glanced at Dennis who shrugged.

"Sorry, boss," Mike said. "But she's being obstructive. Christian Davison went AWOL on an op last week and she's worried that she's going to get into trouble for it. She won't talk to us."

"Tell her that Christian Davison's life is at risk. We need to find him, or he could die."

"What's going on, boss?" Mike asked.

"The Kelvins have got him," she said. "Arthur Kelvin's nephew came to his house posing as a police officer and took him away."

"Shit."

"Exactly."

"I'll tell Stanley. His mate Donna might let us on."

"Just do whatever you have to, Mike."

CHAPTER EIGHTY-NINE

Tina parked her car as close to the entrance to HQ as she could and hurled herself towards the building. She ran up the stairs, cursing herself under her breath. She had no idea how much trouble she was going to be in when the boss got back, but she knew she was going to have to redeem herself. She had to view that CCTV and identify the people on it.

She crashed in through the doors of the team room, pausing for a moment to register how quiet it was. The room was dark, all the computers turned off.

Stop it, she told herself. Was she spooked by an empty room?

She flicked on the lights and threw herself into her chair, turning on her computer. There was an email from the boss, two CCTV videos attached. One was from Davison's house, the other from a neighbour.

She fired up HOLMES and opened the video from the neighbour. She watched it at double speed, her eyes narrowed, her breathing shallow.

She needed to pull herself together. If she was panicking about being in trouble, she wouldn't do her job properly. She pinched the skin on the back of her hand, trying to bring herself back into the moment.

"This is what you do, Tina," she told herself. "Analysing data."

Comparing sources of evidence was what she was good at. Not gallivanting around the county looking for crime scenes, and following up on old operations. That had been a bloody stupid thing to do, but she'd felt so useless sitting here doing nothing.

She paused the video. There'd been a moment when one of the men at the back had raised his helmet.

She squinted and rewound it, slowing it down.

The first man, Darren Kelvin, was in front of him, dressed in a suit.

Arthur Kelvin's nephew. Even Tina recognised him.

But the other one, the man behind him… Tina squinted, watching him lift his helmet and scratch his head.

He had scruffy blond hair and had a tattoo behind his ear. Tina didn't recognise him, but that was the best image she was going to get.

Her breathing was reaching normality now. Her head was in the case again, and not in her own career. That was good.

Tina went to the file for Arthur Kelvin. She needed details of his employees, everybody they'd ever brought in, anyone who'd been suspected of a crime. She'd start with the biggest fish.

She worked her way down, comparing the photos with the still from the video.

She punched the table.

"Got you, you bastard."

She picked up her phone. The DCI answered in two rings.

"Boss," she said, "one of the other men in the CCTV, I've got a match."

"It's alright," the DCI replied. "We already know who it is."

"What?" Tina replied.

"Mike's been on HOLMES for the last fifteen minutes, he's over at the AFOs' base, they gave him access."

"And you asked him to look at the CCTV as well?"

"Yes," the DCI said. "Sorry, Tina. I couldn't wait. Davison's life is in—"

"I understand," Tina said, "So you know it's Stephen Leonard?"

"Yes."

"He was under suspicion last year, the Harry Nevin case."

"It's alright," the boss said. "You can calm down, Tina. You're not going to be in trouble."

"I'm sorry, boss," Tina said.

"You like saying that, don't you? You should focus more on doing your job and less on apologising."

"Sorry, boss."

"There you go again. If you say sorry one more time, then I *will* give you a bollocking."

"So—" Tina stopped herself. "Right, boss. Understood, boss. What's happening?"

"Mike and Stanley are trawling all known premises belonging to Leonard, I suggest you do the same," Lesley told her. "The more heads we've got working on this, the faster we can work out where Davison is. Keep me or Dennis updated and we'll get Uniform visiting all the addresses."

"No problem, boss," Tina put down the phone.

She stared at it for a moment. So Mike had beaten her to a crucial piece of evidence. The boss had pitted them against each other.

Mike, of all people. Why had she been so stupid?

CHAPTER NINETY

Stanley was hunched over Donna's computer, Mike standing behind him. Donna stood near the door, her breathing shallow.

"I'm going to be in so much trouble," she said.

"You could save Christian's life," Mike told her.

"Is it that bad?"

"Let's hope not," Stanley muttered, his eyes scanning the screen.

"What do you reckon?" Mike asked him. "Does it help us narrow down where they might have taken him?"

"Not yet. Give me time." Stanley's cheek twitched.

Mike was itching to take over, to get on the system himself. But Donna would only let Stanley.

His phone rang and he picked it up, grateful for the break in the tension.

"Hi, T," he said. "Are you back at the office?"

"Yeah," she replied.

"How was it staying with your mum?"

"It was fine." Her voice was terse.

"You OK, T?"

"You got me in the shit," she said.

Mike cupped his hand around the phone, looking at Stanley.

"What d'you mean?"

"The boss asked me to look at the CCTV. I didn't get it done as fast as I should have because I was out, at the place where Christian Davison and his team did a drugs bust last week."

"So what did I do wrong?"

"You identified Stephen Leonard before I did."

"Sorry, T," he said. "But I was just doing my job. The boss asked me and Stan to—"

"I know." She sighed, the edge going out of her voice. "I know you were, it's just… I don't need this right now."

Mike turned towards the wall, aware of Stanley and Donna listening in.

"Are you OK, T? Did something happen while you were in Lyme Regis?"

"It's fine. Don't worry about me." She hung up.

Stanley looked up at him. "Everything alright?"

"Fine," Mike replied.

He wasn't about to go into the details of his personal life with the newest member of the team.

CHAPTER NINETY-ONE

Lesley pulled up outside Darren Kelvin's house. She stopped the car and sat for a moment.

"You OK, boss?" Dennis asked.

"Just considering how best to play this."

"He might not even be in."

She turned to him. "If he is, we need a plan of action. If anybody's going to have an alibi sorted out, it'll be Darren Kelvin."

"We've got him on CCTV. No alibi is going to get him out of that."

"True," she said. "But you know the Kelvins, slippery as anything."

Dennis raised his eyebrows. "They're not getting out of this one, boss."

"Let's hope you're right."

She opened her car door and eyed the house as she waited for Dennis to join her.

It was a large detached house in Canford Cliffs, just over half a mile away from his uncle's mansion. Not as grand, but smart nonetheless. She could just about hear the sea in the distance and the ever-present caw of seagulls.

"OK," she said. "Let me lead this."

"Happy on that score, boss," Dennis said.

Lesley gave him a smile. She liked it when Dennis wasn't being argumentative.

She walked up the front drive and pressed the buzzer for the doorbell. After a few moments, a woman came to the door.

"Mrs Kelvin?" Lesley asked.

"No," the woman replied.

"I'm sorry," Lesley said, holding up her ID. "My name is DCI Clarke, Dorset Police. This is my colleague DS Frampton. What's your name, please?"

"Tracy Stevens, what's it to you?"

Lesley frowned. "Ms Stevens, are you Mr Kelvin's girl-friend?"

"No? Who's Mr Kelvin?"

Lesley glanced at Dennis.

"Darren Kelvin, this is his address. We need to have a word with him."

"Sorry, love. I don't know who you're talking about."

"Do you live here?" Dennis asked.

The woman looked at him. "Have I done something wrong? Shit, is it my husband? What's he done this time?"

Lesley tensed. "What's your husband's name?"

"Tom. What's he done?"

"Does he work for one of Arthur Kelvin's companies, by any chance?" Dennis asked.

The woman looked at him. "He's a hotel manager. Big chain, Bournemouth."

Lesley looked at the woman. Was she telling the truth?

"I'm sorry, Ms Stevens," Lesley said, "but do you rent this house?"

"I do. Canford Letting Agency. I've got all the paper-work, pay my rent, pay my water bills, all above board. I've even got a TV licence."

"It's fine," Dennis said. "So Canford Letting Agency is your landlord?"

"Not my landlord, he's some bloke who's working out of the country. But yeah, they're the people I deal with."

"Do you happen to know the name of your landlord?" Dennis asked.

"Sorry, they wouldn't tell me."

Damn. "OK, thanks for your time," Lesley said.

She turned away, Dennis joining her.

"She seems to be telling the truth," she muttered.

He nodded.

Lesley stopped at the car. "If Darren Kelvin doesn't live in that house, where *does* he live?"

CHAPTER NINETY-TWO

"Okay, what now?" Lesley said.

Dennis shrugged. "We need to find out if the rest of the team have found any more potential locations for Davison."

"We also need to know where Darren Kelvin actually lives."

Dennis nodded.

Lesley started the car.

"Where are we going?"

"I don't know," she said, "but I don't want to just sit here. Let's drive into Bournemouth. Call Tina. See if she's got any ideas."

"No problem." Dennis picked up his phone.

"Tina, it's the sarge... OK...Yes." He frowned. "She needs to speak to you, boss." He switched over to hands-free.

"Tina," Lesley said. They were passing Branksome Chine, the road dipping down towards the sea then swooping up and inland again. "The address we've got for Darren Kelvin is rented out. Tenant knows nothing about him. I need you to track down his actual residential address."

"No problem. But I've got the super here. He needs to speak to you."

"Really? Why didn't he call me direct?"

284

"I need to talk to you about Christian Davison," Carpenter said.

Lesley glanced at the phone. "We're trying to locate him, Sir. I'm sure you'll appreciate—"

"DCI Clarke, take me off speakerphone."

Shit.

Dennis made a gesture for her to pull over. She shook her head then parked on the double yellows leading up to the County Gates Gyratory. A car horn sounded behind her.

"Yeah, yeah, whatever," she muttered and got out of the car, grabbing Dennis's phone.

"Sir, I'm alone. What's happened?"

"Christian Davison is already under investigation."

"By whom?"

"Professional Standards, they've been watching him for the last year."

"On what grounds?"

"I'm sorry, Lesley, that's all I know."

"We still need to find him. He's in danger, Sir. If he knows who killed Fogarty and Lawson, he could be next."

"I know."

I know. Is that all he was going to say?

"Will they share their information with us?"

"You know how it is."

Lesley grunted, raising a finger at a car that passed, horn blaring. She'd had plenty of dealings with PSD in the West Midlands. They'd investigated her boss, David Randle. He'd turned out to be involved with organised crime.

Was it all happening again?

Her hand went to the back of her neck. Her old wound was throbbing.

"OK," she said. "What *can* you tell me?"

"Not much. They went to his house yesterday and he wasn't there."

"We already know that."

"Yes."

"Lesley. PSD don't want us interfering with this. It impacts on a major operation."

"Davison could die. He's a serving copper. PSD really want us to leave him to it?"

"No. They want to run the search for him themselves."

Bollocks to that.

"If I happen to find him, Sir, I'm not going to leave him where he is."

"I thought you'd say that."

It was tacit approval. Carpenter was trying to cover his back, but he didn't want Davison's death on his conscience.

"Is that all, Sir?"

"It is."

"Can you put Tina back on, please."

"I asked her to leave the room."

"Can you ask her to call me back then, please?"

"I can. But Lesley, don't do anything stupid."

"No, Sir."

The line went dead.

Damn.

Lesley returned to the car.

"I'm public enemy number one, sitting here," Dennis said.

"Sorry."

"What was all that about?"

"PSD have been investigating Davison."

"We knew that."

"They've been watching him for the past year."

Dennis sucked in a breath. "And Carpenter wants you to back off."

"That's what he's saying. But it's not what he means. Get Tina back on the phone. We need to track Kelvin down."

CHAPTER NINETY-THREE

Christian Davison turned at the sound of movement beyond the door.

He scanned the room, searching again for a potential weapon. But he knew there was nothing.

Of course they'd left the place empty. He was a serving police officer, a trained firearms expert. They knew the first thing he would do on waking up in here was look for a weapon.

He didn't even have anything on him. He was wearing the jogging bottoms and T-shirt that he'd put on when he'd got home last night.

Had it been last night, or longer?

Maybe he'd been here a couple of days, unconscious for half of it.

The door rattled open.

Christian stood up, muscles tense, senses alert.

A man entered, a smirk on his face.

Christian felt his heart dip.

Once again, the man was letting him see his face. And that meant only one thing.

"You," he said. "What do you want from me?"

The man laughed. "I'd have thought that was pretty obvious, don't you?"

Christian backed up, stopping before he reached the wall. His eyes skimmed over the man's body, checking for bulges in his pockets.

The man was slim with dark hair and a thin layer of stubble. He wore an expensive looking leather jacket and ripped jeans, not the suit he'd been dressed in at Christian's house.

There was no sign of anything large enough to cause much damage. But there might be more of them beyond that door.

"Enlighten me," Christian said, trying to sound calm.

The man rubbed his chin. "You're the prime suspect in a murder investigation. Your gun was found on the cliffs above Lyme Regis, where Fogarty and Lawson were buried."

"I know."

"Did you also know that two branches of Dorset Police have been to see you in the last twenty-four hours?"

Christian shrugged.

The man smiled. "The Major Crimes Investigation Team, *and* Professional Standards. You *are* a popular boy, aren't you?"

Christian jabbed his fingernails into his thigh.

"Yes," he lied. But the truth was, he'd had no idea that PSD were on to him.

"You've left me alone for the last ten years," he said. "Why did you come after me now?"

"Jesus Christ, for a copper you're not very bright, are you?"

"Enlighten me," he said, again. Anything to drag this out, to give him time to plan what he would do when Kelvin and his thugs eventually laid into him.

Or was it best to get it over with?

"OK." The man took a step towards him. "That gun of yours, we don't want you telling anybody who used it."

"I don't know who used it."

"Don't talk crap."

The door opened and another man stepped in.

Shit.

Christian recognised him.

"Christian," he said. His voice was low, rough.

"Stephen Leonard."

Leonard smiled. "Glad you remember me after all this time. I hear you've been giving us trouble."

Christian shook his head. "I'll take the blame."

"But that's not what you remember, is it?" the first man said.

"All I know was that I handed it over to Mr Leonard. Just like I promised."

"You were there. You know damn well what happened."

"I was in the back of a van. I didn't see."

Leonard took two steps forward. Christian flinched.

"You're a copper, Christian. Don't tell me you can't remember voices."

Christian shook his head.

"Anyway. PSD, Major Crimes, makes no difference to me," the first man said. "I'm not having you blabbing to either of them."

"It's fine." Christian held his gaze. "I'll tell them it was me. I fired the shots."

"No you won't. You'll cover your own back just like any of you shits would."

"I won't. It was my gun. After ten years they won't know that I didn't have gunshot residue on my skin. They have no reason not to believe me."

"And why would you do that?"

Christian felt sweat drip into the back of his collar. "Because I want to take responsibility for my actions."

No way he was going to tell them the real reason: *because I don't want you to kill me.*

The man laughed. "The prodigal son!" He turned away, and put a hand on the door. Leonard followed him. "I don't believe you."

The door opened. The two men left and two more entered.

They wore forensic suits. Where had they got those?

"Please," Christian said. "Please."

His bowels felt loose. *Hold on to yourself.*

"Just let me go. I'll take the blame."

The men said nothing. Kelvin was gone, the door locked. It was useless.

Christian raised his hands in front of him.

This is it.

He'd been waiting for this for ten years.

"Please," he cried, his voice shaking. "I'll tell them I shot them. I will!"

One of the men reached a hand into an inside pocket and brought out a hammer. Christian felt his insides liquify.

He backed into the wall and slid to the floor, trying not to whimper.

One of the men looked at the other. He made a gesture with his hand, a twisting gesture.

Christian felt his breath catch in his throat.

He screamed as the two men descended on him.

CHAPTER NINETY-FOUR

Lesley had finally allowed Dennis to persuade her to stop driving.

She pulled up in a bus stop near the centre of Bournemouth, bringing another scowl to his face. As she did so, her phone rang.

She hit speakerphone and nodded at Dennis.

"Tina," she said. "How are you getting on?"

"Still no address, sorry."

Lesley drew in a breath. "No business premises, residential addresses? There must be something."

"It's all in his uncle's name."

"Of course." Lesley leaned back in her seat. She rubbed her eyes. She was tired. She had lain awake last night, worried about Elsa.

Her phone buzzed: Mike. "Tina, I'm bringing Mike into the conversation."

"OK." Did Tina sound wary?

"Mike," Lesley said. "What have you got for me?"

"Stanley spoke to Davison's colleague about the drugs bust where he went AWOL. Apparently, they found him talking to some passer-by."

"And an AFO's job is to make an arrest, not to take statements."

"His colleague reckons he knew the guy."

"Have you got a name for the suspect?"

"Stephen Leonard."

"Stephen Leonard? What's he doing getting caught up in a drugs raid?"

"You know him, boss?"

"We questioned him when we were investigating Harry Nevin's murder," Tina said. "He works for Kelvin."

"Exactly," Lesley said. "Tina, that widens our scope. If he knows Davison, then he could be holding him."

Lesley tightened her grip on the steering wheel.

"Leonard was on the CCTV," Dennis said.

"I know."

"Mike, is Stanley there? I assume he spoke to Davison's colleague?"

"Right here, boss."

"Stanley. Did she say anything else? Did they arrest Leonard?"

"He was released without charge last Friday."

"Of course. Tina, get on it. Mike and Stanley, see if you can get anything more from the AFOs. Do they know anything that wasn't logged on the system?"

"Boss," said Mike.

"Boss…" Tina said.

"Yes, Tina."

"There's something else we need to consider."

"Go on."

Silence.

"What is it, Tina?"

"Fogarty, Lawson, Leonard and Kelvin. They've all got one thing in common."

"Christian Davison."

"Not just that," Tina said. "Fogarty and Lawson were partners in what's now Nevin, Cross and Short. Leonard and Kelvin are both represented by that firm." A pause. "Specifically by Elsa Short."

Lesley tensed. "What are you suggesting, Tina?"

"I'm sorry, boss. But we do need to consider that Elsa Short might know where Kelvin could be."

CHAPTER NINETY-FIVE

"Lesley, you do understand that a solicitor's relationship with her client is confidential? I can't pass on client information, no matter what kind of investigation it is."

Lesley was standing outside the car, still parked in the bus stop. A lorry squeezed past, the driver yelling at her, and there was a bus approaching.

She placed the flat of her hand on the roof of the car, her teeth gritted.

"I know, Els, but you're not his solicitor anymore. You got out of there deliberately, because they're dangerous people. And now they've got a police officer. I'm worried they'll kill him because he has information about the murder case."

"Lesley." Elsa's voice was strained. "I can't tell you. It's not just about client confidentiality. What happens if they find out that I passed on that information? What happens if they lead you to Davison and you're able to pin the murders of Fogarty and Lawson on my former clients?"

Lesley scraped her fingers across the roof of the car. "Elsa, do you want a man to die? Do you want the murders of your former colleagues to go unpunished?"

"They weren't my colleagues. And any evidence you get that comes from me will be tainted anyway. The defendant's former lawyer, who's in a relationship with the senior investigating officer, providing evidence for the prosecution? If I were defending Kelvin I'd have a field day with that."

"Come on, Elsa."

A pause. "I understand, sweetie," Elsa said. "But you know I can't reveal client information. It's just not allowed."

"Allowed, my arse," Lesley said. "This is life or death. You know there are exceptions."

Silence.

"Elsa?"

No reply.

"Elsa, please. It's an address. Given enough time, I could track it down myself. But I don't have time."

Lesley turned round to see the bus driver gesticulating at her.

"Shit." She knocked on Dennis's door and gestured for him to slide across the seats. He did so, looked in the rear-view mirror and drove off as soon as she was in the passenger seat, her phone still clasped to her ear.

"Sweetheart," she said. "I know you've been trying to get away from them. I know you want to keep yourself safe. I will make sure that nobody knows where I got this information." She glanced at Dennis who nodded.

"Who in your team have you talked to about this?" Elsa asked.

"Dennis and Tina."

"And can I trust them?"

"I would trust those people with my life." Lesley dragged a hand through her hair. "It's going to be OK, Els. If we can pin these murders on Kelvin and Leonard then you won't be in danger."

A snort came down the line. "You know it doesn't work like that."

Lesley swallowed. "If we don't find Christian Davison, he's going to die. Just like Fogarty and Lawson."

Elsa sighed.

Lesley waited.

"OK," Elsa said. "There's an industrial estate. Nuffield. He's got a unit there."

CHAPTER NINETY-SIX

Tina picked up her phone.

"Tina, it's the DCI. Don't ask any questions. I'm giving you an address. I want Uniform backup there immediately. AFOs as well."

"Is Davison there?" she asked.

"We don't know for sure. But it's an address that belongs to Darren Kelvin. Where are Mike and Stanley?"

"Still at the AFOs unit," she replied.

"Good. You speak to Uniform, I'll speak to them. They'll get the AFO backup organised."

"No problem, boss. How did you—?"

"Don't ask," the DCI said. "And Tina…"

Tina swallowed. This would be about her going out to the drugs bust location. She was about to get removed from the major crime investigations team.

"I'm sorry, boss. I know I messed up."

"It's not that, Tina. The conversation we had about the link with Nevin, Cross and Short, when you suggested Elsa might know something?"

"Er, yes." Tina thought of the tension she'd sensed when the boss had called Elsa from her mum's house.

"It didn't happen."

Tina gripped her phone. "No, boss. It didn't happen."

CHAPTER NINETY-SEVEN

Dennis parked Lesley's car two streets away from Kelvin's unit at the industrial estate. A squad car was already in front of them. Lesley got out just as an unmarked car and a black van arrived behind them.

A woman got out of the car, wearing an AFO's uniform. Lesley approached her, holding out her hand.

"DCI Clarke," she said. "I'm the officer in charge here."

"Ma'am. I'm PS Weathers."

Lesley frowned. "You're Christian Davison's commanding officer."

"I figured he might need a friendly face when we got him out of there."

Lesley grimaced. "Let's just hope we *do* get him out of there."

"Do you know he's in there, Ma'am?"

"Not for sure," she said. "But we've checked CCTV and one of the cars that was outside Davison's house arrived here in the last two hours."

"Is it still there?" Weathers asked.

Lesley nodded. "CCTV hasn't seen it leave. But we need to check the area."

"I'll talk to Uniform, coordinate a sweep."

"You do that."

"Don't worry, Ma'am. We'll make sure we know exactly who's in there before we get close."

"Good. We don't know how many men are in there or what weapons they have." She glanced at the van. "The team you brought with you, are they Davison's colleagues?"

"I came with a different unit."

Thank God. She didn't want personal relationships clouding the officers' judgement.

"Good."

Lesley turned back towards the car. Dennis was approaching her.

"What's the plan?" he asked.

"Uniform and the AFOs are scouting the area first. Once we know who's in there, we'll go in."

CHAPTER NINETY-EIGHT

"You need to keep well back, Ma'am," Sergeant Weathers said.

"I want to get in there. If Davison is hurt—"

"With all respect, Ma'am. He's one of mine. You can trust me to look after him."

"The other men in that building are suspects in a double murder enquiry. It's imperative we don't let them get away." She eyed Weathers, thinking of her earlier operation and the fact she'd allowed one of her team to go missing.

But Lesley knew that an officer who'd recently made a cockup was the least likely to make one again.

Weathers looked into her eyes. "I'll radio you when it's safe for you to enter."

Lesley sighed. "Very well."

"Meanwhile, I suggest you stay here."

They were sheltering behind a row of dusty bushes within view of Kelvin's unit. She was with Weathers and four of her team, plus four PCs.

Dennis was further away, by her car. He was on the phone, briefing Carpenter. She knew she should be doing that herself but she wanted to keep an eye on things here. And she knew that talking to the super right now would cloud her judgement.

She watched the AFOs communicate with each other with silent gestures. Two of them hurried away from their vantage point and around the back of the building, barely visible unless you knew what you were looking for. One of the AFOs still with them gave Weathers the thumbs-up as his radio came to life, then turned the volume down and adjusted his earpiece.

After a moment's intense concentration, Weathers pointed at her colleague, nodded and made a gesture for him to move.

The two of them scuttled towards the building. Three PCs appeared from nowhere, the enforcer held between them. They ran towards the door.

"Police! Open up."

They didn't wait for a response, but slammed the enforcer into the door. It fell back, the locks snapping.

Lesley held her breath.

The PCs pulled back. They ran off to the left and took shelter behind a skip. Three AFOs hurried into the building.

Suddenly, there was quiet. Lesley could hear her own breathing, and the dim sound of Dennis's voice on the phone.

She stared at the door to the unit, her eyes prickling.

The radio she'd been gripping in her hand crackled.

"Ma'am, it's safe for you to come in." It was Weathers.

Lesley turned towards Dennis and gave him the thumbs-up. She ran towards the building.

There was no one in sight. The AFOs were all inside and the uniformed officers were still behind the skip.

She raced through the door, not stopping to feel fear.

The entrance was dingy, paint peeling off the walls. Three doors led off it, all open. She turned in the empty space.

"Sergeant Weathers! Where are you?"

Lesley's radio crackled again.

"Keep to radio comms, Ma'am."

She bent to it, her voice low. "Very well. Who's in here?"

"Just me and three of my guys. No suspects."

"Davison?"

"Here's here, Ma'am."

The radio was heavy in her hand. "Alive?"

"Barely. But yes."

CHAPTER NINETY-NINE

Mike drove towards Poole, following the route that he reckoned the AFOs had taken. They'd been much faster than him, blue lights running and sirens when they'd needed them. But he was doing his best to keep up.

"This way," Stanley shouted. "Turn left!"

"Shit." He'd missed the turn.

Mike slammed on his brakes and reversed. He took the left turn.

"It's over that way," Stanley said, waving his phone in front of him. They hadn't had time to stop and programme the satnav. "Off to the right."

"Bloody industrial estates," Stanley muttered. "Like warrens. There!"

Mike could see the DCI's car up ahead. There was nobody near it.

"Right," he said. "They must be in the building."

"Pull up behind it," Stanley said. "We can follow them in."

"They don't know we're here. It might not be safe."

Stanley grunted. "Yeah, you're right."

Mike approached the DCI's car, slowing to pull in behind it. As he did so, a car sped past in the opposite direction, almost clipping his mirror. A powerful black Audi with recent plates.

Mike squinted at it.

"Fuck me!" Stanley shouted.

"What?"

"That's Darren Kelvin, the nephew."

"Really?" Mike couldn't see into the car, it had passed them now.

"Follow him, Mike. Follow the shitbag."

Mike revved his engine and turned in the road. His brakes squealed and dust surrounded the car.

"Fuck," Stanley breathed. "I've never done this before."

"I thought you were a rapid response driver before?"

"I mean, in an unmarked car."

"Stick the blue lights on," Mike told him.

"We don't want them knowing we're behind them."

"We want to catch up with them. They're not going to miss us."

Stanley did as he was told and Mike hit the accelerator, his senses prickling as they sped out of the industrial estate.

CHAPTER ONE HUNDRED

Every single bone in Christian's body hurt.

He lay still, his eyes squeezed shut. He worked over his body in his mind. There was pain everywhere, muscles screaming at him. But there was no single sharp centre of it. He knew what it felt like to be shot, and this wasn't it.

His mind went back to Kelvin leaving the room.

What had the other two had in their pockets?

Hammers, he remembered. Hammers.

He ran over his body again, his eyes still shut. Hammers wouldn't be quite like being shot, but it wouldn't be far off. He would know if he'd been hit by one.

But there was nothing. No single pain point. Nowhere any worse than the rest of him.

He kept his eyes shut, not wanting them to know he'd come round.

They'd be watching him, one of them at least, sitting in a corner, keeping an eye on him. He knew how these men worked.

He felt something in his thigh, a twinge. He frowned.

Fuck.

There was a point above his knee where the pain *was* worse than anywhere else.

They'd hit him there, hadn't they? His knee would be shattered.

But it was OK. He was still alive. If that was all they'd done, they wanted him to live.

It made no sense. He'd seen Kelvin's face, and Leonard's.

They all knew what had happened ten years ago, and they knew that both PSD and the Major Crimes team were catching up with him.

Surely they wouldn't let him live.

As soon as he opened his eyes, he'd be done for.

There was an itch under his left eye. He wanted to scratch it, but he couldn't let them see that he was awake.

He kept his eyes closed, eyelids screwed tight.

"Christian," came a voice.

A woman?

Sunika?

No. He split up with Sunika ten years ago.

But what if Kelvin had found her? What if he was threatening her?

That was absurd. Sunika had left him. She had another guy now, two kids.

But she was a good woman. She'd left him because of his shifts. There'd been a healthy gap before she'd started seeing Hugh. Or at least, that's what his friends had told him.

If they told Sunika that he was in danger, she would have done whatever they said.

He opened his eyes.

"Sunika?"

A woman was standing over him, her face framed by bright light.

He blinked.

The woman was blonde and tall. She wasn't Sunika.

"Who…?" he stuttered, his voice thin.

She smiled at him. "My name is DCI Lesley Clarke. PSD will be coming to interview you very soon. But I have some questions to ask you. We don't have long."

CHAPTER ONE HUNDRED ONE

Dennis looked up from his desk as the door opened. Mike and Stanley walked in.

"Did you get him?" he asked. "Did you catch up with them?"

Mike shook his head.

Dennis felt his body deflate.

Stanley grinned. "We didn't get him," he said. "But Uniform did. We called for an RRV."

Dennis rapped the desk with his knuckles. "Brilliant. Good work, you two."

Tina was at the desk next to him. She stood up, smiling.

"He drove straight past you?" she asked.

"He did," Mike replied, his face animated. "We were pulling up behind the DCI's car and he just came past us."

"Damn lucky coincidence," Stanley said.

Dennis cleared his throat.

"Where's the DCI?" asked Mike.

"She's at the hospital," Dennis said. "Speaking to Christian Davison."

"PSD still want him?" Stanley asked.

"The boss wanted to speak to him first."

Stanley grunted.

"So where's Darren Kelvin?" Dennis asked.

"Not just Kelvin," Mike said. "Stephen Leonard too."

Dennis felt his smile broaden. "Double trouble. I don't suppose they gave you a confession as well?"

Mike laughed. "No such luck. But hopefully Davison will be able to put them in the frame."

"D'you think he will?" Tina asked. "Given he'll be incriminating himself?"

Dennis looked at her. "I think Christian Davison is in enough trouble already. I'm hoping he'll get an attack of conscience and tell us everything."

"Let's hope so."

Mike moved towards Tina's desk, eyeing her. "Everything OK?" he asked.

She looked down at the desk, not meeting his gaze. "Fine." She glanced at Dennis and he looked away. None of his business.

"Later," she whispered to Mike. "Let's talk later."

CHAPTER ONE HUNDRED TWO

Lesley pulled up a chair. She checked the door to Christian Davison's private room.

There was a uniformed officer standing outside and two AFOs in the corridor. But nobody had registered that the patient had woken up yet.

"PSD will be here very soon," she told him. "They'll want to know how your gun came to be at a crime scene in Lyme Regis. But first I've got some questions for you. I'm the SIO into the murders of Kenneth Fogarty and Catherine Lawson."

He nodded.

Lesley considered the things she needed to know. She didn't have much time.

"First question. Was it your gun that shot Fogarty and Lawson?"

He nodded.

"Are you going to come clean to PSD?"

He stared at her for a moment, blinking. Then he nodded.

"Was it you who shot it?"

She watched for his reaction.

He shook his head. There was no hesitation, no blush, no sign that he was lying.

"So who did fire it?"

"Leonard," he croaked. "I'm pretty sure it was Leonard."

"Pretty sure. Is that all?"

"It was Leonard. He had the gun. He said he was going to shoot the two lawyers."

"Why would he tell you that?"

"They were blackmailing me. I was broke, my divorce… I took money for information, but then, once I'd done that, they had me. It just got worse."

"Why didn't you tell your commanding officer?"

"I thought I could stop it. My job was all I had. Still is."

"You're going to lose it."

"I know. But I'm alive."

The door opened and two men walked in. Lesley didn't recognise either of them.

She stood up. "Who are you?"

The man at the front, tall and well-built with closely cropped black hair, brought his ID out. "Detective Superintendent William Morpeth. Professional Standards Division. Who are you?"

"DCI Lesley Clarke, Major Crime Investigations Team."

"If you don't mind, this is our witness."

Lesley looked down at Christian. "I'll be back. After they've finished with you."

He gritted his teeth and nodded at her. His eyes were red, his face grey.

"You take care of yourself," she told him.

She rounded the bed and stood in front of the superintendent.

"Go easy on him. He's been injured, they struck him in the knee with a hammer."

"You don't need to—"

"And he's been tied up and terrorised for the last twenty-four hours."

The super looked at her. "I know how to do my job, DCI Clarke. Now just leave us to it, please."

CHAPTER ONE HUNDRED THREE

Elsa sat on the sand, staring out to sea, her arms pulled around her knees.

Setting up her own firm wouldn't be easy. She had no contacts down here. She'd come from London and gone straight into the job at Nevin, Cross and Short.

Her contract with the firm prevented her from taking any clients with her. She would have to start afresh.

She preferred to start afresh. She couldn't be sure which clients were associated with Arthur Kelvin. She wanted a new client base as far away from that man as she could get.

She stood up and dusted her jeans down. Lesley would be home soon, and Sharon's train was due in an hour or so. Elsa had plans to take them both out for dinner. A new Italian place on the seafront. It was what they needed, a bit of normality.

She was hoping that Lesley would forgive her for everything she'd done. Everything she'd lied about.

She'd done it partly to protect Lesley, but she had to admit she'd done it mainly to protect herself. There was no way she'd have brought a police officer in on what she'd been planning.

Elsa walked towards the steps leading up to the prom and towards her flat. A man was coming the other way, his head bowed, a dog running in front of him.

The dog rushed towards her and jumped up, paws on her thighs. She laughed.

"You're cute, aren't you?"

The dog looked up at her, tongue lolling. She gave its head a ruffle.

She looked up and her breathing stopped.

The man had been joined by another man, a man she recognised. Short and heavily built with greying hair.

Elsa straightened up, hand still on the dog's head.

"Arthur," she said. "Fancy seeing you here."

The side of his lip curled in a half-smile. "Fancy. You live near here, don't you?"

"I might do."

He laughed. "It's no secret that you've got a flat three blocks back from the seafront. You're not exactly deep undercover."

"Yes," she said, meeting his gaze. "I do live here. I walk along this beach every day."

"Nice for you."

"Not as nice as your house in Sandbanks."

He winked. "True. You'll have to do a bit better for yourself. Why don't you?"

She said nothing. She wasn't about to tell Kelvin her plan to set up a new firm.

"Anyway," he said, "just thought I'd say hello. Tell you to take care."

"I will. Thank you." It was all she could do to keep her voice level.

He leaned in towards her. "Only there's some nasty bastards out there. You know, you need to watch yourself. One of these days you might be walking along this beach and one of them decides he takes a fancy to you..."

She gritted her teeth and stared back at him. *Don't flinch. Don't react.*

"Thank you for the advice," she said.

He cocked his head. "Like I said, you watch out. Don't put yourself at risk. Lock your doors at night. I would hate for anything to happen to you."

He turned and walked away, tugging the dog along on a short lead.

CHAPTER ONE HUNDRED FOUR

Superintendent Carpenter had a visitor when Lesley entered his office.

"Sir," she said, looking between him and the other man. He was older than Carpenter, balding on top with grey hair around his ears. He gave her a stern look.

"DCI Clarke," the super said. "This is Detective Superintendent Phipps, from the Hampshire force."

"Pleased to meet you, Sir."

"He'll be heading up the new investigation into DCI Mackie's death."

"Oh." Lesley swallowed. "Very good, Sir. Will you need my team's input?"

Phipps blinked at her. His eyes were almost unnaturally small. "I imagine we'll be taking statements from some of your team. Those who were here at the time it happened, at least." His voice was thin, grating.

"Yes."

There was something about the man that put her senses on alert. But she had to trust that he'd do a thorough job.

"There's evidence I've been collating and I can run through with you, if you'd like."

He shook his head, giving her a smile that didn't get past his mouth. "As you weren't here at the time, DCI Clarke, I don't think I'll be needing your input. But thank you for the offer."

"Very well." Lesley looked at Carpenter. "We've made three arrests on the Fogarty and Lawson case."

His face brightened. "Three?"

"Well, strictly speaking, we've made two and PSD have made one."

"So PSD have arrested AFO Davison at last?"

"Yes, Sir. He's fully cooperating as far as I'm aware, and I think he'll avoid a custodial sentence."

"He'll lose his job, and he'll thoroughly bloody deserve it," said Phipps. "Stupid bastard."

Lesley said nothing.

"Who are the other two arrests?" Carpenter asked.

She smiled, clenching a fist inside her pocket. "Darren Kelvin, Sir. And Stephen Leonard."

His eyes widened. He glanced at Phipps then composed himself. "Indeed?"

"Yes, Sir. They were spotted by DC Legg and DC Brown, leaving the property where AFO Davison was held. Davison has already provided evidence against them in his written statement, and he'll back it up in court. Leonard shot Fogarty and Lawson. Davison was a witness."

"Davison's evidence is tainted," Phipps said. "He was a co-conspirator."

"I think we can trust him, Sir."

"Good work, Lesley," Carpenter said. "That doesn't get you off the hook for the other things, though."

"No, Sir." She hesitated. "Do you need me for anything else?"

"No." He shooed her away.

She left his office, realising that her palms were clammy.

318

CHAPTER ONE HUNDRED FIVE

"Tina, you shouldn't have," Dennis said.

"My mum sent them. I found them at my flat."

"Then open them!"

Tina grinned. She placed the box of chocolates on her desk and tore off the cellophane.

"Milk Tray," Dennis said. "Your mum's a traditionalist. I approve."

Tina shrugged.

"I didn't know they still made these," Mike laughed.

"Let's make the most of it," Tina said.

"I could get used to your mum," Mike replied, stuffing a chocolate into his mouth.

"That reminds me," she told him. "We're going there for dinner. Week on Saturday. She wants to…" She trailed off.

"What, T?" Mike asked. "You not happy about it?"

"Nothing," Tina said.

There it was again, that atmosphere between the two DCs. Dennis didn't like having courting couples on the team.

The door opened and the DCI entered. "Chocolates. Can anybody have one?"

"My mum sent them, boss. She specifically mentioned you on the card."

"Your mum's alright." The boss peered at the box and then took one out: a strawberry cream, Dennis noticed with surprise.

"So," she said. "I've got news for you all."

Dennis watched her. "We've made three arrests. We already know about that."

"This is something else." Her eyes scanned his face.

"What is it, boss?" He steeled himself. "Is it about DCI Mackie?"

"Carpenter's brought in an investigating officer. Superintendent Phipps. He's from the Hampshire force. Do you know him?"

Dennis felt the ground sway beneath him. He put a hand out and grabbed his desk.

The boss frowned. "Dennis, are you OK?"

"I'm fine, boss. Sorry. Never met the man."

He pulled in a breath. He could feel sweat breaking out on his forehead. His legs seemed to have gone soft.

Superintendent Phipps. He'd come across him before.

"Are you sure you're alright?" the boss asked. She approached him, holding out a hand.

He pushed it away. "I'm fine, boss. I'll be fine."

CHAPTER ONE HUNDRED SIX

Lesley nodded for Tina to come into her office. She'd gone inside and sat down at her chair, anxious to get some rest. But there was a conversation that she needed to have with the DC first.

"Close the door," she said.

"Boss." Tina closed the door and stood leaning against it.

"And relax. Take a seat." Lesley gestured towards the two chairs opposite her desk.

The board was still set up behind them. There was no photograph of Christian Davison, but the investigation wasn't over yet. They would still be looking into the exact details of what had happened ten years ago. She had to hope the CPS would have enough for a conviction. But she was confident that Davison's evidence would be enough to put Leonard and possibly Kelvin away for a long time.

As for Davison himself: well, that was PSD's problem.

"I'm sorry, boss," Tina said, "about me going out to the drugs house."

Lesley leaned on the desk, her elbows on the surface and her hands clasped together. "It was reckless and stupid."

"I know. I wasn't thinking straight."

"I know what you're like Tina, you're keen and you want to prove yourself. But you've already done that. You need to believe that you're good enough doing the work that I give you. You're a valued member of the team. I don't expect you to go galavanting off trying to find extra work for yourself. Particularly work that puts you at risk."

Tina nodded. "I know. I'm sorry. It's just…"

Lesley sighed. "It's just what?" She leaned back in her chair. "Is this about you and Mike?" She'd sensed an atmosphere between them in the team room earlier. As DCI, that was the last thing she needed.

Tina shook her head. "I don't *have* to tell you this yet, boss. Not according to the law."

Lesley frowned. "What do you mean, according to the law? What have you done?"

Tina stared back at her. "I haven't done anything, boss. Don't worry."

"Well, what then? Just tell me, Tina."

Lesley glanced out through the glazed wall separating her office from the rest of the team. Mike was watching them.

"He's worried about you," she said. "Mike."

Tina looked back. "I haven't told him yet."

Lesley put a hand down on the table. "Told him what?"

Tina sat up straight in the chair. "I'm pregnant, boss."

Lesley stifled a laugh. She'd been worried that Tina had got herself mixed up in something illegal…

Pregnancy. That was the last thing she'd been expecting.

She looked out to the team room again.

"You haven't told Mike yet."

Tina shook her head.

"Don't you think you should?"

Tina nodded.

"OK." Lesley dragged in a breath. "What you're forgetting here is that I'm a mum. I know what your rights are. And I know that you don't need to give us official notification yet. But now you've told me, I have to take that into account and do a risk assessment on any operation that you're involved in."

Tina closed her eyes. "I know."

"Mike will work it out, you know."

"Yes."

"When are you due?"

"I'm eight weeks."

"Early days, then. Seven months from now… the autumn."

Tina nodded again. "My mum thinks I'll settle down with Mike."

"But you don't want to?"

"I'm not ready for that."

Lesley looked at her. "Tina, do you want to keep this baby? You know you don't have to. At eight weeks…"

Tina blinked back at her. "I think so."

"Whatever you decide, I'll keep it confidential."

"I know, boss. Thank you. But yes. I want to keep it. It wasn't in my plan but…"

Lesley looked out at Mike again. He deserved to know. But this was Tina's body they were talking about.

She gave Tina a smile. "Being a parent is hard work, but it's very rewarding. I was older than you when it happened to me, already married. Not that that counted for anything in the end. But Mike's a good guy. He'll support you."

"I know, but I just joined the team. This is the worst possible timing."

"Tina," Lesley said, "when it comes to having a baby, it always seems like the worst possible timing. But I think you need to have a bit more of a chat with your mum. Work out what you want to do."

"Yes, boss. I'm pretty sure I want to keep it though."

Lesley smiled. "Well, that's good. An extra member of the team."

CHAPTER ONE HUNDRED SEVEN

Lesley opened the door to the flat and was immediately accosted by a body throwing itself at her.

"Whoa," she said, almost tumbling to the floor.

"Mum!" cried Sharon. "I've missed you."

Lesley held her daughter at arm's length, surveyed her for a moment, then pulled her in for a hug.

"I missed you too, sweetie. But it's only been ten days."

"I know," Sharon said. "But I want to move down here. I'm going to in the summer."

Lesley clutched her daughter's arm. "Let's not make any rash decisions just yet."

Sharon shook her head. "It's not rash. It's what I want to do. I want to live here with you and Elsa."

"You do?"

"She's got her mind made up." Elsa stood in the doorway to the living room, a tea towel in her hands. "And she's like you, Lesley. When she's made a decision, there's not much talking her out of it."

"How would you feel about that?" Lesley asked Elsa.

Elsa grinned. She approached Sharon and put her hand on her shoulder. Sharon turned to her and wrapped an arm around Elsa's waist.

"I'd love it," Elsa said.

"Me too," added Sharon.

Lesley looked at the two of them. They were so natural together. She was amazed at the way that Sharon had adapted to Elsa's presence in their lives. The way the two of them had bonded.

"What about your dad?" she asked.

"He's fine with it," Sharon said. "Now that he's not with Julieta he's working all the time. To be honest, I think he'll be well shot of me."

"Don't talk like that," Lesley said. "Your dad loves you."

Sharon shrugged. "He has a funny way of showing it."

"He loves you," Lesley repeated. "You just need to make a bit of an effort. Remind him that he has a family from time to time. Academics like to get lost in their work. A bit like us coppers."

Sharon shrugged. "Anyway," she said. "I brought something with me."

She turned away and disappeared into her bedroom. After a moment she called out. "Mum! Need a bit of help here!"

Lesley looked at Elsa, who shrugged. She followed Sharon into her room. The girl's suitcase was open on the floor and wires spilled out of her laptop bag on the desk. She'd put up two new posters. What time had she arrived?

Lesley sat down on the bed. Sharon had bought a new duvet cover, too. She really was making herself at home.

"Are you sure?" she said. "You really want to live with me and Elsa?"

Sharon was turned away from her, rooting through a rucksack. "Yes, Mum. I'm sure. Elsa's pretty cool."

Cool. Did sixteen-year-olds say that these days?

"Here it is." Sharon turned to her, brandishing a box. "I bought a cake for Elsa's birthday."

Lesley clapped her hand to her face. "It's tomorrow. I left her present at work."

"She won't mind. You know Elsa."

"Still…"

"Help me with this, Mum. I've brought candles, too."

Lesley smiled as her daughter brought the cake out of its box and started sticking candles into it.

"Don't we need a plate?"

Sharon stopped what she was doing. "Good point. Can you sneak one in?"

Lesley laughed.

"What's going on in there? Can I help?" Elsa called.

Sharon stood up. "Nothing! Stay out!"

"OK. I'll make some coffee."

"It's OK," Lesley said. "We'll use the box as a plate."

"OK." Sharon started tearing into the cardboard. At last the cake was ready.

"One moment." Sharon delved into her bag and brought out a lighter.

"Where did you get that?"

"Don't worry, I didn't buy it. I nicked it from Dad."

Lesley stifled a laugh.

"Come on." Sharon stood up, balancing the cake in one hand and grabbing Lesley's arm with the other.

Lesley followed her daughter out of her room and into the kitchen, where Elsa was getting mugs out of the cupboard.

"We've got something for you. Or rather, Sharon has."

Elsa turned. Her face lit up. "Sharon, a cake. How kind!" She eyed Lesley. "You forgot, didn't you?"

"No." Lesley scratched her cheek. "I might have left your present at work, though."

Elsa leaned over and kissed her cheek. "It's fine. You've been busy." Her expression flickered, just for a moment.

"You OK?" Lesley asked.

"Fine. Sorry."

"You'd tell me if you weren't?"

Elsa looked back at her for just a moment too long. "I'm just preoccupied with the new business, that's all. Ignore me, this cake is more important."

Lesley nodded.

Sharon lit the candles and they sang *Happy Birthday*.

Elsa gave Sharon a hug. "It's fabulous, sweetheart." She looked at Lesley. "Your daughter is one hell of a woman."

"She takes after me."

Sharon gave her a mock slap on the bum. Lesley laughed.

"So when will you be able to retrieve my present?" Elsa asked.

Lesley looked at her. Elsa took a bite of the cake and licked her lips.

"I've got something better than a present."

Elsa cocked her head. "Surely we can leave that till later?" She glanced at Sharon, who was stuffing cake into her mouth and heading for the sofa.

"Not that," Lesley said, her eyes widening. "Something else. Something better."

She looked at her girlfriend, taking her in in a way she'd never done with Terry. Elsa's eyes sparkled. Her dark hair was soft and shiny. Lesley wanted to wrap her fingers in it and pull Elsa to her.

Elsa smiled. "Have you found out how old I am yet?"

"Thirty-nine!" Sharon called from the sofa.

Elsa shook her head. "Close."

"Forty?" Lesley asked.

Elsa nodded. "The big four-oh," she whispered.

"Why didn't you tell me?"

"Because it makes me feel old."

"You're not old."

A shrug. "So what's this thing that's better than a present?"

Lesley felt her body dip. She stopped herself. *No. Too traditional.*

"Els," she said. She licked her lips.

Elsa leaned forwards, her gaze on Lesley's mouth. "Yes?"

Lesley swallowed the lump in her throat. "Elsa, will you marry me?"

I hope you enjoyed *The Fossil Beach Murders*. Do you want to know more about DCI Mackie's death? The prequel novella, *The Ballard Down Murder*, is free from my book club at rachelmclean.com/ballard.

Thanks,

Rachel McLean